A jolt of electricity sizzled through Cooper, sending a thousand watts of need racing through his system. He crushed his lips to Piper's.

The heady sent of roses and jasmine filled his senses. His blood roared through his veins pounding out a deafening beat.

"What the hell is going on?" Piper's brother's voice thundered around the room.

Cooper's eyes widened. "Calm down, Shane."

Shane invaded his space and glowered at him.

Piper snapped, "I am a grown woman. I can, and will, kiss whoever I want, whenever and wherever I deem fit."

Shane stared at her, a stunned expression on his face. "Are you telling me that you two..."

"Are together." Piper looped her arms around his waist.

Cooper liked the feel of her hands on him. The rightness of it.

"Come again?" Shane's eyes bugged out. He shook his head, a perplexed expression on his face. "No way. I don't believe it."

Piper looked at him and grinned. "I guess my brother here needs more convincing." She rose up on her tiptoes and yanked Coop's head down to hers.

Dear Reader,

What happens when your mother won't stop fixing you up with every eligible bachelor in town? Out of desperation to stop the endless stream of potential husbands, you strike a deal with your sworn enemy to act as each other's significant other for the next five weeks.

The trouble is, said enemy is sinfully sexy, devilishly handsome, and his kisses are to die for.

Sparks will fly...

Thank you for picking up this copy of *A Deal with Mr. Wrong*—book two in my Sisterhood of Chocolate & Wine series! For those who don't know me, I'm Anna James. I write contemporary romance, and although I've been writing for years, this is my first series with Harlequin. I hope you enjoy *A Deal with Mr. Wrong* as much as I enjoyed writing it. I'd love to hear what you think of Cooper and Piper's story. Please share your thoughts with me on Facebook and Twitter (annajames.author, @authorannajames) or drop me a line through my website, authorannajames.com.

Happy reading,

Anna James

PS: If you haven't read book one yet, you can pick up a copy of *A Taste of Home*, Layla and Shane's story, at Harlequin.com.

A Deal with Mr. Wrong

—

ANNA JAMES

HARLEQUIN
SPECIAL
EDITION

Recycling programs
for this product may
not exist in your area.

ISBN-13: 978-1-335-59453-2

A Deal with Mr. Wrong

Copyright © 2024 by Heidi Tanca

For questions and comments about the quality of this book,
please contact us at CustomerService@Harlequin.com.

Harlequin Enterprises ULC
22 Adelaide St. West, 41st Floor
Toronto, Ontario M5H 4E3, Canada
www.Harlequin.com

Printed in U.S.A.

Anna James writes contemporary romance novels with strong, confident heroes and heroines who conquer life's trials and find their happily-ever-afters.

Want to learn more about Anna and her books?

Sign up for her newsletter: authorannajames.com.

Follow her on Instagram: @author_anna_james.

Books by Anna James

Harlequin Special Edition

Sisterhood of Chocolate & Wine

A Taste of Home
A Deal with Mr. Wrong

Visit the Author Profile page at Harlequin.com.

For my cousin, Sue. Thanks for all your love, your support and your encouragement. I miss you.

Chapter One

Piper Kavanaugh pulled her Honda Fit into the parking lot of the old, colonial mansion and parked in an empty space. Grabbing her purse, she exited the car and walked over to the side entrance to the building that would take her to the second floor and the three thousand square feet of space that would become her gallery.

Her gallery. Something she'd imagined opening ever since she visited the Museum of Modern Art in New York City as a little kid.

She grinned. That dream was about to become a reality now.

She punched in the code on the keypad and opened the door, making sure to relock it behind her. The room was empty now, except for the dining tables scattered throughout the space.

One of the first orders of business would be to put up walls separating the private dining room that was part of the Sea Shack restaurant that Layla Williams, the current owner of the mansion, ran on the first floor, from the grand staircase that led to the entrance to her gallery on the second floor.

Piper climbed the stairs, stopping at the top to fish out the keys Layla had given her from her purse.

She'd replace this standard wood door with something more appropriate for her gallery entrance. Perhaps a double door with glass panes? Yes. That would work.

"Piper," a familiar voice called.

She glanced over the rail to the room below and waved. Her older sister stood at the bottom of the stairs with a big grin on her face. "Hey, Mia. Come on up. Wait. How'd you get in?"

Another thing she'd need to change when she was open for business, since patrons would access her gallery directly from the parking lot and not— "Did Layla let you in from the restaurant?"

Mia nodded. "I hope you don't mind. I wanted to surprise you."

"No. Not at all." She'd never mind a visit from her sister, but the two businesses needed to be independent of each other. That included access.

Mia took the stairs two at a time and threw her arms around her when she reached the landing. "You're finally here."

Piper grinned and eased out of her sister's embrace. "The New Suffolk building department finally approved my renovation plans yesterday." Months after she'd submitted the layouts.

Mia laughed. "You know how small towns are."

"Local governments are all the same. It's called bureaucracy."

"When did you get in?" Mia asked.

Piper glanced at her watch. "A few hours ago. I grabbed the red-eye out of LAX last night. Mom picked me up at the airport in Boston this morning. I picked up the car you helped me find at Mom's place. Drove over to my new apartment and dumped my bags, grabbed a quick shower and came straight here."

"You must be exhausted," Mia said.

"Nah." Piper waved off Mia's concern. "I'm too excited. And I grabbed a quick catnap on the drive from the airport to Mom's. Now come on, let's go inside." Piper smiled a mile-wide grin.

How lucky was she to find the perfect place for her gallery on a trip home to see her family a few months ago? Especially since she'd been searching for a location for some time.

Really lucky—or maybe it was fate? Dad would have said the latter. A sad smile crossed her face. He'd always believed in that stuff. As for her...not so much. She believed you carved out your own path in life.

Piper waited for the gut-clenching grief to choke her, like it always had before when she thought about her father. It didn't happen. Her stomach wasn't tied up in knots.

A mix of surprise and relief flooded through her. Surprise because she'd carried her grief with her for so long it was like a physical weight on her shoulders, and relief because that burden was now gone. Unlocking the door, she stepped inside and Mia followed.

"So, what do you think?" Piper gestured around the massive space with its classic crown molding and oak plank flooring. Her chest filled to bursting point. It was just as she remembered. "It's pretty great—right?"

"I'm just glad you're home to stay." Mia slung an arm around Piper's shoulder.

"Me, too." She missed the closeness she and Mia had shared growing up together. They'd been each other's confidantes throughout childhood.

Mia locked her gaze on Piper. "Ten years away was too long."

Piper sighed. Leaving right after high school graduation had seemed like her only option at the time. Life in

New Suffolk had been suffocating. She could...breathe in Los Angeles.

"I've missed having my little sister around," Mia continued.

"That won't be a problem anymore." With the help of a great counselor, she'd worked through the loss of her father. Yes, the ache was still there, but the anger and grief that consumed her in the years after his death had finally faded. Coming home now seemed right.

She mock-punched her sister in the arm. "Pretty soon you're going to complain I'm around too much."

Mia grinned. "Not a chance. So, what are you going to do with all this space?"

Piper laughed. "You always did like a renovation project. Tell me again why you're teaching instead of going back to TK Construction?" Her sister had been happy working at the family-owned construction company started thirty-five years ago by her father and his best friend, Ron Turner.

Mia shook her head. "This is about you, not me. Now, come on. Out with it. What are your plans for this place?"

Piper wouldn't press her sister further. Now was not the time. Once she settled in, she'd invite Mia over to her place. They'd have a bottle of wine and maybe some pastries from the Coffee Palace and she'd get Mia to open up.

"I'm going to close this area off." Piper walked over to the kitchen Layla's grandfather had installed when he'd made this upstairs an open-concept apartment for himself and his wife. Lucky for her he'd retired and moved to Florida a couple of years ago, when Layla bought the mansion. "Although I'll keep the island and turn it into a small bar." Fingers crossed the state would issue her permit to serve alcohol on the premises before her grand opening in a few weeks. She couldn't imagine hosting a show without serving something sophisticated to drink.

"This big space—" she wandered back into the living room, where they'd come in "—needs to be divided into smaller sections so I can display different art collections at the same time.

"I need to reconfigure the master bedroom to allow access to the bathroom from the main hall. That way I'll have two for public use. I'll use the remaining part of that room for my personal studio."

She couldn't wait to get back to painting and sculpting again—managing Blue Space gallery, in Los Angeles, over the past few years had made it difficult to pursue her own creativity.

"I assumed TK Construction will do the work?" Mia asked.

"Yes. I'd do the modifications myself if I had more time." Her father had made sure all three of his kids could swing a hammer. "But since I'm in a rush, I hired the best in town."

Mia glanced at her watch. "Hey, I've got to get to the Coffee Palace. My shift starts in fifteen minutes."

That was another thing she and her sister would talk about. Mia working part-time at the Coffee Palace made no sense. At least not to Piper. "No worries." Piper picked up the cylinder containing the final floor plans for the gallery renovation. "I need to get going, too. I'm supposed to meet Mom at the diner. I'm going to give her these—" she tapped the cylinder "—and we're going to have lunch."

"That's right. She mentioned meeting up with you for lunch today when we spoke earlier." Mia looked her in the eye. "She's really happy you decided to come home. She's missed you."

"I know. And I'm glad I'm home, too." It felt good. Piper glanced around the space. It felt…right to come back now. "To new beginnings." She lifted her to-go coffee cup in the air.

Mia nodded and touched her cup to Piper's. "Cheers. I've really gotta go." She gave Piper a quick hug and started toward the exit. "Oh, one more thing." Mia stopped and turned to face her. "Big Brother is playing tonight at Donahue's."

Her eyes widened. "Nick Turner's band?"

Mia laughed. "Yes. They've gotten really good in the last few years."

"They must have if they're playing venues. What time does the band go on?"

"Eight."

"Sounds great. I'll see you there."

Mia gave her a thumbs-up. "Bye." She gave a little wave before she left.

Piper slung her purse and the cylinder containing the gallery floor plans over her shoulder. Stepping into the small hall, she locked the door and headed out.

Outside, the January cold surrounded her and she shivered. She was going to miss the warmer climate in LA, for sure, but at least the sun was shining. It took the edge off the frigid temperatures.

Piper walked along Main Street and passed the town entrance to the beach. The scent of salt and sea filled the air. In the summer months, umbrellas would dot the sand as far as the eye could see. Hordes of tourists and locals would bronze themselves beneath the sun and frolic in the salty ocean. Not a soul could be seen on the shore today. She passed by several tourist shops with signs in the windows indicating they were closed for the season. Crossing the street when she reached the New Suffolk Bank, she stepped inside the nearby diner.

Mom waved from a booth in the rear.

She strode over and dropped a kiss on her mother's cheek. Removing her winter parka, she slid into the booth opposite her.

"Don't you look lovely." Mom smiled.

Piper glanced at herself. The black trousers and teal long-sleeved, fitted, button-down cotton blouse with matching belt and low black pumps were more casual than the work attire she would normally wear, but this was small-town Massachusetts, not Los Angeles. "Thanks. I've made arrangements to meet with an artist later this afternoon whose work I want to feature in the gallery, so I wanted to change out of my comfy travel clothes."

"I already ordered our meals," Mom said.

"Oh, great." She grabbed the tube containing her floor plans. "I'm surprised you wanted to go over these here instead of the TK offices."

"I don't anticipate any significant changes since the last time we reviewed them. This way we get to have lunch together."

Piper smiled. Yes, it was good to be home. She handed the cylinder to Mom. "And these are perfect as is."

"Great. I'll take a look at the schedule and let you know who's available to start the renovations."

"No need." Piper waved off the notion. "I already spoke to Levi. He can start the day after tomorrow."

She and Levi Turner had kept in constant communication over the past few months so he could hit the ground running as soon as the building permits were approved.

"Okay." Mom nodded her head. "I'll give him the plans. He'll let you know if he has any questions."

A waitress approached with three dishes in her hand. "A Greek salad with chicken for you." She placed one of the plates in front of Piper. "And the same for you." She set an identical dish in front of Mom.

"I see you're planning to have leftovers." Piper pointed to the to-go container the server handed mom.

"Yes." Mom chuckled.

"Where would you like this?" The waitress gestured to the third plate.

"You can set that right here." Mom pointed to the empty space beside her.

"Who's that for?" Piper asked when the waitress left. "Is someone else joining us?"

Instead of answering, Mom stood and waved her hand in the air, as if trying to get someone's attention.

A tall man, in his late thirties if she had to guess, appeared in front of the table. He wore a gray suit with a white dress shirt and a gray-and-red striped tie. Formal attire for the diner, if you asked her.

"Hello, Jane." The man smiled.

"Blake." Mom slid out of her seat. "Please, join us. I hope you're in the mood for a turkey club."

"Oh." Blake gave a hesitant nod. "Sure. Sounds great."

Piper crooked a brow and sent an inquiring glance at her mother as Blake slid into the booth. She mouthed silently, "What's going on?"

Mom flashed an I-have-no-idea-what-you're-talking-about smile.

"You must be Piper," Blake said.

"I am." She offered him her hand and he shook it.

"Blake is the new bank president," Mom said.

Why was the new bank president joining them for lunch?

"I'll let you two talk." Mom dumped the contents of her plate into the plastic container the server had handed her earlier. She grabbed her purse, the salad and the tube containing the gallery floor plans. "See you later."

"Wait." Piper's eyes bugged out. "Where are you going?"

"I need to get back to the office." Mom flashed a quick smile and bolted before Piper could object further.

What the hell? She turned her attention back to Blake. "I'm sorry about that."

"It's no trouble. I'm sure she wanted to give us some privacy to discuss matters."

Discuss what matters? What was going on? She drew in a deep breath and blew it out.

Blake removed the turkey from the sandwich and set it aside. "I'm a vegetarian," he explained. "But I didn't want to be rude to your mother."

Great. Just great. You missed that little nugget, Mom. Your investigative skills are failing you. "I can order something else for you, if you'd like."

"No, thanks. This is fine." He lifted the sandwich, pausing before he bit into it. "So, what questions did you have?"

"I'm sorry. You have me at a disadvantage. I don't know what you're talking about."

His brows furrowed. "I'm here to talk to you about what types of business accounts we offer so you can find the type that best suits your needs."

"I opened my business accounts at your bank a few months ago." She'd worked with one of his employees last summer when she'd come home to meet with the town's planning and zoning department. Piper dug into her purse and withdrew the business card the man had given her and handed it to Blake.

"Ah." Blake nodded and handed the card back to her. "Your mother must not have known. We talked when she came in yesterday and she was under the impression you could use some advice."

Piper's gaze widened. Her mother knew damned well she'd already opened her business accounts. She'd gone with her to do some banking that very day.

"She suggested we meet for dinner—"

A red haze filled her vision. She didn't hear the rest of what Blake was saying.

Piper couldn't believe it. She'd been back in New Suffolk for less than twenty-four hours and her mother was up to her old tricks. Again.

How dare she try to set her up? With the bank president, no less.

Mom had made it her mission to find Piper a husband, even though that was the last thing she wanted. Why couldn't her mother understand that?

Blake shot her a quizzical glance.

Piper sighed. "I'm sorry this misunderstanding has inconvenienced you, Blake." She would read her mother the riot act for sure. For all the good it would do.

"It's no trouble." Blake grinned. "After all, I got a free lunch." He pointed to his plate. "I should get back to the bank."

Piper flashed a nervous smile. "Of course. Thanks again for coming this afternoon. And again, I apologize for the misunderstanding."

Blake smiled. He rose from the table and headed out.

Piper grabbed her cell and called her sister. "Did you know about this?" she demanded when Mia answered.

"Know about what?"

Piper dragged a hand through her hair. "That this lunch with Mom was really a setup?"

"What are you talking about? A setup for what?" Mia asked.

Piper explained.

"Oh, no. She's at it again," Mia said.

"Yes. How am I going to stop her?" Piper wasn't interested in dating Blake, or any of the others her mother had tried to set her up with over the years.

Mia sighed. "She just wants you to be happy."

"I *am*." Which was more than she could say for her mother. Piper couldn't imagine loving someone as much as her mother had loved her father. Fifteen years after Dad's death, she was still devastated by the loss.

"I don't need a man to make me happy." No way would she end up like her mother.

Cooper Turner concentrated on the files in front of him. Once again, his gaze strayed to the upper right corner of his desk, like a grisly image you couldn't turn away from. The large white envelope embossed with a lace pattern taunted him.

He refocused on the task at hand. His response for the wedding wasn't due for another week. Not that he could decline the invitation. He'd agreed to be Everett Burke's best man months ago, but things had changed since then. Now he couldn't bring himself to drop the response card in the mail.

Cooper closed his eyes and allowed his shoulders and back to melt into the soft, cushioned leather of his chair. He drew in a deep breath and exhaled, enjoying the moment of peace and quiet after another chaotic day at work.

"You're still here." Levi's voice echoed in the now-empty Turner Kavanaugh Construction headquarters.

Maybe his brother would go away if he didn't acknowledge him? Cooper kept his eyes closed and remained still.

"I know you can hear me and I'm not going away," Levi continued.

He let out a muffled curse and opened his eyes. "It's seven thirty. Shouldn't you be home with your son?"

"Noah is with his mother tonight. I don't have to be anywhere right now." Levi arched a brow. "What are you doing here this late?"

"I'm working." Coop gestured to his desk.

"We both know you're caught up on all of your projects."

He wouldn't deny it. There was nothing that couldn't wait until morning.

"Come out with me tonight. We can go to Donahue's."

He shook his head. "I'm not in the mood."

"I get it." His brother shuffled into the office and dropped down in the chair in front of his desk. "You've been in a funk since Rachel broke things off with you. That's normal. I went through the same thing when Wendy and I split, but you have to get on with your life."

He dragged his fingers through his hair. None of it made any sense. They'd spent two fantastic years together. Why had she ended things between them?

"You can't keep hiding out here," Levi said.

What his brother didn't know—what no one knew—was he'd planned to ask Rachel to marry him. The receipt for the diamond solitaire set high on a thin platinum band still sat in his wallet as a sad reminder.

What a fool he'd made of himself. There he'd sat at a table for two at the little hole-in-the-wall Italian restaurant they'd found on their first date. Rachel had fallen in love with the romantic ambience. He'd loved the food. Of course he'd booked a table at her favorite place to pop the question.

He'd started the evening with such optimism. The waiter would bring Rachel's favorite starter. The lightly breaded fried calamari with capers in a tasty lemon sauce was his favorite, too. They'd enjoy their favorite meals: vegetable lasagna for her, chicken piccata for him. Rachel would ask him for a bite of his chicken and end up eating his meal because it tasted much better than hers, and he'd eat her lasagna, but he wouldn't care. He'd get down on one knee after they'd eaten their cannoli and the restaurant owner would bring a chilled bottle of his best champagne to celebrate their engagement.

He should have left after thirty minutes of waiting but he'd stayed. An hour later, he'd convinced himself she'd left the office late and was stuck in traffic, even though all his calls to her went straight to voice mail. The waiter approached at some point with a large vase of water—for the two dozen red roses he'd brought, so they wouldn't wilt any more than they already had.

He'd never forget the look of pity on the owner's face when he came over to inform him they were closing soon.

Cooper shook his head. He'd trashed the flowers and tipped the waiter two hundred bucks for the bread and bottle of wine he'd consumed. It was the least he could do for taking up a table for four hours on a Saturday night.

Rachel's text came as he sat in the cab on his way back to the upscale hotel in Boston on the water—so much for the romantic evening he'd planned for the two of them. He hated sentences that started with *we need to talk*, especially when they came from a woman.

It's me, not you, she'd told him.

Yes, he was a fool all right.

"Big Brother is playing tonight. You know how Mom likes us all to go when Nick's playing," Levi said.

Coop snorted. "You're as bad as Mom with the guilt."

"Whatever works, bro."

Coop heaved out a resigned sigh. "Fine. Donahue's it is. Maybe we can get a quick game in before Nick starts playing."

"Sounds good. Let's get out of here." Levi jerked his head toward the exit. "I'll even buy the first round, cuz I'm such a nice guy."

"Yeah, right." Coop rolled his eyes skyward. He rose, flicked off the light on his desk and followed his brother out.

"Wanna ride?" Levi asked as they strode to the parking lot.

"Nah. I'll take my own car." Coop waved off the offer. That way he could leave whenever he wanted to.

"Okay. See you there." Levi slid behind the wheel of his SUV and started the engine.

He did the same and pulled out of the TK Construction parking lot.

Coop pulled his car into the parking lot at Donahue's a few minutes later. He hated driving his Camaro in the winter weather and couldn't wait for the repair shop to finish fixing his truck. It was just his luck that someone slammed into his F-150 when it was parked at the mall a few weeks ago. Whoever hit him hadn't bothered to leave a note. Worse, the repair shop was having trouble locating the parts they needed to fix his vehicle.

This time he'd take every precaution to protect his car. He pulled into a spot far away from all the others.

He hopped out and headed toward the back entrance.

"Wait up, Cooper," a voice called from behind him.

Every muscle in his body stiffened. He knew that voice all too well. He turned. "Rachel." His heart slammed against his chest hard enough to break a rib. Damn it. He should have known she'd show up tonight. Thanks to him, Big Brother was one of her favorite bands, too.

"No Tom tonight?" He couldn't hide the sarcasm in his voice. It still stung, even after all these months, that she dumped him for his best friend. Talk about a kick in the teeth.

"He's working late. I'm meeting a friend of mine from work. Um, about Tom—"

She raised her left hand. That was when he saw it. "What the hell?" He stared at the massive rock on her third finger. "You're engaged to Tom?"

She jerked at the anger—or shock?—in his tone. "Yes. He asked me a few days ago."

Coop didn't know what to say. The woman he'd wanted to marry planned to marry someone else. His heart iced over and it would stay that way.

No way would he ever let another woman get close enough to melt it.

Piper heard the din of the crowd as she approached the front entrance to Donahue's Irish Pub. She stared through the glass door. The place was packed. Grabbing the handle, she pulled the door open and stepped inside. She peered around. The long, glossy wood bar sat to her right with a couple of dozen high wood chairs. Four square, high-top tables stood in a not-so-straight line in the center of the room. Booths with green leather benches lined the outside perimeter of the room and three round tables in the back. Three pool tables stood in the space to her left.

The place looked exactly the same as it had the last time she came here. Right down to the sports paraphernalia that covered every inch of the walls, except for the spots where beer signs hung. However, the owner had finally upgraded the old televisions to flat screens.

It seemed surreal to be back in New Suffolk again. Time seemed to have stood still here while the rest of the world marched on, or maybe it was just that Los Angeles had been the complete opposite of life in this sleepy seaside town.

Still, she liked the fact that things stayed the same around here. Took comfort in the fact that people here built businesses that lasted, like Donahue's Irish Pub, and the Coffee Palace. She would, too.

"Hey, Piper." Nick Turner came up and gave her a big bear hug. "Welcome home. Glad you made it tonight."

She grinned. "Thanks. I'm looking forward to hearing you guys play."

Nick released her and draped his arm around the petite blonde who stood by his side. "You remember my fiancée, Isabelle, don't you?"

Piper nodded. "We met last spring." When she'd come back for her sister's thirtieth birthday party. "It's nice to see you again."

"You, too." Isabelle seemed…uncomfortable. Yes, that word best described the vibe she gave off.

"Hey, I've got to get back to the band. We're starting in a few minutes. Oh, Abby said you were going to join them. She's with Elle, Layla and your sister at one of the tables in front of the stage," Nick said.

"Great. Thanks." She had been wondering how she was going to find them with all the people here.

"Catch you later." Nick grasped Isabelle's hand and strode toward the back of the room.

Piper followed suit. As she walked through the crowd, she spotted a group of guys she remembered from high school. As she got closer to their table, she heard one of the guys chanting, "Chug, chug, chug." The others joined in, except for one guy who lifted his growler and slugged the entire sixty-four ounces of beer in one shot.

Piper rolled her gaze skyward. Of all the foolish, juvenile... This wasn't high school anymore. They were adults. "At least some of us are," she murmured to herself.

She caught a glimpse of Elle Patterson waving at her out of the corner of her eye and headed over to where she sat.

"Good. You found us," Mia said when Piper sat in the only empty chair at the table.

"How are you settling in to your new place?" Layla asked.

"Great. I'm going to love living in your old apartment above the Coffee Palace," Piper answered.

"And I love having a new neighbor now that Layla has moved in with her hot EMT." Elle sipped from her glass of white wine.

"Eww." Mia made a face. "That's our brother you're talking about."

"Yeah." Piper plucked up a tortilla chip covered with gooey cheese from the plate of nachos in the center of the table. "It's hard to think of Shane as 'hot.'" It was also a little weird that her brother's girlfriend was *her* friend, as well. Not to mention her business landlord.

Funny how that had never happened before, given New Suffolk was such a small town, and their closeness in age—the three of them were only a little more than a year apart—but it hadn't.

She glanced around. "Which server is ours? I'd like to order a glass of wine."

"Yes. I need a refill." Layla lifted her empty glass. "Oh, there she is."

The light glinted off Elle's necklace as she waved to their server.

The woman nodded as she passed by with a full tray.

"I love your choker," Piper said to Elle.

"Oh, thanks. I got it at the jewelers in town. You know, the one next door to the diner. Now that the son has taken over, they're finally selling some modern pieces."

Piper nodded. "I'll check it out."

"In the meantime…" Abby propped her elbows on the table and laced her fingers together. Attention trained on Piper, she said, "I want to hear about the gallery you're opening."

Elle nodded. "Me, too."

"What do you want to know?" Piper asked.

"What made you decide on opening a place here?" Abby tucked a lock of titian hair behind her ear. "I mean, you can't compare New Suffolk to Los Angeles, or New York."

"True," Piper agreed. "But our quaint little town has a lot to offer. Sandy beaches in the summer, the harvest celebration in the fall and Christmas festivities throughout December. All of these events bring tons of people here each year, and I plan on taking advantage of that."

"And don't forget the annual ice art festival in the middle of February," Elle added.

"Exactly." Piper grinned. "That event is gaining in popularity. Groups from all over the East Coast come to New Suffolk during that time."

"Your plans sound awesome," Elle said. "I'm so excited for you."

"We're all happy for you," Abby agreed. "We need more female-owned businesses in this town."

"Like you," Mia said. "And Layla, of course."

"That's right." Abby grinned. "Everyone loves coffee. And the amazing French fusion food Layla cooks."

"I know I do." Piper lifted both arms in the air and lowered her palms to the table. "All hail the Coffee Palace and The Sea Shack."

Everyone laughed.

How lucky was she to have found such a great group of friends since she'd decided to return home? They'd included her in their circle and offered their friendship and support the moment she'd met them.

"So, when is the grand opening?" Elle asked.

"The first day of the ice art festival," she answered.

"That's only five weeks away," Abby gasped. "How are you going to do it? You're going to have to renovate the space to make it work for what you want to do and all of the local construction companies are booked for months," Abby continued. "I tried getting someone in to make a few minor changes to the Coffee Palace last month and no one was available until this summer."

"You should have told me." Mia turned her attention to Abby. "Our family co-owns TK Construction. I know they're busy, but I'm sure someone can help you before then."

"You own TK Construction?" Abby asked.

"Technically my mother and Ron Turner own the

company," Piper said. "Ron and my father started the business almost thirty-five years ago."

"I never knew TK stood for Turner Kavanaugh," Elle said.

Piper picked up another tortilla chip from the plate. "Most people don't, since it's just initials."

"Any chance you can ask someone from TK to come out and give me an estimate?" Abby asked.

"Sure." Mia smiled. "It's too bad we didn't know earlier. Piper could have asked our mother to set something up for you when she had lunch with her today."

Piper cringed as she remembered the fiasco with the bank president. "I could have, if I'd actually had lunch with Mom."

"Oh, right." Mia sighed.

"Did something happen?" Layla asked. "Is Jane okay?"

"She's fine." Piper rolled her gaze skyward and related the story.

Abby, Layla and Elle chuckled.

"Do you have any idea how embarrassed I was?" Piper asked.

"I can only imagine," Elle agreed. "Do you think he realized what was going on?"

"He didn't let on if he did." She shook her head.

"Unfortunately, this isn't the first time Mom has tried this," Mia said.

"Oh, do tell." Layla grinned.

Piper rested her elbows on the table and steepled her fingers. "The most recent time was last year. She tried to set me up with one of my coworkers when she came out to LA to visit me. And yes, *he* definitely understood what she was up to."

Abby doubled over laughing. "Oh, God. I would have been mortified."

Heat flooded her face just remembering George's re-action. "What's even worse is that he was interested." He'd confessed to having a crush on her for a long time.

"But you weren't," Elle stated.

"Actually, I was. He was pretty damn hot." Piper grinned. "But I got the feeling he was looking for something long-term, and that was the last thing I wanted." She shrugged. "I'm not looking for anything serious right now." *Not ever.* "I just wish my mother could understand."

"Maybe you should find a fake boyfriend," Elle suggested. "That would get your mother off your back."

Her eyes went wide. "That's not a bad idea."

Mia shook her head. "It won't work. Mom would double down on her efforts the minute Piper ended the relationship."

Mia was right. Piper's shoulders slumped. Mom was relentless.

The server breezed by their table again without stopping.

Piper stood. "I'm going to go to the bar. Anyone else want anything?"

Elle and Layla rattled off their requests.

"Coming right up." Piper made her way through the crowd to the bar and placed her order.

A man stepped up beside her while she waited for the bartender to return with her drinks. Her pulse soared. With those bulging biceps on display and that thick, wavy golden brown, hair...he looked like a Greek god. Not to mention that hard-core five o'clock shadow. *Oh, yeah. Sexy as all get-out.* She wasn't looking for Mr. Forever, but he could be Mr. Right Now.

"Hey, Cooper. What'll you have?" the bartender asked.

Cooper? No. It couldn't be. She jerked her gaze back to the man and stared.

"I'll take a Macallan on the rocks," the man said.

Shit. She'd know that voice anywhere. "Cooper Turner," Piper blurted.

He didn't respond.

Maybe she was wrong? This wasn't the tall, gangly geek with shaggy hair she remembered. Not with those broad shoulders and lean, narrow hips. Lord have mercy!

The man shot a side-glance her way. "Piper Kavanaugh." He couldn't hide the disdain in his voice. "Heard you were back in town." He looked none too pleased about it.

"Yes." She'd known they wouldn't be able to avoid each other the way they had during her few and brief visits home over the years, but she'd hoped to evade him for at least a little while. She should have realized he'd come to see his brother play, but she hadn't given it any thought when Mia had mentioned Nick's band was playing tonight.

Cooper grabbed his glass, slugged down the contents, and walked away without another word.

The old anger and resentment roiled around inside her as potent as ever.

What had she expected? That he'd welcome her with open arms—like his brothers had? *Hah!* Cooper Turner didn't care about anyone but himself.

This was the guy who'd played countless pranks over the years and left her to take the blame when things went wrong.

Her father had loved him like another son. And Cooper…couldn't even pay his respects when Dad passed.

He thought no one had noticed him leave—moments

after he and his family had arrived—and go skateboarding in the funeral parlor parking lot during Dad's wake.

Her lips tightened into a thin line. *She* had.

Piper shook her head. How could he have done such a thing?

Cooper stopped walking when one of the guys she'd recognized from high school grabbed his arm and shoved a chair at him. He placed his empty glass on the table and picked up the beer one of the other guys slid toward him.

"Chug, chug, chug," the guys started chanting.

Cooper grinned and lifted his growler.

She ripped her gaze away. He might be gorgeous and sexy, but it was clear to her he was still the same jerk she remembered.

Chapter Two

Piper walked into the TK Construction offices the next morning at eight o'clock sharp. She couldn't be late for her meeting.

"Hi, Piper." Laura Hawkins smiled at her as she approached the reception desk. "Welcome back. It's so nice to see you again."

"It's nice to see you, too. Your hair looks fantastic."

Laura grinned and touched her fingers to her short bob with blond highlights. "This is my post-divorce hairdo. My friends say it takes twenty years off me. I guess that means I can pass for a woman in her mid-thirties." Laura winked.

"Maybe even younger." Piper nodded. "Is my mother in her office?" She'd called this morning and asked if they could meet at the Coffee Palace for breakfast to discuss a couple of things regarding her layouts. Piper assumed Levi must have had questions when he'd reviewed her final plans. Given what happened at the diner yesterday, Piper wasn't taking any chances. She'd insisted they meet at the TK offices. Once bitten, twice shy.

"Let me check." Laura picked up the phone on her desk.

Piper peered around the lobby as she waited. They needed to redecorate. It hadn't changed since she was last here years ago, except… She walked over to where two large photos sat mounted on the wall that stood to the left side of the double glass doors separating the lobby from the offices. Each sleek metal frame held an image of an ice sculpture. The first was a massive dragon with its wings spread wide and the second an enormous, graceful swan.

"Your mom will be out in a minute." Laura came to stand beside her. "Aren't they fantastic?"

"Yes," Piper agreed.

"This one won first place at the festival last year." Laura pointed to the dragon.

Piper could see why. The details on the piece were incredible. The scales on the beast looked almost lifelike. "Who is the artist?" A TK employee maybe, or it could be an artist TK had sponsored. She wondered if it were too late to find her own artist to sponsor?

Laura opened her mouth to speak just as her mother burst through the double doors.

"Sweetheart." Mom hugged Piper and gave her a quick peck on the cheek. "You're right on time. Come on back." She yanked open one of the glass doors and gestured for Piper to precede her.

Piper stepped into the hall and Mom followed.

"Head into the conference room. We're set up for you in there."

"You don't need to do that. Your office is fine. It's just going to be you, me and Levi, and the table in your office is big enough to review the drawings." Piper stopped short and turned to face her mother. "Oh, and by the way. I won't be having dinner with the bank president."

Her mother shot a perplexed expression in Piper's direction. "Excuse me?"

"Are you going to deny you tried to set me up with Blake?"

"I don't know what you're talking about, darling." Jane darted into the conference room.

Piper gritted her teeth and followed her in. "You need to stop—" She froze when she spotted Cooper sitting at the conference table. Dressed in a pair of tan trousers and a navy button-down shirt, he looked even yummier than last night.

No, no, no. Jerk. *Remember? Get a grip.*

Piper sucked in a deep, steadying breath. "Where is Levi? I thought we were meeting with him this morning."

"We can finish up later, Jane." Cooper stood and headed for the door.

"Stop," Mom commanded.

Piper gawked at her mother. What was going on?

Jane pointed to the table. "Please have a seat, Cooper. You, too, Piper."

Her gaze narrowed. What was her mother up to now? She wasn't going to stay here and find out. "I only have thirty minutes before my next meeting." Piper glanced at her watch. Okay, that was a little white lie. She wasn't supposed to meet with a sculptor, whose work she wanted to feature when she opened her gallery, for another couple of hours, but... She headed toward the exit. "I'll find Levi and—"

"Levi isn't here," Mom cut in.

Piper executed a 180-degree turn. "What do you mean? I thought we were supposed to go over the floor plans for my gallery?"

"That's what I'm trying to do. Now—" Mom huffed out a breath "—if you would both sit down, we can get started."

"What are you talking about, Jane?" Cooper began.

"Mom, Levi should be here for this," Piper reiterated.

This *couldn't* be what she thought it was. Why would Mom even suggest such a thing? Okay, Mom didn't know about what Cooper had done at her father's wake, no one in her family did, but she did know about all the jerky pranks he'd played on her over the years.

Why would her mother believe Piper would agree with her suggestion?

"You." Mom pointed to Cooper and spoke in a calm, rational manner. "Are the only TK employee who has availability in your schedule to accommodate Piper's tight timeline."

Piper shook her head. "But Levi said…"

Her mother propped her elbows on the table and steepled her fingers. She looked Piper in the eye. "He is already slated for another project. Which he would have realized if he'd double-checked the schedule before making a commitment to you."

"What about—" Cooper began.

Mom held up a hand. "All the crews are out on other jobs right now. I wish I had an alternative, but I don't. Unless—" she peered at Piper "—you're willing to hold off on your renovations until someone else becomes available."

Piper dragged a hand through her hair and blew out a breath. "You know I can't do that." She'd already lost months due to permit delays. Not to mention all the money she'd paid out in rent for a business that wasn't generating any income. Thank goodness her boss had allowed her to stay on at her job in LA until things got straightened out here; otherwise she would have gone under before she'd ever opened her doors. "The gallery needs to open at the start of the ice art festival." She couldn't afford to wait any longer.

Cooper leaned back in his chair and folded his arms in front of his chest. "Then I guess you're stuck with me." His tone challenged her to deny it.

She couldn't, even though she wanted to.

They'd have to spend almost every day of the next five weeks together. Piper groaned. She opened her mouth to object, but her mother cut her off before she could say anything.

"This is the *only* solution I can offer you. We hadn't anticipated taking on this extra work right now. I know it's not your fault the town took so long to approve your permits, but the timing sucks for TK."

Piper gritted her teeth. What choice did she have if she wanted to make her new business venture a success? *None, that's what.* "Okay."

Cooper nodded. "I'll order the materials today." He extended his hand to her.

Piper hesitated for a brief moment, then pressed her palm to his. A bolt of electricity shot through her. Cooper felt it, too, if his surprised expression was anything to go by. She jerked her hand away.

Lord help her. She'd just made a deal with the devil.

Thirty minutes later, Piper exited the TK Construction offices. She glanced at her watch. She had plenty of time to grab a coffee before her meeting with the sculptor.

Piper drove the short distance to the Coffee Palace and parked in an empty space on Main Street. She walked inside.

"Hey, Piper." Elle smiled. "What can I get for you today?"

"I'll take a large toasted almond coffee." She glanced at all of the pastry trays. "And one of those chocolate cupcakes." She'd need to run five miles to work off the calories for the copious amounts of creamy frosting alone, but it would be so worth it.

Mia walked into the front of the shop from the kitchen. "Hey, sis. How did your meeting with Levi go? Oo-oh, not so good, if the look on your face is anything to go by."

"Levi has been assigned to another project. Cooper will be completing the renovations for the gallery."

"Oh, boy," Mia said.

"Why is that a problem?" Elle asked.

Mia snorted. "Piper and Cooper don't get along."

Elle propped her hands on the counter and sent an inquiring glance Piper's way. "Oh, do tell, because last night, I was pretty sure you felt differently."

"What?" Mia's jaw nearly hit the floor.

Elle smirked. "I saw Piper checking him out when she was standing at the bar."

"Ah…" Mia still wore a stunned expression. "I think you need to explain."

Piper sucked in a deep breath and exhaled slowly. "There's nothing to explain. Cooper and I don't get along. Never have. Never will."

Mia chuckled. "You guys have rubbed each other the wrong way since you were in diapers." She turned to Elle and grinned. "Apparently Cooper stole one of Piper's toys and she's never forgiven him."

Piper straightened her shoulders. "That was the first of many indiscretions over the years."

"This is true. Let's see. Whoopee cushions left on the teachers' chairs and fake tarantula spiders let loose in the cafeteria come to mind." Mia turned thoughtful. "Some of the more memorable offences included setting alarm clocks to go off at various hours in the early morning during the eighth-grade class trip to Camp Jewel, and, oh, the toothpaste cookies—I can't remember when that happened."

Piper's lips tightened. "Home Economics, freshman year. We thought he was being nice when he offered them to our team."

Elle grinned. "Cooper sounds like quite the prankster."

"Oh, yes." Mia snapped her fingers. "The water balloons he and his friends dropped on you guys at what's-her-name's sweet sixteen. And of course, there was the skunk incident."

"Skunk incident? What happened?" Elle's gaze widened and she rubbed her hands together. "Details, please."

Piper shot Mia an I-am-going-to kill-you look.

Mia smirked. "Have you ever been over to the Turner house?" she asked.

Elle shook her head.

"They have a lot of acreage and in the back, near the property line, there's an open field. We used to ride dirt bikes—"

"You and Shane used to ride with Nick, Levi and Cooper," Piper corrected.

Elle studied her from head to toes, taking in her persimmon-colored stretch sheath dress and her cream leather boots. "Definitely not a mini bike kind of girl."

Piper straightened her shoulders. "Absolutely not."

"Anyway," Mia continued. "We used to have bonfires on the weekends in the cooler months as well. A bunch of kids from school would come and we'd all hang out. It was tons of fun."

"It was," Piper agreed. "Until Valentine's Day my senior year of high school."

"So, what happened?" Elle looked from Piper to Mia and back to Piper again.

Piper heaved out a sigh. "As usual, we were all hanging out at the bonfire all afternoon. It was about four o'clock and a bunch of us girls were getting ready to head home and get ready for the Seniors' Sweetheart Dance."

"Some of the guys, including Cooper, had been riding around on the dirt bikes earlier," Mia added. "Apparently, one of the guys dared Cooper to jump over the fire on his bike."

Elle shook her head. "Please tell me he wasn't foolish enough to agree."

"No can do, girlfriend," Piper scoffed. "The fool backed up the bike and turned the throttle full force. He headed straight for the flames."

"But he chickened out at the last minute," Mia said. "He swerved around the fire."

"Driving at top speed. A bunch of us were in his path. He came straight at us."

Elle's eyes widened. "Oh my God. Did he run into you?"

"No." Piper shook her head. "Everyone ran for it and luckily no one got hurt." Although they would have if Cooper hadn't ditched the bike to avoid crashing into them. Not that Cooper would have cared. He'd hadn't given a damn about anyone else. He'd bolted instead of sticking around to make sure everyone was okay.

Not true.

Cooper had left to go to the hospital. She and her friends may not have been injured, but he'd suffered a concussion and a broken arm.

Which she hadn't learned until the next day, so yeah, that evening, she'd thought him heartless.

Looking back on it now, *she* was the one who hadn't cared. Worse, she'd been a complete jerk to him, too.

Piper clenched her hands into tight fists. She was just so damned angry with him. All the pranks he'd played on her over the years. Not paying his respects at her father's wake. It had all melded together that evening and, well, she'd lost it with him. Big-time.

Not one of my finer moments. Piper sighed.

Elle's brows furrowed. "So, where does the skunk come in?"

"Remember how Piper said everyone ran for it?" Mia asked. Not waiting for Elle's answer, she added, "Piper ran into the shed at top speed.

"Fun fact." Mia's eyes danced with delight. "One of the common places skunks make their winter dens are in sheds."

Elle gasped. "You got sprayed." She doubled over in a fit of laughter.

Piper rolled her eyes. "I stunk to high heaven, even after I washed with peroxide and tomato juice."

"That tomato juice thing is just a myth." Mia grinned. "It doesn't take away the smell."

"My date dumped me. No one would get near me." Piper gritted her teeth. Was it any wonder she and Cooper didn't get along? "Worst Valentine's Day ever."

"I don't know, I still think you have the hots for Cooper." Elle flashed a smug smile.

An image of him formed in her head. His sexy smile sent shivers down her spine. "Not in this lifetime."

"Thanks a lot, Levi." Cooper marched into his brother's office in the TK Construction building. Bright sunlight filtered in the small space through the shuttered blinds, casting a glow on the potted plants set on a bookshelf near the window. The faint sound of rock music played from the computer set atop his brother's gleaming metal-and-glass desk. "I thought you were going to handle Piper's gallery renovations."

Levi held up his hands as if surrendering. "I thought I was free, but Jane already had me scheduled to handle a new client. I'm sorry."

Cooper dropped down into the seat opposite his brother. "Let me take the new customer." *Please.*

"I can't. It's the Xaviers. I did their kitchen reno about five years ago. They're remodeling their master bed and bath and asked for me by name."

"Come on." Coop scrubbed his hands over his face. He looked up at his brother. "Is there really no one else who can do this?"

"You're it. Everyone else is tied up on another job."

"I *so* don't need this right now." Coop shook his head.

"What's up?" Levi propped his elbows up on his desk.

Coop closed his eyes for a moment and sucked in a deep breath. "I saw Rachel at Donahue's last night."

His brother nodded. "Yeah. I saw her, too. I was hoping that with all those people there you might have missed her."

He shook his head. "No such luck. I ran into her in the parking lot on my way in. She and Tom got engaged a few days ago."

Levi's gaze widened before he pinned a neutral expression in place. "Good riddance."

He let loose a derisive laugh. "Leave it to you to give it to me straight."

Levi shook his head. "The woman cheated on you for more than two months before she finally ended things."

"I know. I know." He dragged a hand through his

hair. His head understood that it was over between them, but his heart… Wasn't involved anymore. He'd been upset when Rachel shared her news last night, but truth be told, he'd forgotten about her the minute he spotted Piper. God, she'd always been beautiful, but the woman she'd turned into… Long blond hair kissed by the sun, sky blue eyes, curves in all the right places…

What was wrong with him? He was *not* interested in Piper Kavanaugh. The woman was wound tighter than the Timex watch his father wore.

"I agree," Levi smirked. "Rachel is pretty uptight."

He jerked his gaze to his brother. "What are you talking about?"

Levi stared at him as if he were delusional. "You just muttered something about her being wound tight."

He hadn't realized he'd said that aloud. "I was talking about Piper."

Levi's brows furrowed. "How did we go from Rachel to Piper?"

He'd been thinking of her. How the smile she'd flashed at him when he first stepped up to the bar… could light up the darkest skies.

No, no, no. Once she'd recognized him the brilliance had faded to distain. Suddenly everything was his fault again.

His mind drifted back to that night she'd been sprayed by the skunk.

Cooper blinked and opened his eyes. Multiple faces filled his view. What was he doing lying on the ground?

Everyone was shouting at the same time. "Are you all right? Are you hurt?"

The bike. He'd dumped it to avoid hitting the group of girls. What an idiot he'd been to allow those guys to goad him into jumping the fire.

Levi appeared. He pushed all the others out of the way. "Can you sit up?" he asked.

He pushed up to a sitting position. Stars exploded in front of his eyes. His left arm throbbed.

Levi must have realized what happened. He removed Coop's helmet for him, muttering to himself about how Mom and Dad were going to kill him for letting his little brother pull such a crazy stunt.

"Help me up." Cooper extended his right hand to his brother and cradled his left arm against his chest.

Levi pulled him to his feet.

Everyone started clapping and he grinned.

Everyone started talking again. His head started to pound. He felt like he was going to get sick.

Levi looked at him and said something about getting him to a doctor. They started toward the house.

Piper appeared in front of him, blocking the path. She looked like...her whole world had come crashing down on her.

She started screaming at him, and if looks could kill, he'd be a goner for sure.

Cooper couldn't make out most of what she was saying but juvenile, it's your fault, and ruined everything came through loud and clear.

He started walking again. Levi's arm was around him propelling him forward.

Levi said something to Piper. It made her even angrier.

"I hate you, Cooper Turner," she said.

She looked as if she meant every word.

"Hello, Earth to Cooper." Levi waved his hand in front of Coop's face. "You still with me?"

Cooper blinked. "Yeah. Sorry."

"Where'd you go?" Levi stared at him as if he were trying to determine if he was okay.

You don't want to know. Cooper waved off the question. He focused his attention on his brother. "How the hell am I supposed to work with her?" She hadn't given a damn that he'd broken his arm in two places and received a mild concussion when he'd hit the ground all those years ago.

Levi shrugged. "You're a smart man. I'm sure you'll think of something."

He straightened his shoulders and gave his brother a pleading smile. "Can you at least talk to Jane for me? Have her reassign me."

Levi arched a brow. "What makes you think she'll listen to me any more than you?"

"I'm desperate here."

"For crying out loud." Levi rolled his gaze skyward. "Piper is not that bad."

"Are you kidding me?" Coop jumped up from his seat and started pacing back and forth. The girl had all the compassion of a snake about to eat its prey.

"Okay, okay." Levi spoke as if he was trying to placate a child. "I'll admit Piper can be a little…standoffish sometimes."

Cooper stopped midstride and turned to face his brother. He crossed his arms in front of his chest. "Well, that's a polite way of putting it." He'd have said she was arrogant, unfriendly and, yes, downright rude *all* of the time.

"I'm sure you'll figure out something."

Cooper shook his head. Convincing his brother to help him get out of this *was* his plan.

"It's only five weeks. What's the big deal?"

Thirty-five days of her hostility, the condescending attitude, that's what. "She has no sense of humor."

"Fine." Levi heaved out a sigh. "So she doesn't like to laugh."

"She needs to lighten up," Coop continued. "Have a little fun."

Levi threw his hands up in the air. "What does it matter? We're asking you to renovate her place, not date her."

Date Piper? A shiver of excitement ran through him.

He stiffened. *No way. Never gonna happen.* Not in this lifetime or any other.

Chapter Three

Piper grabbed her backpack and purse and headed out of her apartment. The overhead light lit the staircase as she walked down to the parking lot behind the Coffee Palace. Darkness still filled the early-morning sky. She wouldn't see the sun for at least another two hours this time of year.

She hurried to her car and drove the short distance to the mansion that housed her gallery.

Parking by the side entrance, she hopped out of the car and headed to the door.

Twin beams of light pierced the darkness. A moment later Cooper slid from the driver's seat of his car. She couldn't help admiring the sleek lines of his vintage Chevy Camaro. And the turquoise color with the two white stripes across the hood... Yeah, that was pretty hot.

"Hey." He wouldn't look at her. His body language indicated he'd rather be anywhere else but here with her.

"Morning." She practically choked out the word.

Piper blew out a breath. This wasn't going to work if this was how it was going to be between them. She tried again. "Thanks for agreeing to five a.m. starts."

"Not like I had any choice in the matter."

She gritted her teeth. The gallery was located above The Sea Shack, Layla's restaurant. Of course Layla would want the construction noise to stop when her customers were dining. They needed to start early in the day in order to finish up by noon.

"So…" Cooper arched a brow. "Are we going to stand here all morning chitchatting, or are you going to unlock the door so we can get started?"

Piper threw her hands up in the air. The man made it his mission in life to drive her crazy. "You are impossible."

He rolled his eyes. "Can we get to work now?"

Piper wanted to scream. She stabbed the combination of numbers on the keypad that unlocked the door and shoved it open. "Please." She gestured for him to precede her. "Don't let me hold you up." *Immature and juvenile. That's what you are.* She huffed out a breath.

He marched up the stairs, turning to face her when they reached the top. "I am neither immature nor juvenile," he shot at her.

"What?" How could he know what she was thinking?

He glared at her. "Are you going to deny that's what you just called me?"

Crap! She'd said that out loud? Not the smartest thing to do. Piper's shoulder slumped. Why was she letting him get to her? She folded her arms across her chest. "Nope. That's what I said. I call it like I see it."

"What are you talking about?" He mimicked her stance.

Besides the eye rolling of a few minutes ago? "You downed a whiskey the other night at Donahue's and followed it with a sixty-four-ounce beer chaser. Are you going to deny that?" She arched a brow.

His hands clenched into tight fists. "There you go judging me again. Did you ever stop to ask yourself why I would do such a thing?" He didn't wait for her to answer. "No, of course not. Once again, the Ice Queen convicts without knowing any of the facts." He walked away from her.

Ice Queen? Was that how he saw her? Her stomach twisted. No. He was just trying to make her mad. It was what he did. Piper glared at his back. "Fine. By all means, explain." She couldn't hide the sarcasm in her voice.

He turned back to face her. A muscle in his neck jerked. "I don't need to."

Of course not.

"I don't need your help today. I can handle the framing myself."

Her mouth fell open. He didn't want her around? No problem, because being here with him was the last thing she wanted. "Great. Have at it." Piper gestured to the pile of two-by-four planks stacked in the middle of the room.

She stormed down the stairs and exited the building. The slamming door punctuated her mood.

Piper drove the short distance back to her apartment. She glanced at the dashboard clock before hopping out of her car—5:30 a.m. The Coffee Palace would be open now. She walked around to the front of the building and entered the coffee shop.

"Hey, Piper." Elle waved from behind the counter. "What can I get you this morning?"

"A toasted almond coffee with cream and two stevia." She eyed the pastry trays. "And a chocolate cream–filled doughnut. Make it two." It was that kind of day.

"Two?" Elle eyed her curiously. "Are you okay?"

Piper blew out a breath. She was letting Cooper get to her again. She needed to clear her head. Only one way to do that. A jog on the beach. "On second thought, cancel the doughnuts."

Elle nodded. "A toasted almond coffee coming right up."

Five minutes later, Piper exited the Coffee Palace and made her way up to her apartment. She changed out of her jeans and sweatshirt and into a pair of fleece-lined yoga pants. Layering a moisture-wicking long-sleeved shirt under a zip-up jacket, she shoved her feet into her running shoes. She shrugged into a safety vest—it was still dark out—grabbed a water bottle, and headed out.

Piper set a brisk pace as she walked along Main Street. She didn't mind the cool temperature this morning. She might have goose bumps now, but she'd be sweating in a few minutes. She passed the New Suffolk Bank, the police station and the row of boutiques, turning when she reached the entrance to the town beach.

She peered around. Stars still twinkled in the clear dark sky, and the seagulls squawked in time with the waves crashing on shore.

She'd love to run like the wind with the sand beneath her feet. Having the entire beach to herself was what she needed right now.

But she'd settle for pounding the pavement on the main road until the sun came up. Piper retraced her steps and broke into a light jog when she reached the road. She'd forgotten just how beautiful New Suffolk could be at this time of year with the holiday lights still displayed on storefronts and streetlights.

She lengthened her stride, but even with all of the beauty surrounding her she couldn't find the serenity she desperately craved. Thoughts of Cooper kept intruding.

She wasn't an Ice Queen. She cared about others.

She'd even given him the benefit of the doubt and he refused to explain.

Not true, a little voice inside her head persisted.

Piper sighed and slowed her pace. Okay, so maybe she had convicted him without due process.

No maybe about it. She'd assessed the situation at face value. Acting as judge and jury, she'd found him guilty as charged. He was right about that.

Crap.

What was she going to do now?

Cooper hummed along to the music as he tapped the nails into the studs. Nailing them in at a forty-five-degree angle would provide the flexibility he needed to slide the frame into place. He'd shore it up after he confirmed the position was correct.

All of a sudden, the music stopped.

Why had the Bluetooth disconnected? He stuck the hammer in the looped holder attached to his belt and walked over to where he'd left his cell phone on the kitchen island.

Piper came into view.

Son of a gun. He so didn't need this right now. He'd had enough of her condemnation over the years.

Okay. Maybe, just maybe, he'd deserved some of it. As an adult, he could see how some of his childhood antics could've rubbed her the wrong way.

Still, she never stopped to consider what other people were going through.

His stomach plummeted as he remembered the service for her father.

Coop tugged at his tie as he walked into the building. It felt like a boa constrictor around his neck. And the suit jacket... He was going to sweat to death if he couldn't take it off soon.

"Stop fidgeting." Nick elbowed him in the ribs.

"Give him a break." Levi shoved Nick's arm away. "He's already green, if you haven't noticed."

Nick shook his head. "For Pete's sake, we're not kids anymore."

Maybe not, but at thirteen, Coop wasn't an adult either. He glanced back at the car. Maybe he could wait in there while Mom, Dad, Nick and Levi went in? No one would even notice he wasn't there, would they?

Nick grabbed the collar of his coat and Cooper jerked to a stop. "Don't even think about it."

"Lay off, Nick," Levi said.

"You think I want to go in there?" Nick pointed to the two-story brick Georgian manor that loomed in front of them. "Well, I don't, but we have to."

Coop's stomach churned. How could he face the Kavanaughs—especially Piper—when he was responsible for Victor's death?

He hadn't caused the heart attack, but if he'd called 911 faster, instead of freaking out when Victor fell to the ground, he might be alive today.

Dad turned to face them. "That's enough, boys." *He looked madder than he had when Nick and Levi got caught skipping school last year so they could go to the beach.*

Hands on her hips, Mom added, "Stop your arguing. You should know better."

They walked the rest of the way in silence.

The smell struck him when they stepped inside. Like they hadn't opened any windows since the turn of the century. All the dark wood made him feel like the walls were closing in on him. His insides lurched. He hated antique furniture, at least he did now.

Piper looked at him as he came into the room. *Your fault.* That's what the look on her face said. Sweat poured off him. He couldn't breathe.

Coop raised his hand to his tie again, but stopped when Levi glared at him.

They waited for what seemed like hours to go through the receiving line. Hushed whispers were the only sounds he heard.

It was their turn to kneel on the pew in front of the casket.

Nick and Levi dropped down.

Dad motioned for him to join them.

Coop swallowed hard.

It was one thing to be prepped for what he'd experience—Mom and Dad had done their best to explain what was going to happen since neither he or his brothers had ever been to a wake before—and something a hell of a lot different to go through it.

His stomach heaved. Cooper covered his mouth and bolted outside.

Dad found him puking in the bushes on the other side of the parking lot a few minutes later.

He helped him clean up and told him he didn't have to go back inside.

But Dad did.

How was Dad supposed to say goodbye to his best friend? How were any of them?

Coop wasn't sure how long he'd been sitting in Mom's Pathfinder, but the parking lot was almost empty now, so he figured it had been a while. When were his parents and brothers going to come back?

He stared at the massive brick building. All he wanted was to get away from this place. Now.

Coop needed to do something. Sitting here... His mind kept drifting back to that day. If he'd gone with Dad and Nick to grab lunch, he wouldn't have been there, but he'd stayed behind to help Victor tack up the Sheetrock on the wall they'd just framed.

When Victor fell to the ground... Tears flooded his eyes. No, no, no.

He jumped out of the SUV and dug around in the back for his skateboard.

The only thing he thought about was holding his balance as he glided back and forth across the parking lot.

Coop sucked in a lungful of much needed air. Finally, he could breathe.

He spotted Piper descending the stairs to the parking lot. The look on her face... His stomach plummeted.

Yep, she definitely blamed him for what had happened to her father.

"Cooper." Piper waved a hand in front of his face.

He blinked and looked around the space. *The art gallery.* Piper's place. He blew out a breath. He couldn't stop her from being here, but he wasn't going to allow her to start in on him again. He'd had enough of that over the years.

"You turned off my music." He wasn't accusing, just stating a fact.

She shrugged off her zip-up jacket and laid it on the counter next to his phone. "I called out to you a couple of times but you didn't answer."

He couldn't help noticing how the yoga pants and long-sleeved top she wore displayed her curves to perfection. Coop blew out a breath. *No, damn it.* What was wrong with him today? "What do you want?" He dragged a hand through his hair.

"To apologize."

Cooper stared at her and he was pretty sure his mouth was hanging open. No. He must have misunderstood what she'd just said. "Excuse me?"

Hands on hips, she shot him an annoyed glance. "I'm not going to say it again."

"For what?" He wasn't trying to be sarcastic. He just couldn't believe what he was hearing.

Piper looked him in the eyes. "You were right. I shouldn't have said what I did earlier."

"Um…thanks." He couldn't think of anything else to say. The truth was, he might have jumped to the same conclusion if he'd witnessed what she had. He'd downed the whiskey, after all.

"I didn't drink the beer." Coop wasn't sure why he told her that. He didn't owe her an explanation.

Piper's brows furrowed. "But I saw you—"

"I set it down without drinking any." It would have been foolish, and yes, juvenile. She was right about that.

Piper blew out a breath. "I was wrong to assume. I'm sorry."

His jaw nearly hit the ground. He couldn't help it. "I appreciate you saying that."

She opened her mouth. Closed it without saying anything, then opened it again. "I think we should call a truce." Her words came out in a rush.

His mouth gaped open. He couldn't have heard her right.

"We're both adults now. We shouldn't be sniping at each other."

She was right about that.

"I'm not proposing we become best friends. That's never going to happen."

She was right about that, too.

"But I do think we can be civil to each other while we're working together."

Could they? Neither of them had managed it thus far. Then again, neither of them had tried.

"What do you say?" She shot him a hopeful glance.

If she was willing to try, he could, too. "Count me in."

Chapter Four

The next morning, Piper stepped out onto the patio at the gallery that overlooked the ocean.

The stars had disappeared and hints of light touched the early-morning sky. She closed her eyes and breathed in the cold, salty air.

She couldn't remember the last time she'd experienced this sense of serenity.

"So this is where you disappeared to."

She opened her eyes and Cooper came into view.

"Yes." Piper crossed the deck and leaned her elbows on the railing.

"What are you doing out here?" he asked. "It's cold." Cooper ran his hands up and down his coatless arms.

"I haven't seen an East Coast sunrise in quite some time." She might have been up in time to see it yesterday morning, but with all the arguing they'd done, she'd missed it.

Piper returned her attention to the view. The stars had disappeared now and streaks of blue and yellow had appeared.

Seagulls squawked in the light breeze while the waves crashed on the shore below.

"It's beautiful." She'd never appreciated that before. What teenager did? But now... She loved the peace and tranquility. The quiet beauty. Yes, she was glad to be home.

"Morning is always my favorite part of the day." Cooper moved beside her and mimicked her stance. "It's a new beginning. A time of possibilities."

She turned to face him. "I never thought of it that way before, but you're right." Piper lifted her mug to her lips, but no coffee came out when she tipped it. She peered inside. "Ugh. Empty." *Damn.* That was the last of the thermos she'd filled this morning before leaving her apartment.

"There's more inside if you want some." Cooper pointed his thumb behind him.

She eyed him curiously. "Are you offering to share your coffee with me, Cooper Turner?"

He let loose a chuckle. "I believe I am."

"Thank you." A rush of warmth flooded through her. "That's nice of you." She wouldn't have expected that from him, given their history. They might have called a truce yesterday, but there was a big difference between being civil to each other and being nice.

"You're welcome." His genuine smile sent another wave of heat rushing through her.

"Um…" She jerked her gaze away from him. "I'm going to grab another cup." She brandished her empty mug for effect.

"It's just regular, not the flavored stuff you seem to prefer."

She stopped midstride and turned to face him. "How do you know I like flavored coffee?" It wasn't something she'd told him.

He pointed to her cup. "I could smell it when you were drinking earlier."

"Oh." That made sense. Piper started walking again.

"There's cream in the fridge and some sugar packets on the counter, too," Cooper called.

"Great. Thanks." Piper slid the door open and stepped inside.

She stepped up to the kitchen island and poured the hot liquid into her cup. Cooper was being nice to her. She didn't know what to make of this new development. Not that she was complaining. It was just...foreign. They'd sniped at each other for so long now, she hadn't been sure they'd be capable of anything else. He'd proved her wrong.

"Ready to get back to work?" she asked as she heard Cooper enter behind her.

His long legs crossed the room quickly. "Yes. Did you want to frame another wall or put up the Sheetrock on the ones I built yesterday?"

Piper pursed her lips as she considered. "Let's do the Sheetrock. That way I can tape the seams this afternoon." The work would be quiet enough so as not to disturb Layla's customers dining on the first floor.

He nodded. "That'll work. Let's get started." He walked over and grabbed a four-foot-by-eight-foot sheet off the stack.

Piper joined him and lifted one end while he boosted the other. They carried it across the room and into the hall they'd formed to create access to the second bathroom.

As much as she'd wanted to put up the walls to separate Layla's private dining room from what would become the entryway for her gallery, they didn't have enough time to construct and finish them before Layla opened for business at eleven thirty. They'd have to wait until Sunday, when the restaurant was closed for the day, before that could happen.

They'd nailed in four sheets, enough to cover one side of the wood frame, when Cooper's phone rang.

He pulled it from his holder. Stabbing the screen, he lifted it to his ear.

Piper walked into the main room to give him some privacy.

Cooper appeared a few minutes later, walked toward the grand staircase that led downstairs to the private entrance they used to access the gallery, and disappeared.

Piper stared, dumfounded, at the spot where Cooper had been standing a moment ago. "What the hell?" He'd left in the middle of what they'd been doing without so much as a word, let alone an explanation. Of all the irresponsible, negligent...

There you go judging him again.

Crap. The little voice in her head was right. She'd jumped to conclusions without bothering to ask if there was a reason he'd do such a thing.

She'd done a lot of that over the years. Not once had she stopped to consider if there was a reason why he'd acted the way he did.

She was starting to think that she'd earned the Ice Queen title fair and square.

Piper didn't want that name anymore.

So what was she going to do to change it?

Coop hit the redial button on his cell as soon as he reached the parking lot.

"Hey, man," Everett answered.

"What's up? It's like seven thirty in the morning." A light breeze blew, sending a chill through him. Damn. *Should have grabbed my coat.* He started walking to stay warm.

"It's after eight," Everett retorted.

Coop frowned. They must have been working longer than he'd thought.

"Don't tell me I'm interrupting your beauty sleep."

Coop let out a soft chuckle. "If I recall from our college days, you're the one who needed beauty sleep, not me. I've been at work since five."

Everett let out a groan. "That's cruel and unusual punishment."

"That's why you're a desk jockey and I'm boots on the ground. So, what's going on?"

The long silent pause made his gut tighten.

"So…" Everett dragged out the word.

His insides churned. "Spit it out, Ev. What gives?" Coop knew instinctively that this call had something to do with his ex. It was why he'd bolted before taking the call.

"We received Rachel's response card last night. She's bringing Tom."

His hand clenched around the phone. "Yeah. I know." That's why he didn't want to go to this shindig.

"There's more," Everett continued.

He gritted his teeth. "I already know she and Tom got engaged."

"That's good." Everett's relief was palpable. "Not for you. I meant that you already know."

His blood boiled just thinking about how the two of them had deceived him.

"You know that if it were up to me, I'd disinvite her to the wedding," Everett said.

That wasn't going to happen. Rachel was Everett's fiancée's cousin—and the maid of honor.

How the hell was he supposed to get through the day with her by his side? How was he supposed to act like everything was fine between them, when it wasn't? Just thinking about how she'd cheated on him with his best friend made Coop's stomach churn.

"I'm sorry, man." Everett's voice was full of compassion.

Great. Just great. The last thing he needed was people feeling sorry for him.

"It's fine." He clipped out the words.

"You're sure? You're…ah… Not gonna bail on me, are you?"

If only that were an option. Coop sighed. "Not unless you want me to."

"No way, dude. You and I go way back. We pledged together. Got through rush week together. Not to mention all the antics we pulled over our four years of college."

Coop smiled, remembering all the fun they'd had together over the years.

"I want you to be my best man," Everett insisted. "That's why I asked you."

Coop dragged his hand through his hair and nodded. "I won't let you down." Rachel and Tom be damned. He could handle this. He had to.

"Good," Everett said. "You had me worried. We haven't received your response yet."

"I'll be there," he said.

"Are you bringing a plus-one?" Everett's voice was filled with hope.

"Yes." Who that would be, Coop couldn't say, but no way would he show up alone. It was bad enough Everett felt sorry for him. He didn't want the rest of the groomsmen or his frat brothers to feel that way, too.

"You're seeing someone." Everett whooped. The sound of a hand slapping a tabletop echoed down the line. "I knew it. The Cooper Turner I know wouldn't let a breakup get him down for long. Way to go, bro. So, what's her name? What does she look like?"

Crap. What was he supposed to say now? He had no

prospects on the horizon. He hadn't even thought about finding a date. "I gotta go now. Talk later."

"Wait a minute. I want to know about the woman you're bringing. Who is she?"

He sure as heck didn't know the answer. "You'll meet her at the wedding." He blew out a breath. "I really need to get back to work. I walked out in the middle of something." Piper was going to rip him a new one for walking out in the middle of what they'd been doing.

She might be justified in this case. He should have said something, even if all he'd said was he needed to take the call.

You never explained about anything you were going through. Not once.

How could he blame Piper for jumping to conclusions over the years? He couldn't.

"Fine. But don't think you're off the hook regarding this mystery woman, especially once Annalise finds out. She's gonna want to meet her. She's still feeling bad about how things turned out with you and Rachel."

"It's not her fault." Annalise might have set him and Rachel up, but she wasn't responsible for Rachel's actions. "I was the one who introduced Rachel to Tom." Coop's hands clenched into tight fists. More than twenty-five years of friendship and comradery ended in the blink of an eye.

I fell in love. Tom had made a point of telling him that. Like that fact justified the two of them sneaking around behind his back.

"Let's do dinner together soon. I'll check with Annalise and get back to you." Everett's words pulled him from his thoughts.

He needed to find a date for this wedding. Fast. "Talk

soon." He ended the call before Everett could say anything more.

Coop shoved the phone back in its holder. It was time to face Piper's wrath. He looked around. Hell, he'd walked all the way to the center of town while he and Everett were talking. Which meant he'd be further delayed getting back. *Crap.*

He started back toward the gallery, passing the post office and the library. The aroma of freshly ground coffee hit him as he approached the Coffee Palace. Maybe Piper would be in a better mood if he brought a peace offering? Regardless, he could use another cup of caffeine.

Coop walked inside. He peered around. Most of the tables were full, but no one stood in line to order. He approached the counter.

"Hi, Cooper." Mia smiled at him.

"Hey." His brows furrowed. "What are you doing here?"

She let out a soft chuckle. "Ah, I work here."

"Still?" he asked. "I thought you were teaching at the private elementary school in the next town over."

"I am. I'm only here when school is on break." A delicate flush stained her cheeks. "We're off for the Christmas holiday until next week. We go back later than the public schools."

Coop frowned. Was she struggling financially now that she and her husband had split? Working at TK Construction would pay more than her teaching position and whatever she was making here combined. So why was she killing herself with two jobs?

"Right." He eyed her curiously. "You know we'd love to have you back at TK Construction." His father had been disappointed when she stopped working after her second daughter, Brooke, was born, although he'd respected her decision to stay home and raise her children.

"Thanks. I appreciate that. Mom and your dad told me the same thing."

"Perfect. You can start today." He grinned. "As a matter of fact, I've got a job for you right now. You can help Piper renovate her gallery. You could always swing a hammer with the best of them."

"Hey, no stealing my employees, Turner." Abby walked in from the kitchen and flashed a grin.

"You don't have to worry," Mia said to Abby. To him, she added, "Even if I was interested in going back to TK, which I'm not, I couldn't work on the gallery renovation. You start way too early for me. I have to get the kids off to school most mornings."

He sighed. "You are always welcome back at TK if you change your mind."

"I know, and I appreciate that. So, what can I get for you?" Mia asked.

He ordered his usual. "Large regular coffee with half-and-half and two sugars." He may as well grab something to eat as long as he was here. "And a bacon, egg and cheese breakfast sandwich, too."

"Is that all?" Mia asked.

Coop shook his head. "I thought I'd pick up something for your sister, too. What type of coffee does she like?"

Mia gawked at him. "A large toasted almond—light." She arched a brow. "She'd also appreciate a ham, egg and cheese croissant to go with it."

Cooper laughed. "Okay, sure. Why not." This was a peace offering, after all.

Mia shot him a curious glance. "It's awfully nice of you to bring something for Piper."

"Contrary to some opinions, I'm a nice guy." Coop grinned and waggled his brows.

Mia chuckled. "Yes, you are." She handed him his

drinks and indicated he'd need to wait a few minutes for the rest of his order.

Fifteen minutes later, Coop entered the old mansion and took the elevator to the second floor. He found Piper kneeling on the floor over a couple of wood studs with a tape measure in her hand.

She looked up when he called her name.

"You're back. Good. I got to work on the next wall while you were gone. If it's all right with you, we can finish this one, and then go back to Sheetrocking."

"Yeah, sure. No problem." He stared at her, waiting for the lecture to come, but she just got back to measuring the boards. "Um, sorry I ran out on you."

"No problem. I figured you needed to deal with whoever called you."

He nodded. "It was Everett. He's getting married in a few weeks. I'm his best man." Why was he telling her this? He sounded like a bumbling fool. "Here." He thrust the foam cup at her and the bag containing her food.

"What's this?" Her brows drew together in a deep V.

"It's a toasted almond coffee with extra cream and a ham, egg and cheese croissant. Mia said that's what you like."

"Yeah." She stared at him as if he were an alien who'd just landed on the planet. "It is. Thank you."

Heat crept up his neck and flooded his face. Why he was so pleased with her response, he couldn't say. He just was. "You're welcome." Coop grinned.

Maybe there was hope for them yet.

No, damn it. There was no *them*.

He didn't want there to be.

Chapter Five

"Why are you ignoring me?" Coop's brother Nick walked into his office at TK Construction on Wednesday evening.

Coop's brow furrowed. "What are you talking about?"

"I texted you an hour ago and called twice in the last fifteen minutes. Why haven't you answered?" Nick flashed an exasperated look at him.

"I haven't received any texts or calls all afternoon." He glanced to his right, ready to pick up his cell and prove his point, but it wasn't there. He scanned the entire desktop. It wasn't anywhere. Coop patted the holder attached to his belt. No luck. He flashed back to earlier today. *Crap.* "Sorry. I must have left my phone at the gallery." He stood. Closing his computer, he disengaged it from the docking station. "I need to go and grab it." He shoved his laptop into his backpack and started toward the door. "What did you want?" he asked his brother.

"Are you still planning to go to Levi's to watch the game tonight?" Nick asked.

"Yeah. I'll see you at eight."

Coop stepped outside. Clouds covered the early evening sky, leaving a blanket of inky darkness behind. He shivered as he hurried to his vehicle. Hopping inside, Coop drove the short distance to the old, colonial mansion that housed Piper's gallery. The parking lot was packed, which meant Layla's restaurant must be busy. He pulled his Camaro into an empty spot near the side entrance and hopped out.

Punching the code in on the keypad, he pulled open the door and hurried up the stairs two at a time. He spotted his phone where he'd left it—next to the circular saw in the far corner of the room.

Coop grabbed it and thrust it in his belt holder.

He heard muffled music coming from the opposite side of the space. Was that the soundtrack from that Disney movie his nephew, Noah, liked to watch?

He listened again. Magic carpets and genies. Yes, definitely children's songs. Who was here and why were they playing kids' music? Cooper headed in the direction the sounds came from to investigate.

A squeal of laughter came from the room Piper had designated as her studio. The music came from there, too.

Coop arched a brow. What was she doing? More laughter filtered into the hall. Muffled voices, too.

"Piper?" He knocked on the closed door.

No response.

"Hello?" He thrust the door open and walked in.

Piper whirled around and stared at him, a startled expression on her face.

"Uncle Coop!" A paint-covered Noah smiled. "What are you doing here?"

"I have the same question." Piper shot him a curious glance. She grabbed her mobile from the table that stood in the far corner of the room. The music stopped.

"I forgot my phone." He tapped the holder on his belt. "Came back to get it. What's going on in here?" He stared at walls covered with various streaks and stripes and four equally colorful children.

"We're helping Auntie Piper decorate her studio," Aurora, Piper's eldest niece, said.

"It's really fun," Kiera, the youngest of the three girls, added.

"Yeah," Brooke, the middle sister, agreed. "Do you want to help?"

"I…ah…" He didn't know what to say. He doubted Piper would appreciate anything he contributed.

"You can grab a brush and some paint from the table if you want," Piper said.

He trained his gaze on her. Something flickered in her expression. Curiosity, maybe? He wasn't sure, but at least it wasn't the condemnation he usually saw when she looked at him. He supposed that was a good thing.

"Look what I did." Noah dragged him over to where he'd drawn a few squiggly lines in various colors. "Piper said I could write my name so everyone knows who painted it."

Cooper studied the oversize letters. "You did a great job, buddy."

"Yes, they all did." Piper pointed to the rest of the pictures. "I'm so proud of all of you."

His nephew and her three nieces beamed.

Coop frowned. Why were the kids even here?

"Hey, Coop." Levi appeared by his side.

"Daddy!" Noah raced toward his father. "We had so much fun today with Piper."

"Whoa." Levi held him at arm's length. "You've got wet paint all over you. I don't want it on me."

"Hey, Levi." Piper waved. To Noah she said, "Go and change into the clothes you were wearing earlier."

"But I don't want to go home yet," Noah protested. "Aurora, Brooke and Kiera get to stay."

"No, they don't." Mia walked into the room. "Go and

get changed, girls. You've got swim lessons in twenty minutes."

A round of grumbling ensued.

Piper laughed as she herded them toward the door.

"Thanks again for volunteering to watch the girls this afternoon." Mia started cleaning up.

"And thanks for including Noah," Levi said.

Coop frowned. He wouldn't have expected the uptight woman he knew to go out of her way to do such a thing. Let alone allow the kids to splatter paint all over her walls.

"You're a lifesaver." His brother helped Mia put things away. "I can't believe I forgot to hire a sitter. My mother told me last week that she couldn't watch Noah, but with the holidays, I forgot to call someone."

"You're welcome. It was no trouble. I had a lot of fun with them. Check out the artwork they created." Piper walked to the front of the room where three easels sat.

There was more than just the walls? Coop followed Levi and Mia to where Piper stood.

"We went over how to draw some basic shapes and this is what they came up with." Piper pointed to the first canvas. "Noah created these fish out of ovals and triangles."

Coop's gaze widened. "Hey, that's pretty good for a five-year-old."

Piper nodded. "Yes. It is."

"This must be Kiera's drawing." Mia pointed to the second easel. "She loves flowers. And Brooke loves butterflies." She examined the last canvas. "Where's Aurora's drawing?"

"She opted for a different media for her project." Piper grinned and pulled out her cell. She stepped close to her sister. "Look at these." She swiped her finger across the screen.

"Oh my gosh, that's a great picture of Brooke and Kiera," Mia said. "This one's great, too." Mia scrolled through what he assumed were more photos.

Cooper studied her. Piper hadn't just watched the kids today, she'd taken the time to do things with them and teach them something, too.

"She's a natural," Piper said. "You should have seen the smile on her face as she was taking the pictures. You would have thought I'd given her a million dollars when I gave her my phone and told her to have at it."

"I had no idea," Mia said. "Can you teach her?"

"Absolutely. I'd be happy to." Piper let out a little chuckle. "Although don't be surprised if we surpass what I know sooner, rather than later. She's a quick study."

Mia hugged her sister. "You're the best. I'm so glad you're home."

The kids rushed into the room, each trying to talk above the other.

"Okay, okay, girls." Mia held up her hand. "First, I need you to help Auntie Piper finish tidying up." She glanced at her watch. "We need to leave in five minutes if we're going to make it to the YMCA in time for your swim lessons."

"You, too, sport." Levi pointed to Noah.

"Come on, guys." Piper sang a song about everyone helping to put things away and the kids joined in.

Coop marveled at how good she was with children. Even more surprising, she seemed to enjoy being with them. The persona didn't fit the woman he had believed her to be.

"Thanks for your help, guys." Piper capped the last paint jar.

Noah ran over to her and threw his arms around Piper. "I had so much fun today."

"I'm so glad." Her smile lit up the room.

"Me, too," Noah said.

"I'll see you guys later." Piper hugged Noah tight, and then her nieces.

"Let's go, girls. Chop, chop." Mia clapped her hands together.

"We're going to head out now, too." Levi motioned for Noah to join him. "Thanks again, Piper." He waved and headed out the door.

"Bye, Auntie Piper," the three girls called together.

Piper waved as they exited.

When they were alone, Piper turned to him, hands on hips. "Why are you staring at me?"

Coop hadn't realized he was. "Sorry." He'd been trying to reconcile the Piper he remembered with the woman who stood before him, and couldn't.

"That doesn't answer my question. You've obviously got something to say, so you might as well say it."

All right, then. "I can understand why you'd watch your nieces for the afternoon, but why Noah? You barely know him."

She gawked at him. "What did you expect me to do, leave him in the dungeon all alone?"

She was talking about the converted conference room at the TK Construction offices. He and his brothers and the three Kavanaughs would go there on days off from elementary school, and early closings, if no one was available to watch them. The six of them had nicknamed the place the dungeon because they hated their time spent there. He smiled to himself. Looking back, it wasn't as bad as he'd once thought. They'd had a television, an air hockey table and lots of video games to play.

Piper crossed her arms and glared at him. "Of course

you did. After all, I'm the Ice Queen. I'm not capable of caring or compassion."

He might have believed that once upon a time, but what he'd witnessed here today proved otherwise. "No. I was clearly wrong about that."

Dead wrong.

Chapter Six

"Thanks again for meeting with me today. I appreciate you taking time out of your Saturday afternoon to accommodate my schedule. It was a pleasure meeting you," Talia said.

"You, too." Piper smiled at the woman standing a few feet away. "And you're welcome." This appointment had been well worth the time. She was looking forward to featuring Talia's work in her gallery. Piper glanced around the studio. The woman was quite a talented sculptor. "I'll be in touch with the details as we get closer to our grand opening." She gave a little wave and exited Talia's studio.

A cold midday breeze struck her the moment she walked outside and she shivered. Would she ever get reacclimated to the cold January weather in New England? She zipped up her parka and tied the pashmina scarf Mom had given her for Christmas around her neck.

Hurrying to her car, she climbed inside and started the engine. Cool air blasted her. She shut the vent until the car warmed up.

Piper pulled out of the parking lot that housed the building where Talia's studio was located. Humming along with the radio, she headed toward town.

Her cell rang. She pushed the phone button on her steering wheel and connected the call. "Hi, sis. What's up?"

"Have you eaten lunch yet?" Mia asked.

"No." She glanced at the clock on the dashboard. It was already one thirty. No wonder she was hungry.

"Me either. I just got off my shift at the Coffee Palace, and for once, Kyle is around."

Piper cringed. She'd never liked her brother-in-law. Kyle had always been pleasant to her—to everyone in her family—but there was something about him that had rubbed her the wrong way from the start. Personally, she was glad her sister was no longer married to him.

"He has the girls, so I'm free as a bird. Want to meet me for a bite to eat?"

Piper turned left onto Rainbow Road. "Sounds good. Where do you want to go?"

"How about Layla's place? Maybe after we eat you can show me the progress you've made on the gallery. I can't wait to see what you've done."

She chuckled. "I knew it. You can't help yourself. You love the construction world."

"What I like is transforming a space, or in the case of a new build, creating a vision," Mia corrected.

Piper shook her head. "If you like it so much, why don't you go back to TK? I'm sure Mom and Ron would love to have you back."

"That was a long time ago." Was that a hint of regret in Mia's voice? "I have other priorities these days and their names are Aurora, Brooke and Keira. Teaching fits the girls' schedule. Besides, I spent all that time and money getting my teaching certificate. It would be a waste if I didn't use it."

"Maybe, but there's something to be said for being happy."

Mia sighed. "I'll live vicariously through you for now. So, Layla's place?"

She and Mia needed some alone time. Something wasn't right with her sister and she needed to figure out what it was. "You bet. I'll see you in about ten minutes. I'm coming from a meeting with an artist on the other side of town."

"Perfect. I should arrive around the same time. Grab a table if you get there first."

"See you there. Bye." She ended the call.

Piper continued driving toward town. The four new houses that sat side by side under various stages of construction caught her eye. She tried to remember what was there before. The Walker property, if she remembered correctly. At least it used to be. Three old barns in major disrepair had once stood where the new houses did. Yes. That was it.

Those structures had always reminded her of the old outbuildings at Ron and Debby Turner's place. She'd always loved the century-old dwellings. Could remember playing hide-and-seek in the Turner barns when they were little kids and they'd go over for big family barbecues during the hot summer months.

Maybe that was why some of the kids had started hanging out at the Walker property after Ron and Debby had stopped the bonfires at their place.

After Cooper had gotten hurt their senior year.

Piper sighed. She'd been so...furious and upset that evening. All her plans had turned to dust.

The truth was, she'd been looking forward to that evening with Tom Anderson. It was the first time, in a very long time, that she'd let someone in. Let herself feel something for someone else.

Losing her dad... Piper shuddered and stopped that thought in its tracks. It hurt too much to feel.

She'd really gone off on Cooper that night. No wonder he thought of her as an ice queen. He'd suffered a broken arm and a concussion and she hadn't given a damn about anyone or anything but herself.

Piper gasped when the Homes for Humanity sign came into view. Wait. The four houses were Humanity homes?

She turned around and drove back to where the sign stood.

Piper grinned. Yes. Homes for Humanity was building homes in New Suffolk. Dad would have been thrilled. He, too, had believed everyone should have a decent place to live, and he'd helped the nonprofit build homes throughout the state for as long as she could remember. Piper was sure he would have continued to volunteer if he was still alive today.

She pulled into the parking area to turn around. The turquoise-colored car parked separately from the others in the parking area caught her attention as she backed up and turned toward the road. Was that Cooper's car? She looked in the rearview mirror to see if the car had twin white stripes across the hood, but she couldn't tell from this vantage point. It couldn't be Cooper's, could it? Piper dismissed the thought. She couldn't imagine Cooper volunteering his time for such a cause.

Not the old Cooper, anyway. But the current version…

She couldn't say. Piper didn't know him well enough. Why that thought made her heart pang, she wasn't sure, but it did.

She arrived at The Sea Shack a few minutes later. Parking in a free spot in the parking lot, Piper hopped out of her car. The Coffee Palace bag and the commercial coffeemakers she'd purchased earlier today sat in the back seat. She decided to bring the bag containing the coffee and one of the makers up to the gallery now, so she wouldn't have to juggle all three of them tomorrow morning. Opening the rear passenger door, Piper grabbed the packages and nudged it shut with her hip.

"What have you got there?" a familiar voice asked.

Piper turned and spotted Mia parked one spot away from her. "Some things for the gallery. I thought I'd run them up before we had lunch."

"Looks like you have your hands full. Let me help." Mia rolled up her car window. Sliding from the driver's seat, she pressed her key fob and locked her vehicle. She slung her purse over her shoulder and reached for the box Piper held. "This is going to make a *lot* of coffee."

"A lot of people come to shows." Wine and beer weren't the only beverages she'd serve her customers. Piper unlocked her car and grabbed the other coffee-maker from her back seat. "I need to make sure we don't run out."

They entered through the side entrance and into the room that Layla used as a private dining space.

"Let's take the elevator." Piper gestured to the door that looked like a closet to the right of the grand staircase.

Mia opened the door with her free hand. "You're lucky Layla's grandfather had this installed when he and his wife used the second floor of the mansion as a residence."

Piper nodded. "I wouldn't have rented the space if it wasn't here. I wouldn't have the proper accessibility required by the state."

The elevator door opened a minute later. They exited into the hall that led to the main space if you turned left, and her studio if you turned right.

They headed toward the main space.

Piper set her box and the bag of coffee on the island and Mia did the same.

Mia glanced toward the main space. "You haven't gotten much done in here yet."

Piper chuckled. "First off, it's only been a few days. Second, we've been focusing on creating access from the hall to what was the primary bedroom en suite. Modifying that bathroom so that it's only a sink and commode is taking a lot more work that I thought."

Mia slanted a sidelong gaze at her. "Are you sure it's not taking longer because you and Cooper can't get along?"

"Actually, Cooper and I called a truce. We're both adults now and we're managing to work together just fine." Piper burst out laughing at the shocked expression on her sister's face. "You might want to pick your jaw up off the ground."

"I can't help it. You couldn't have surprised me more."

"We're not bosom buddies, if that's what you're thinking." She still didn't *like* him. Images of his handsome face and sexy smile flooded her brain. Her pulse kicked up a notch.

No, no, no. Piper turned away to hide the color she knew had stained her cheeks.

"Still…" Mia flashed a smug smirk. "Levi and I thought you two would have killed each other by now."

"Gee, thanks." Piper rolled her eyes skyward. She walked back to the island that would soon be converted to her bar. Grabbing the bag from the granite surface, she placed the four bags of grounds into the cupboard.

"Why is the stove pulled away from the wall?" Mia asked.

She spared a quick glance into what was currently the kitchen. "I can't keep it. As a business, I don't have a permit to cook up here. My insurance company wants it gone."

"What do you plan to do with it?" Mia asked.

"Layla suggested I donate it." She shot her sister a quizzical look. "Unless you want it. I'm sure she wouldn't have a problem with that."

"No." Mia shook her head. "I was going to propose the same. There's a donation center over in Carver. The money earned from the donations people make goes to support the Homes for Humanity houses."

She nodded. "Perfect. And it's so close by, too." Piper sucked in a breath and released it. "Speaking of Homes for Humanity. I noticed they were building a few homes on the outskirts of town."

Mia grinned. "Yes. They started those projects a couple of months ago."

"Is Cooper one of the volunteers?" Her insides jumped and jittered. Why was she so nervous about asking such a simple question?

"I assume so. He's been helping build Humanity homes for a long time now."

He has? Her brows furrowed. "How long?"

"Ever since he was old enough to volunteer."

Piper shook her head. "No way." You had to be sixteen to help build Humanity homes. That would have meant he started while they were in high school. "I would have known."

Mia's expression turned contemplative. "Not necessarily."

"Oh, come on. I lived here back then." She definitely would have known unless… "He didn't want me to know? Why?"

Mia pulled a face. "Do you really have to ask?"

Her shoulders fell. No. She didn't. They'd hated each other back then.

"It was his way of honoring Dad," Mia said. "You know how close they were."

Yes. Dad was Cooper's godfather. They'd shared a special bond. That was why it had been so hard when she'd caught him skateboarding at Dad's wake. Dad had loved Cooper like another son, and Piper thought Cooper couldn't have cared less about Dad.

"I wish I'd known." Piper dragged her hand through her hair.

"Would it have made a difference back then?" Mia's soft voice thundered in the silent room.

Yes. No. The truth was, Piper wasn't sure. She'd been caught up in her own grief back then. And Mom's depression… It hit all of them hard. Mia, Shane and especially her. At least it felt that way. It was as if she'd lost both her parents.

Was it any wonder why she wanted no part of a serious relationship after watching what her mother went through?

"Piper?" Mia waved a hand in front of her face. She repeated the question.

She sucked in a deep breath and released it. "I don't know."

Ice Queen. Oh, yes. Cooper had been more than right about that. Lord, no wonder he'd hated her back then.

Hates. Present tense. As in, still does.

They might have called a truce, but she wasn't under any illusions his feelings about her had changed.

Her stomach plummeted.

Chapter Seven

The aroma of fresh coffee brewing hit Cooper the minute he walked through the main entrance of the gallery on Sunday morning. That was the good news. The bad news was it smelled like the toasted almond flavor Piper preferred.

Tapping his backpack, he sighed. At least he had a thirty-ounce YETI full of the regular brew he enjoyed. He'd made it fresh this morning before he'd left the house. It would have to do.

"Hey, Cooper." Piper walked into the main space from the hall that led to her studio. She flashed a smile in his direction.

What was it about her smile that sent a flood of warmth rushing through him every time he saw it? Coop gave himself a mental shake. So what if she had a nice smile? *A great smile.* He shouldn't be wasting time thinking about it now. He shouldn't be thinking of Piper in any way, shape or form, other than as a client, because that was what she was, for all intents and purposes. A TK Construction customer. No more. No less.

Focus on the job and nothing more. "You're here early." It was barely five in the morning.

Piper nodded. "I got here about an hour ago. I needed to finish sanding the walls so I can paint later. I ran out of time yesterday."

A part of him felt bad for leaving her to work alone, but no way would he cancel on the Humanity crew. They counted on his help.

"I had meetings with a couple of artists I'm interested in featuring once the gallery opens."

"How'd that go?" he asked. Part of him still couldn't believe he was standing here talking to her like she was an old friend.

A client, he mentally corrected. He was making small talk with a client. That was all. He would do that from time to time with other TK customers. It was appropriate to do this with Piper, especially since they were also working together.

It helped that they'd been getting along great these past few days. Who would have guessed that getting along with her was much easier than he'd expected? Not him. That was for sure. But here they were.

Piper smiled and his heartbeat kicked up a notch. That was another thing that had surprised him these past few days. How much she smiled. He couldn't remember ever seeing the old Piper smile—not at him, anyway.

The woman before him smiled a lot, and the happiness that radiated from her when she flashed those pearly whites… It stole the breath from him.

You're not supposed to be thinking about her smile. But he couldn't help it. He liked seeing it. It brightened his day.

"Great, thanks. I'm going to showcase both of them during the festival." She snapped her fingers. "That reminds me. I've got another artist I need to interview. I tried to set up the appointment for after we finished up here, but her schedule is full for the next few days, so I've got to speak with her this morning. I'm leaving at ten thirty. I should be gone about an hour and a half at the most."

He nodded. "No problem. I can handle things here while you're gone." *Look at us, communicating like normal people.* He chuckled to himself.

Cooper set his backpack on the workstation and yanked out the thermos.

"There's a fresh pot of coffee for you on the kitchen island." Piper pointed a thumb over her shoulder.

He glanced over. Two coffeemakers stood side by side on the counter top.

"Where'd these come from?" Coop pointed to the coffeemakers as he walked to the island and inhaled the aromatic brew.

"I bought them at the store yesterday afternoon, after my meetings. I'll need them for when we start having shows. The coffee is from the Coffee Palace. Toasted almond for me and a pound of Abby's special blend for you. It's a medium dark roast. She thought you'd like it."

Of course he liked it. He ordered a large every time he visited Abby's place.

"I figured it would be easier than having to bring it in each day," Piper finished.

"Thank you. That was really nice of you." More than nice. She'd gone out of her way. For him. He wouldn't have expected her to consider his preferences.

Now who's judging who?

This was the same woman who'd included his nephew in the fun and games she'd played with her nieces the other day so he wouldn't be left out.

The old Piper might have been an ice queen, but the woman who stood before him now was anything but.

"You're welcome." Piper wiggled her brows. "Let's face it. We both go through a lot of java each day."

He laughed. "Yes, we do." A love of caffeine was another thing he'd realized they had in common.

Coop spotted the stove in the middle of the kitchen. "What are you doing with this?"

"Shane is going to stop by later with his truck and he's going to take it to the Homes for Humanity donation center for me. There's one close by."

He shot her a quizzical glance. "How did you know that?" The store she referred to had only opened a short time ago.

Piper cocked her head to the side. "Mia told me about it." She waited a beat and added, "She also told me that you've been a Humanity volunteer for years."

"Yes." It might have started as a way to honor Victor in the beginning, but somewhere along the line things had changed. Coop loved the work and the charity's mission. He continued volunteering because it was something he wanted to do.

A soft smile filled her face. "That's really great." She walked over to where he stood and captured his hands with hers. Giving them a gentle squeeze, she said, "Thank you."

Her sincerity sent a flood of warmth rushing through him and filled his chest to bursting point.

Focus on the job. No more, no less. Coop walked over to the island. He spotted two large mugs resting beside the coffeepots. "I see you grabbed these, too." One cup had a picture of a harried cartoon with the caption I Drink Coffee for Your Protection, and the other had a bunch of flowers on it with the inscription A Cup of Happy. He grabbed the cartoon character mug and held it up in the air. Nodding, he said, "This is rather appropriate."

Piper laughed. The sweet sound surrounded him like a soft cloud of silk.

Coop did his best to ignore the fluttering in his stomach and filled the mug. "Thanks again for doing this."

"You're welcome. Shall we get started on the wall to separate Layla's private dining room from the gallery entrance?" She gestured to the stack of wood studs lying on the floor.

He gave her a thumbs-up and walked to the pile. Grabbing a board, he started measuring.

A few minutes later, he caught Piper staring at him, an odd expression on her face.

"What?" he asked.

She looked like a kid who got caught stealing a cookie from the cookie jar. "You were whistling."

Coop shook his head. "I don't think so." He never whistled—unless he was happy.

"You were whistling. No doubt about it." Piper grinned.

Holy crap. He gawked at her, nonplussed.

"Cooper. You're here." Jane Kavanaugh walked into the gallery from the main entrance on Monday afternoon.

His brows furrowed. "Yes. Why are you so surprised?"

"Don't you usually wrap things up by this time so you don't disturb Layla's customers dining downstairs?"

He nodded. "I'm just finishing up now."

Jane peered around the space. A look of concern crossed her face, but she said nothing.

She was probably thinking they hadn't made any progress over the last few days, but she couldn't see the walls he and Piper had created to allow access to the bathroom from the main hall, or the new entrance they'd created to Piper's art studio.

"Is there something that I can do for you?" His gaze shot to the man who stood next to Jane. Tall and lanky, he was dressed in a pair of dark tapered pants with a matching button-down shirt, his long, dark brown hair tied back in a ponytail. He didn't look familiar.

Why was he here with Jane?

None of my business.

"Is Piper around? I wanted to speak with her," Jane asked.

Coop shook his head. "Not right now. She said she had an appointment this morning and would be back around noon."

"Yes. She mentioned that when we spoke earlier." Tapping her watch, she added, "It's almost ten after."

Coop arched a brow. "I'm sure she'll be back any minute."

Jane walked over to where he stood by the workstation. "You can go ahead and call it a day. I'm sure Piper won't mind. We'll just wait here until she returns. It won't be a problem."

Coop frowned. Was she trying to get rid of him? "Okay. If that's what you want."

Relief flooded through Jane's features. "I know you have better things to do with your time than sitting around and waiting for Piper to return."

"Rii-ight." He dragged out the word. Why was Jane acting so…not normal? "Let me just finish up what I'm doing and I'll head out. Help yourself to some coffee if you want." He pointed to the kitchen island that was partially visible from where he stood.

"Sounds good." Jane flashed a tight smile and walked away.

Coop frowned. *Definitely not normal.* He needed to finish up and get out of here. He grabbed another stud from the pile on the floor and laid it across the workstation. Grabbing the tape measure, he began measuring.

"Hey, Mom," Piper greeted. "What are you doing here?"

His gaze strayed to where Piper stood a short distance away. He swallowed hard. Gone were the jeans she'd worn when she'd walked out of here earlier. She'd replaced them with a slim-fitting black pencil skirt. A wide fabric belt was cinched around her narrow waist. The sweatshirt she'd worn had disappeared as well. In its place was a white, figure-hugging blouse. And those heels… How she managed to stand upright, let alone walk in them, was beyond him, but they made her legs look great.

His heart beat a rapid tattoo.

No, damn it. He needed to concentrate on building the frame for the next wall, not gawk at Piper.

"Hello, I'm Piper Kavanaugh." She extended her hand to the guy.

She didn't know the man standing next to her mother either? Why had Jane brought him here?

"This is Donny," Jane said. "He's my friend Miriam's son."

Dead silence followed Jane's introduction.

What was going on? He shot a covert look in Piper's direction. She stood stiff as a board.

Coop gave up all pretense of working. Whatever was happening here was much more interesting.

Piper jerked her gaze to Donny. She was none too happy, if the tight smile on her face was anything to go by. "It's nice to meet you."

"You, too." Donny shook Piper's hand.

"Donny is an artist," Jane said.

Comprehension dawned. Jane's friend had probably asked her to introduce her son to Piper in the hopes that Piper would look at his work. Best-case scenario,

Piper would display his art—whatever that might be—in her gallery.

He almost felt sorry for her. Almost.

"I'm a computer programmer," Donny said.

Coop frowned. Why would Jane say he was an artist if it wasn't true? It didn't make any sense.

Jane patted Donny's arm. "But you like to paint." It was a statement, not a question.

"Um, yeah." Donny flashed a nervous smile.

Something weird was happening. Piper seemed to know what it was, if the expression on her face was anything to go by, but she seemed helpless to stop whatever it was.

"You have a great smile." Jane turned her attention to Piper. "Don't you think?"

Coop's jaw dropped. Why on earth would Piper care if Donny had a great smile or not? Why would Jane even say such a thing?

"And you're a snappy dresser, too," Jane added.

Donny brightened. "Thank you, Mrs. Kavanaugh."

"Mom—" Piper began. She looked like she was about to explode.

"Donny, tell Piper about the paintings you showed me." Jane's words came out in a rush.

Donny turned his attention to Piper. "It would be better if I could show you."

"What a great idea," Jane enthused. "As a matter of fact, you could grab a bite to eat on the way. Why don't you go and do that now? You know, I have a table booked downstairs at Layla's restaurant for twelve thirty. You two can take it. I'm sure she won't mind if you're a few minutes early."

Coop's jaw dropped. He couldn't help it. Now he understood why Donny was here. Jane wanted to set him up with Piper.

A loud clang filled the now-silent space. He glanced down. Damn. He'd dropped the tape measure he'd been holding. Coop bent to pick it up. When he stood up again, Piper was staring at him. Her face flushed fire-engine red. She probably hadn't realized he was still there.

Piper marched over to him and dragged him down the hall and into her studio. "Stay here."

"Not a chance." He wasn't some minion she could order around. Coop headed toward the door.

"Please." Her shaky voice stopped him dead in his tracks.

He turned around and faced her. The breath caught in his throat. She looked like she wanted to crawl under a rock and die. He knew that feeling all too well. The embarrassment and mortification he'd experienced when he'd learned of Rachel and Tom's affair... Coop blew out a breath. He wasn't about to kick her when she was down. He wasn't a teenager who played pranks anymore. "Okay." He nodded. "I'll stay."

Relief flooded her features. "Thank you."

His hand brushed hers as she passed by him on her way to the door.

Sparks of electricity zipped down his spine from the accidental touch.

She stopped and stared at him.

Something hot and needy pulsed between them. His heart slammed against his chest.

Her lips parted and a soft little gasp came out of her mouth.

White-hot heat pooled low in his belly.

Piper jerked her gaze from him. Holding her head high, she strode from the room.

Coop stared at the closed door. What the hell had just happened?

* * *

Piper sucked in a deep, steadying breath as she walked along the hall toward the main part of the gallery. She was losing her mind. Yes. That had to be it. It was the only reason she could come up with that would explain why she'd almost grabbed Cooper Turner and started devouring his mouth like a starving person feasting at an all-you-can-eat buffet.

One minute she thought she might burst into tears—she'd never been this angry and frustrated in all her life—the next minute Cooper's hand brushed against hers. It was the lightest of touches, but the intense, fiery need it ignited inside her…holy hell. She'd never experienced anything like it before.

"Hey." Donny flashed a nervous smile and gave a little wave as she walked down the short hall to where he stood.

"Hi. Sorry for disappearing on you like that." Piper peered around the empty space. "Where's my mother?"

"She got a phone call and had to leave."

"I see." Her hands clenched into fists. She'd bet the commission from her first sale after the gallery opened that mom had bolted to avoid a confrontation. Well, that wouldn't save her. Not this time. She was going to march down to the TK offices right now and lay down the law once and for all. Piper had had enough of her interfering to last a lifetime.

Donny eyed her curiously. "I…ah…guess you didn't know we were coming."

She shook her head and gave him an apologetic smile. "No, I didn't. I'm so sorry."

"That explains why your mom was acting so weird. Did you still want to have lunch together?" Donny's voice sounded hopeful.

What was she supposed to say now? She didn't want to hurt him. He was as much of a victim of her mother's manipulations as she, but she didn't want to lead him on either.

"Sorry, dude." Cooper strode into the room like he owned the place. "She already has lunch plans. With me."

Now it was her turn for her jaw to drop.

Donny jerked his attention to her. "Is that true?"

It was now. She'd buy Cooper whatever he wanted to eat this afternoon for throwing her this life preserver. "Yes. As you said, I wasn't expecting you."

"Well." Donny looked from her to Cooper and back to her again. "Maybe another time?"

"I don't think so, pal." Cooper walked over to where she stood. He flashed a brilliant smile and draped an arm around her shoulder.

It took every ounce of inner strength she could muster not to gasp at him.

Donny stared at them for a moment. "I guess I misunderstood."

Piper shook her head. "This is my mother's fault, not yours. I'm so sorry."

Donny nodded and left without another word.

Piper let out the breath she was holding and added some much-needed space between her and Cooper. She peered over at him. She still couldn't quite believe what he'd done for her. "Thank you."

"You're welcome." His expression turned quizzical.

Piper could only imagine what he must be thinking. Lord, how was she going to put a stop to Mom's matchmaking ways once and for all? Talking to her wasn't going to help. She'd already tried that.

"Does she do that often? Your mom, I mean." He shook his head. "If I hadn't witnessed it for myself, I wouldn't have believed she would do such a thing. It's so unlike the Jane Kavanaugh I know."

Piper nodded. "She does this a lot. Twice since I came back to town and I've been back less than a week."

Cooper's eyes rounded. "I don't understand. I've never seen her do this before. Shane never mentioned her doing anything like this and neither has Mia."

"That's because she's never done it to them."

Cooper shook his head. "So, why you and not them? It doesn't make any sense."

She might as well tell him. She probably owed him that much for bailing her out with Donny. "Shane and Mia both got married."

Piper couldn't help but laugh at the expression on his face.

"Let me get this straight. She wanted you to marry Donny?"

"He was potential husband material, in her mind," she corrected.

Cooper nodded. "But you're not interested in getting married."

"Exactly. But she thinks if she keeps presenting good prospects—or what she believes are good prospects—I'll somehow change my mind."

His brows drew together in a deep V. "So, why don't you just tell her you're not interested?"

Piper snorted. "You don't think I've tried that? Repeatedly? When I confront her, she tells me she has no idea what I'm talking about. I bet you a hundred bucks she'll do the same thing when I try and talk to her about what she did this afternoon." She started pacing back and forth across the room. "I'm beginning to think Elle was right."

"About what?" he asked.

"About finding a fake boyfriend to get my mother off my back."

His disapproving glance made her hands clench into tight fists.

Piper glared at him. How dare he condemn her? "Obviously, you disagree."

"Actually—" His cell started to buzz. Cooper grabbed it from the holder and glanced at the screen. He uttered a muffled curse.

"Don't let me stop you from getting that." She was going to find her mother and head back. It was well past noon now. They couldn't do any more construction today. She headed down the hall.

"Wait a minute," Cooper called.

"Hey, Piper. Are you here?" her brother called.

"Yes." She pivoted and returned to the main space. Shane came into view a moment later.

"Hi." Shane came over and kissed her cheek. He turned his attention to Cooper. "What's up?"

"Finishing up for today." Cooper gestured around the space.

"Thanks for coming," she said to her brother. "The stove is in there." Piper pointed toward the kitchen.

"Okay, but first I've got a surprise." Shane waggled his brows. He turned toward the entrance. "You can come in now."

Her brows drew together in a deep V. "Who are you talking to?"

The door to the main gallery entrance opened and her brother's best friend, Jax Rawlins, walked in.

Piper grinned and walked over to meet Jax as he stepped through the door. "What are you doing here?"

"Just taking care of a few things here in town. Bumped in to Shane at Donahue's and he told me what you're up to. Figured I'd stop by and see how you're doing." He threw his arms around her and gave her a big bear hug.

"I'm great. How about you?"

"Doing well." He eased her back, but left his arms loose around her waist. "Look at you." He winked. "Lookin' good, baby."

She grinned. He wasn't too shabby himself. As a matter of fact, with that sexy smile he was aiming at her, he was pretty hot.

Shane cleared his throat. He tapped Jax on the shoulder. "You know that's my baby sister, right?"

Piper glared at Shane. "Knock it off already. I'm not a kid anymore. I'm a grown woman."

Shane straightened his shoulders and smirked. "You're still my baby sister."

Jax let go of her and held up his hands as if surrendering. "I know. Best friend code."

"What does that mean?" Piper asked.

"You can't go after your best friend's sister," Shane answered.

Jax nodded. "He's one hundred percent right."

Piper shook her head. "That's the most absurd thing I've ever heard."

"It's true." Cooper walked over to where she, Jax and Shane stood. He extended his hand to Jax. "It's good to see you."

Jax grasped his hand and clapped him on the shoulder. "You, too, Turner."

Shane's phone rang. He pulled out his cell and glanced at the screen. "I've got to take this. I'll be right back." He exited the gallery.

"So…" Jax winked at her. Draping his arm around her shoulder, he said, "Talk to me, beautiful."

She laughed. "I see you're still a terrible flirt."

Jax pounded a fist to his heart. "You wound me, woman."

"Oh please. I know you." He'd been her brother's best friend for more than twenty-five years. "You've left a trail of broken hearts all over town. Heck, all over the country, now that you're a famous photographer."

An idea hit her. He'd make a *great* fake boyfriend. He was sinfully handsome, sexy as all get-out, and the best part...like her, he'd never been interested in a serious relationship. She arched a brow and shot him a curious glance. "How long are you in town for?"

"A couple of days, then I've got a bunch of shows back-to-back, so I'm traveling for the next month. I'm back in New Suffolk for a few days in the middle of February. Why?"

Oh, yes. He was perfect all right. No one would be surprised when he dumped her for someone else and left her brokenhearted. She grinned like a Cheshire cat and placed her arm around his waist. "I've got a proposition for you."

"Oh yeah?" He sent her an inquiring glance. "What is it?"

She winked and gave him her best sexy smile. "Come with me and I'll tell you about it."

Chapter Eight

"Wait a minute," Cooper called as Piper dragged Jax down the hall toward her studio.

Piper looked over her shoulder at him, but kept going. "I'll be back in a minute."

No. That wouldn't work. She was going to ask Jax to be her fake boyfriend. He was sure of it. That was the last thing Coop wanted—because he wanted her to be *his* fake girlfriend.

His phone rang again. He didn't have to look at the caller ID to know who it was. It was Everett's ring tone. He knew Ev was calling to set up a time when he and Annalise could get together with him and his new girlfriend. Coop hadn't made any progress in finding anyone.

When Piper had told him about Elle's idea of a fake boyfriend, he thought they could help each other. Was about to suggest as much when Shane and Jax had showed up.

"This can't wait. It's important," he insisted.

Piper looked annoyed, but she gave him a reluctant nod. Turning to Jax, she said, "Can you give me a minute? I promise this won't take long."

Jax nodded. "Sure. No problem."

Piper grasped Jax's hands and squeezed them. "Please don't leave before we have a chance to talk."

Jax gave her a speculative glance and nodded. "I'll

be in the other room." He jerked his head in the direction of the main space.

Piper thrust open the door to her studio and gestured for Coop to proceed her in.

He stepped inside.

She followed and closed the door. "Okay. What's so important that it couldn't wait a few minutes?"

Coop opened his mouth, but no words came out. Was he really considering Piper Kavanaugh, of all people, to be his fake girlfriend for a few weeks?

Coop started pacing from one end of the room to the other. They'd been at each other's throats less than a week ago. How could they possibly pull this off?

He peered around the room. The art projects Noah and her nieces had painted a couple of nights ago were still on prominent display.

He'd been wrong about her. The old Piper may have been an ice queen—*no maybe about it*—but the grown woman who stood before him was anything but.

"I don't have time for games." Piper threw her hands up in the air and headed toward the door.

Crap. "You need a fake boyfriend, right?"

She turned back to face him. "That's none of your business." She folded her arms across her chest.

Coop blew out a breath. "Just hear me out, please."

"Okay. Fine. Yes. I need a fake boyfriend. What of it?"

"How about me?" His words came out in a rush.

She stared at him as if he were delusional. "Ha ha. So funny." Piper shook her head. "Look. I appreciate you bailing me out with Donny, but come on… I need a real solution to my problem."

"I'm serious. We could be the perfect solution for each other."

He almost laughed at the confused look on her face,

but he figured she wouldn't appreciate it. "A situation has developed and I find myself in need of a temporary girlfriend. For the next few weeks, to be exact. It wouldn't require much commitment on your part. One, maybe two outings with some friends of mine, and a date for a wedding I'm in the first week of February."

A thoughtful expression appeared on her face. "So, you're talking two or three dates?"

She was considering his proposal. He wanted to pump his fists in the air.

She cast a curious glance in his direction. "Would you be willing to include a lunch or something with my mother—you know, to make it look real?"

Hell, yes. He'd do whatever she needed. "I can do that. Do we have a deal?" He flashed what he hoped was a winsome smile.

Her face fell. "Oh my God. What am I thinking?" Piper dragged a hand through her hair.

Coop wouldn't give up now. He needed this to work. He was running out of options. "Piper." He moved closer.

The air between them thickened, sparking and crackling with energy.

Piper stared at him. Her eyes turned a smoky shade of gray.

His heart rate kicked up a notch.

"Who would believe you and I are an item?" Her voice was a soft caress against his skin.

A shudder ran down his spine.

Coop swallowed hard and fought the overwhelming urge to close the infinitesimal distance between them. "Donny found it plausible."

"He doesn't know our history." A lock of hair fell forward as she shook her head.

He reached out and tucked the strands behind her ear. Coop closed his eyes for a moment and enjoyed the feel of the soft, silky tresses against his calloused fingertips.

She drew in a swift breath. "We don't even like each other."

"You're right." He gave a sage nod.

"We can barely tolerate being in the same room together." Her lips parted and the way she was looking at him, like maybe he could make her wildest fantasies come true...

All sense of reason vanished. Coop snaked an arm around her waist and hauled her up against him.

"Cooper!" Her cry sounded desperate. She wrapped every inch of her supple form around his body and held on tight.

A jolt of electricity sizzled through him, sending a thousand watts of need racing through his system. He crushed his lips to hers.

"Oh God." Her mouth ravaged his while her hands explored every inch of him.

The heady sent of roses and jasmine filled his senses. His blood roared through his veins, pounding out a deafening beat.

"What the hell is going on?" Shane's voice thundered through the room.

Oh, shit. Coop jerked away from her. "I...ah..."

Jax chuckled. "You two need to get a room."

"Like hell they do." Shane grabbed two fistfuls of Coop's T-shirt and dragged him close.

His eyes widened. He'd never seen Shane so mad.

"Stop it." Piper pushed her way between them and shoved her brother hard. Caught off-balance, he fell backward and hit the floor. "You're acting like a caveman, for goodness' sake."

"It's not her fault," he blurted. He didn't want Shane to be mad at Piper. He'd started this and he'd take full responsibility.

Piper looked him in the eye. "While I appreciate you trying to help, I don't need you to defend me or take the blame on my behalf. Neither of us has done anything wrong."

"Like hell he hasn't." Shane stood and pointed at him.

Piper turned to her brother, who was walking toward them again. "This is none of your damned business."

She was right, but that fact wouldn't stop Shane from butting in. He wanted to safeguard his sister. Coop couldn't blame him. Family meant everything to Shane. He'd do anything for them.

He admired Shane's protective nature.

Shane advanced on him, growling like a grizzly bear protecting its cub.

Coop didn't flinch, but it was a near thing. "Calm down, Shane."

Shane invaded his space and glowered at him.

Coop stood his ground.

"How dare you walk in here unannounced and uninvited and start yelling like you're some lord and master?" Hands on hips, head held high, Piper looked magnificent.

Shane blinked and turned to face her. "You're my little sister," he announced, as if that explained everything.

"I'm not a kid anymore. I'm a grown woman. I can, and will, kiss whoever I want, whenever and wherever I deem fit. You have no say in the matter. Do I make myself clear?"

Shane stared at her, a stunned expression on his face. "Are you telling me that you two…" He didn't complete the rest of his sentence.

"Are together." Piper looped her arms around his waist.

He liked the feel of her hands on him. The rightness of it.

Wait. What? Coop frowned. Where had that thought come from? The only thing between them was a little lust. Pure and simple.

"Come again?" Shane's eyes bugged out.

Coop released the breath he was holding. "We haven't told anyone yet."

"You two... Are you really..." Shane shook his head, a perplexed expression on his face. "No way. I don't believe it."

Piper looked at Coop and grinned. "I guess my brother here needs more convincing." She rose up on her tiptoes and yanked his head down to hers.

"Okay, okay." Shane held up a hand. "I believe you."

Jax smirked. "All that anger you directed to each other over the years was really just pent-up sexual frustration."

"You're not helping." Shane clapped his hands over his ears.

"I'm not trying to help." Jax grinned. He turned to Piper. "I've got to get going, but I'm on board."

"What are you talking about?" Shane asked.

"Piper said she had a proposition for me," Jax said.

"Um, about that..." Heat crept up Piper's neck and flooded her cheeks. "You don't have to worry about it anymore."

Jax's brows furrowed. "Are you sure? I don't mind doing a show here at your gallery. That is what you wanted, right? Why you asked me when I was going to be back in town?"

Piper walked over to where Jax was standing and

linked her arm through his. "Of course. What else could I want?"

She turned an even brighter shade of red. Coop chuckled.

"Great. I'll give you a call and we can settle the details before I leave." He gave her a quick kiss on the cheek.

"Jax." Coop practically growled the name.

Piper gave him a what-the-heck glance.

He was only playing the part of her besotted boyfriend. He wasn't *really* jealous.

Liar.

"Sorry. Old habits die hard." Jax grinned and released Piper's arm. "I'll talk to you later." He waved and exited the room.

Shane looked at Coop and then at Piper. He shook his head, a dumbfounded expression on his face. "I should get going, too."

"I'll see you out." Piper ushered her astounded brother through the door. She glanced back at Coop and mouthed a silent "Stay here."

Coop stayed put and waited for her to return. He heard their muffled voices and the noise when they moved the stove onto the dolly. The sound of the elevator car a moment later signaled Shane's departure.

Coop paced back and forth across the space. What if she said no?

What if she said yes?

Anticipation hummed and buzzed inside him.

Shit.

Chapter Nine

Piper's mind raced as she walked alongside her brother. She'd just kissed Cooper Turner—and liked it. More than just liked, if she was being honest. How was that possible?

One minute she was explaining why his crazy idea of having a fake relationship with each other wouldn't work and the next...

Driving need thrummed through her body and all she wanted was for him to ravage her like there was no tomorrow. She would have begged him to do as much if Shane and Jax hadn't walked in when they did.

Thank goodness for small favors. Her brother had saved her from making a complete fool of herself. Piper shuddered.

They stopped when they reached the kitchen.

"So…" Shane grabbed the dolly and moved it behind the stove. He looked Piper in the eyes. "You want to tell me what that was all about in there?"

Piper locked her gaze with his and folded her arms across her chest. "No." How could she when she wasn't sure herself?

"Come on. I walk in there and Cooper, of all people, looks like he's about to—" Shane didn't finish the sentence.

A shiver raced down her spine as she filled in the blank. *No, no, no.* "I'm a grown woman, Shane."

He moved the stove onto the dolly and secured it with straps. "You're my baby sister. I don't want to see you get hurt."

She grinned. "That's not going to happen." It's not like she was going to fall for Cooper.

"You don't know that. I like Cooper. He's like a brother to me, but he's also a guy. I saw the way he looked at you." Shane shook his head. "I don't like it."

Despite her objections, she was happy Shane had her back.

Another reason it was great to be home. She'd missed her family. Missed the closeness she'd shared with Mia and Shane. But she wasn't about to allow any of them—not her brother, not her sister, and especially not her mother—to interfere with her love life.

Her mother, of all people, had no right. Talk about the pot calling the kettle black. She wanted Piper to fall in love, when she had never moved on and done the same. *Fifteen years* since she'd lost her husband. And Mom hadn't so much as glanced at another man. No, Piper could and would decide relationship matters, or lack thereof, for herself.

"You have nothing to worry about." She kissed her brother's cheek.

Cooper Turner wasn't a love interest. He wasn't even a *like* interest. They couldn't stand to be around one another.

Okay, that wasn't true anymore. The truth was, he wasn't as hard to be around as she'd once imagined. This past week had proved that. They'd worked well together and the days had flown by.

"You two really like each other?" Shane asked.

"Yes." She could admit that Cooper, the man, wasn't

at all like Cooper, the boy, who'd been the bane of her existence ten years ago.

And she wasn't anything like the young woman who thought cutting herself off from everyone and everything she'd once held dear was her only option. She was ten years older. Ten years wiser. She'd learned to deal with the loss of her father and was starting to see the past from a new perspective.

"This thing with Cooper... It's what you want?" Shane pressed.

Piper nodded. "It is." With any luck, Mom would stop the husband search once and for all.

"Okay." He sighed. "I guess I can get used to you guys together."

Piper laughed because Shane's expression conveyed anything but confidence.

"Thank you." She threw her arms around him.

"For what?" Shane asked.

"For being my big brother. I couldn't ask for a better one."

"You got it. I'm always here for you."

"You always have been."

Shane arched a brow and slung an arm around her shoulder. "You know I'm going to kick Cooper's ass if he hurts you."

She grinned. "I know."

Shane released her and grabbed the dolly handles. "I'll see you later. Oh, and tell the rest of the family so they don't find out about you and Cooper the way I did." He shook his head. "Sooner rather than later."

"I will." Piper walked beside him as he strode to the elevator. "Thanks again for taking the stove."

The door opened and Shane moved inside. "You're welcome."

The car door closed.

Piper glanced down the hall at her studio. "Here goes nothing."

Cooper paced back and forth across the room as she entered. He stopped short when he saw her.

He trained his gaze on her. "Well?"

"We have a deal."

Cooper flashed a smile that made her go weak in the knees.

He strode toward her. Would he kiss her again? A frisson of pleasure washed over her. Who knew the man could kiss like...like all her schoolgirl fantasies come true.

Just thinking about it now... Piper fanned herself. She touched her palms to her cheeks. Lord, they were hot as Hades and probably fire-engine red.

Heaven help her, she wanted his lips on hers again. Wanted to drown in the sweet pleasure rushing through her veins. The—

No, no, no. Not happening. Not again.

Something flickered in his gaze. He felt it, too. The heady beat of desire that pulsed between them. Her heart beat a rapid tattoo.

"So... What should we do now?" Cooper dragged a hand through his already disheveled hair.

She'd done that. Messed up those short soft tresses with her hands. She licked her suddenly dry lips.

Get a grip.

"We should tell our families about us, and not let them find out like Shane did." Piper shuddered. How were they supposed to do that? Her mother and Mia would be as shocked as Shane. She could only assume all the Turners would react to the news in the same fashion.

Cooper nodded. "Yeah. That makes sense."

"Any ideas on how we should break the news?" she asked.

"I know that Shane finding us…" He twirled his finger in the air.

A shiver ran down her spine at the thought of what they'd been doing.

"That wasn't ideal, but in the long run, I think it was a good thing. He witnessed…" Cooper blew out a breath. "You know what your brother saw. What I'm trying to say is…"

Piper sucked in some much-needed air and blew it out slowly. "We made our claim credible."

He stopped and looked her in the eye. "Yes. Let's go to the TK offices. We can kill two birds with one stone."

"You want to tell our parents first?" Piper swallowed hard. Never in her wildest imaginings would she have ever come up with a scenario where she'd tell her mother she was dating Cooper Turner. She shook her head. What was she supposed to say?

"I was thinking more like we could get them in the same room and tell them together. That way we make sure we get our story straight. The last thing we need is for you to say one thing and me to say another."

She nodded. He had a point. They needed to be on the same page with this.

"Ready?" Cooper held out his hand to her.

She grasped his palm in hers and ignored the tingles racing up and down her arm. She looked at him. "As I'll ever be."

Cooper nodded. "Let's do this."

They exited the gallery space and walked down the grand staircase to the first floor.

Piper slanted her gaze to their joined hands. His

large hand engulfed her much smaller one. His grip was strong but gentle at the same time. She liked it.

Good grief. She'd fallen down the rabbit hole, head-first, and knocked herself silly. Yes, that must be why she was thinking such ridiculous thoughts.

He dropped her hand when they exited the building. She missed the sensation of his calloused palm against her softer skin.

Earth to Piper. Come in, Piper. This whole thing is a farce—remember? A part they'd each agreed to play. A means to an end.

"My car or yours?" she asked. "We should drive together. Like you said, we need to get our story straight."

"I'll drive." He jerked his head toward his Camaro.

"Heck, yes." She'd admired it the moment he'd pulled it into the parking lot on the first day they'd started construction. "Who wouldn't love to ride in this baby? She's gorgeous. What year is she?"

He looked at her, nonplussed. "You like my car?"

Piper laughed. "Heck, yeah. It's cool-looking." And just a little bit sexy, or maybe that was the guy driving it. She shook her head. *Down the rabbit hole, all right.* "It's a classic—right?"

He nodded. "1968."

"It's in perfect condition."

Cooper chuckled. "You should have seen her when I first got her a couple of years ago. I rebuilt the whole thing."

"That's impressive."

He flashed a cocky grin. "I'm a man of many talents."

The sensation of his lips sliding over hers while his hands touched every inch of her flooded her brain. Piper sucked in a deep, steadying breath. *Oh my, yes, you are.*

Cooper unlocked the car and held the door open for her.

A gentleman. She approved. "Thank you." Piper slid onto the cool leather seat.

Cooper slid in beside her a moment later.

"I know it's cold out, but can you put the top down? We could crank up the heat to keep us warm." Piper sent him a winsome smile.

"A girl after my own heart, but we're not going to be able to talk if I do that."

Damn. He was right, and they needed to talk.

"Another time?" he asked.

"Sounds good."

He started the car and pulled out onto the main road.

"So, how are we going to explain—" She couldn't bring herself to say the words so she just pointed to him and back to herself again.

"I've been thinking about that." His sexy grin sent her heart thudding and her stomach flip-flopped.

"Jax's explanation is out of the question."

He laughed, a deep, rumbly sound that vibrated through her in the most delicious way. "Don't worry. I wasn't about to suggest we tell our mothers that."

Thank God for small mercies. Piper shook her head. "Good. So, what are we going to tell them?"

"Keep it simple and believable. After spending so much time together over the last week, we realized we have a lot in common."

That made sense and it was true, too.

Cooper continued. "The more we talked, the more we liked each other."

Piper sucked in a deep breath. That was true, too. The more she got to know Cooper Turner, the more she did like him.

Chapter Ten

Cooper pulled his car into a parking space at the TK Construction offices a few minutes later. He removed the key from the ignition and looked at her. "Ready?"

Yes. No. Lord, she didn't know if she could go through with this. Piper sucked in a deep breath to steady her jangling nerves.

Nerves. Yes. That was all this jumping and jittering inside her was.

Cooper looked her in the eyes. "Think about Donny if you need to stiffen your resolve."

No way did she want to go through another setup again. It wasn't fair to her or to any potential guy Mom chose to match her up with.

"We've got this. Together." Cooper reached for her hand and gave it a firm squeeze.

He was right. They could do this.

Piper nodded. "Let's get this over with." She jumped out of the passenger seat and shut the door.

They reached the front entrance and walked inside.

"Where's Laura?" she asked. The receptionist desk was vacant.

"She takes a late lunch." Cooper glanced at his watch. "She should be back in a few minutes. Don't worry. We can still get into the office."

Cooper held his badge to the scanner by the double

glass doors. Pulling the door on the right open, he gestured for her to go through.

Piper walked past the conference room and down the quiet corridor that led to the executive offices. She stopped at her mother's, but found the room empty.

"She's not here." Piper wasn't sure if she was mad or relieved.

The faint sound of female voices drifted into the corridor.

"That sounds like your mom." Cooper gestured to an office farther down. "She's in my mother's office. Come on." He grabbed her hand and practically dragged her along.

"How mad was Piper?" Debby asked.

Piper stopped short at the mention of her name.

Cooper turned because she'd jerked his arm, hard, with her sudden halt.

"Hold on," she whispered in his ear. Piper wanted to hear what they were saying. They were talking about her, after all.

"Pretty mad, if the look on her face was anything to go by," Mom said. "She figured out what I was up to pretty fast. I really thought she'd have a lot in common with Donny."

It was bad enough that Mom tried to play matchmaker at Piper's expense, but to brag about her exploits to Debby... Piper's hands clenched into tight fists.

"I told you—you were too hasty. You didn't even give her and Cooper a chance," Debby said. "I still think they belong together. We just need to give them a little more time together to realize it for themselves."

Debby Turner thought they *belonged* together? Her jaw dropped. Lord, the woman must be a card short of a full deck if she thought that.

Cooper's hand clenched around hers. She turned and saw the same stunned expression on his face that must be on hers.

"Maybe you're right," Mom agreed. "I just hope they don't realize what we've done. It was pretty risky making them work together."

"Desperate times call for desperate measures," Debby quipped.

Cooper blew out a harsh breath.

Piper turned to him. "*Be quiet*," she mouthed. She couldn't believe what she'd just heard. How dare they conspire against her and Cooper! What right did they have?

"That's it," Cooper whispered in her ear. "I'm going to give them a piece of my mind." He started toward the open office door.

"No. Wait." She tugged him back to her. "I've got a better idea. Come with me." Piper walked back the way they came.

"But!" Cooper protested.

"No buts. We need to get out of here before anyone spots us. I'll explain everything when we get back to your car."

"This way." He marched them to the side exit. "We don't want to risk running into Laura."

Once outside, they hurried to Cooper's car and jumped inside.

"Quick. Get us out of here. This car is way too conspicuous." Piper started laughing. She couldn't help it. The whole situation reminded her of a television sitcom.

"What's so funny?" Cooper looked at her as if she'd grown two heads. "I'm furious with the two of them. I would think you would be, too."

"Oh, I'm pissed off. Believe me. They have some

nerve messing with our lives, but confronting them doesn't solve our problem. I've tried that before with my mother and she acts as if she has no idea what I'm talking about. What we need is to make sure they never try this again. With either of us."

Cooper pulled out into traffic. "How are we going to do that?"

She grinned and patted his knee. "You, my friend, are going to break my heart."

Coop jerked his attention from the road for a brief minute to look at Piper. "I'm going to what?"

Her soft chuckle sent shivers zinging up and down his spine.

"You heard me right."

He shook his head. "I don't get it."

Piper covered her heart with her hands. "When you break things off with me, I'm going to be so devastated that both our moms will feel guilty for throwing us together. If they see how upset I am, they won't try it again. With either of us."

He was all for that. No way did he want his mother, or anyone else, for that matter, playing matchmaker for him. But… "I'm going to need a good reason to dump you."

"I know. You can say you fell for someone else. An old girlfriend, maybe? You know someone who you had a relationship with in the past. You called it quits, but with some time and distance you've both realized how right you were together."

An image of Rachel floated into his mind. The idea of reconnecting with her now made him nauseous. "No." His forceful decline had her eyes going wide.

"Okay." She nodded. "No problem. We've got a little

time to figure it out. We just need to make sure we're on the same page about it."

Coop blew out a breath and tried to calm the churning in his stomach. "So, what are we going to do about telling our families?"

"I haven't figured that out yet." Piper's stomach rumbled audibly.

Coop slated a quick glance in her direction and smiled at the pink staining her cheeks. "Hungry?"

"Yes. With everything going on today I missed lunch."

"I never ate either. Have you had one of Layla's burgers since you've been back?"

"I have not. Are they good?" Piper asked.

"They're the best in the state. Today is your lucky day, because I'm treating."

"Then maybe I'll have two."

He caught her smirk out of the corner of his eye and laughed.

Coop pulled into a parking spot at the restaurant a few minutes later.

Exiting the car, they walked toward the entrance.

Coop couldn't be sure how they ended up holding hands. Maybe his hand had been by his side and Piper reached for it, or it was the other way around. Either way, he liked the feel of her slender fingers entwined with his.

He pulled open the door and they walked in. Approaching the hostess, he asked for a table for two.

"It's a forty-five-minute wait," the woman said. "Would you like to wait in the bar?"

Piper looked at him and gave a brief shake of her head. She pulled him aside. "Let's go somewhere else."

They were on the same page. "How about the diner in town?"

"Perfect." Piper smiled. "I'll drive. I'm going to come back here anyway to finish up some of what we were working on in the gallery earlier, so I can drop you off."

"Or we could walk. It will probably be faster than driving between here and there. The stoplights on Main Street will delay us for sure. Not to mention finding a parking spot. Even at—" he glanced at his watch "—one thirty on a Monday." He gave her his best winsome smile.

She looked at him as if he'd lost his mind. "It's cold out there."

"By Southern California standards, maybe, but forty-five degrees Fahrenheit is downright balmy for New England in January. Come on." He held out his hand. "It won't take long."

She let out a resigned sigh. "I see you're still a big fan of walking places."

"I am," he nodded. "I problem-solve when I walk."

"Fine." Piper zipped up her coat and threw the hood up over her head. "Problem-solve how we're going to convince people we're a real couple, especially our families."

"Yes, ma'am." He gave a jaunty salute.

They exited Layla's restaurant and headed toward town.

If he was going to come up with a solution to their problem, he needed to know the facts. "What did you say to Shane about us?"

Piper looked at him. "Not much, really. He was still reeling from finding us..." She gave a little twirl of her finger. "Well, you know what he saw."

Coop's pulse quickened just thinking about their interlude. *So not the time.* "Did you mention anything about the length of time we've been seeing each other?"

"I've only been back in New Suffolk for a few days." She shook her head. "Lord, how are we going to convince anyone we're for real?"

He'd thought about that. "What if we told everyone that we reconnected last April when you were here for Mia's thirtieth birthday party, and we found we had more in common than we realized."

She stared at him. "But I never saw you."

"You never saw me at the party." He'd stayed away on purpose to avoid her. It was what they both did on those few occasions when she came to town over the years. Sometimes he begged off if the families got together and sometimes Piper would. "But you were in town for a couple of weeks, weren't you? We can say we ran into each other and got to talking."

She shrugged. "I guess that could work, but we're going to need a little more than that."

"Agreed. You came back last July, right?"

Her eyes widened. "How did you know that? I was only in town for four days to see if I could expedite getting the building permits for the gallery."

"My mother told me." He snorted. She always told him when Piper came to town. He used to think it was because she wanted to give him a heads-up so that he could avoid running into her while she was here, but after her comment to Jane earlier, he wasn't so sure. Lord, why would she believe he and Piper belonged together? That made no sense. They'd been at odds with each other for as long as he could remember. What could she possibly know that he didn't?

Coop gave himself a mental shake. Why was he

wasting time even thinking about it? Mom was wrong. End of story.

"Did you stay with your mom during that time?" he asked.

"I stayed at her house, but she wasn't there the last couple of days. That reminds me, have you met her friend Chris? Mom said they met at book club last spring."

"No." Coop shook his head. "What does this Chris have to do with what we're talking about?"

"She's the reason Mom wasn't home. She and Chris went to Cape Cod for a few days. Neither Mia or Shane have met her either, so I was wondering if you have."

"I haven't," he confirmed. "But I know your mom is really into her book club. Maybe Chris is a new member." Coop shrugged. "If you're concerned, ask her to introduce you."

Piper grinned. "I can definitely do that now that I'm back in New Suffolk."

He steered the conversation back to the problem at hand. "Is it plausible that we ran into each other again the times you were here?"

"I didn't socialize much, but yes, I suppose it would have been possible. Maybe we ran into each other at town hall? I spent a lot of time waiting to see the planning and zoning commissioner."

He grinned. "We had a cup of that sludge that passes for coffee."

"That's good." She nodded. "But when did we start dating?"

"When I came out to LA."

"You were in LA last summer?" Her eyes rounded.

"No, but my fraternity brother, Jack, lives out there.

I could say I went out to see him the second week of August."

She shot him a curious glance. "Why the second week of August? That's rather specific."

"Because I took off for a couple of weeks during that time period, and I didn't mention where I was going." He'd been down in the dumps about his breakup with Rachel and had needed to get away.

Coop continued, "So I decided to look you up while I was there."

"Now, why would you do that?" She looked him in the eye.

He shrugged. "Things seemed to be better between us after we talked in July so I thought I'd say hi while I was in town."

Piper nodded. "Okay, so we got together while you were in LA and we talked some more and…" She shot a sideways glance at him.

"We went out a few times. Got to know each other better and decided to keep seeing each other since you were moving back to New Suffolk. We didn't say anything because we wanted the opportunity to see where the relationship was going without interference from our families."

"Amen to that." Piper grinned and pumped her fist in the air.

He chuckled. "I thought you might like that reason."

"Oh, yes. And what you just said could work, but what about what happened between us that day at TK when my mother told us we had to work together?"

"It wasn't that bad," he said.

"Really, 'cause I'm pretty sure I tried to walk out." The tone of her voice dared him to deny it.

"All right. I still need to think about how to finesse that," he admitted.

"You'd better think fast because we've already reached the center of town. The diner is only a block away." She pointed up the street.

Coop grinned. "We can keep walking."

"You can keep walking. I'm starving. I'm going to the diner." Piper stopped short. "But first." She gazed at the jewelry store window display. "I forgot this place was so close to the diner. Elle told me they feature some pieces made by a local artist."

"Did you want to go inside?" he asked.

"Not now. I'll come back later when I have more time. That's her stuff next to that gorgeous engagement ring on display." She pointed to an eclectic diamond solitaire with a thin strip of gold that was shaped like a curlicue, with the stone mounted between the bottom and top points.

"You like that ring, huh?" Cooper chuckled.

She smiled. "I do. I mean it's gorgeous. Classy. Understated." She flexed her left hand out in front of her and glanced at her third finger, as if she were imagining what it would look like there.

He chuckled. "I thought you didn't want to get married."

Color invaded her cheeks. "I don't. Definitely not."

"Then why are you admiring engagement rings?" *Damn.* The words slipped out of his mouth before his brain could engage. He shouldn't have tried joking with her. She used to hate when he did that. He held his breath, waiting for her condescending reply.

Piper let out something between a laugh and snort. "Touché."

He grinned. He couldn't help it. He liked this friendly

rapport they were developing. "It's definitely not a tra-ditional diamond solitaire."

Piper laughed out loud. "If you haven't noticed, I'm not traditional either."

"That's okay. I like unique."

She flashed that gorgeous smile again and every-thing seemed right with his world.

"Piper Kavanaugh, is that you?" A short, rotund woman approached them.

"Do you know her?" Coop didn't recognize her.

"Hellen Francis. She's Mom's next-door neighbor. White colonial house on the right."

He nodded. "The nosy neighbor with the cardboard-tasting sugar cookies." He hadn't seen her for years.

"Yup," Piper whispered to him. "I can't believe you remember her cookies. She used to use them as an ex-cuse to come over and find out what was going on."

"They were pretty bad."

Piper wiggled her brows. "No kidding."

Hellen stopped in front of them. "Yes, it's you, Piper."

Piper smiled. "Hi, Mrs. Francis."

"I think you're old enough to call me Hellen." She pulled Piper against her chest and wrapped her arms around her. "It's so good to see you again. Your mother told me you were moving home, but she didn't tell me you were already back."

"It's only been a few days." Eyes wide, Piper looked at him and mouthed, "Help."

Coop grinned. "Hello, Mrs. Francis." He extended his arm toward the woman in the hopes that she'd re-lease her death grip on Piper to shake his outstretched hand. "I'm Cooper Turner. Do you remember me?"

"Ron and Debby's youngest. Of course." Hellen released Piper and grasped his palm with hers. "I didn't recognize you. It's been a while since I've seen you."

"Yes," he agreed. "It has been."

"What are you two doing here?" Hellen eyed them curiously.

"Just a little window shopping." Piper pointed behind her.

Hellen looked at the display. *"Oh!"* Her eyes widened and she shot Piper a coy smile. "I see." She winked and said, "Well, I won't keep you anymore. You have a good day." She gave a little wave and continued down the street.

"Bye," he and Piper called in unison.

"That was interesting," he said as they watched her retreating form.

"Come on, let's get going." Piper started toward the diner.

"So…back to the problem at hand." Coop heaved out a sigh.

"You've come up with a solution?" She chuckled. "Boy this walking thing really works for you."

"If you are referring to that day at TK, we can say we had a fight. And we were still annoyed at each other when your mom dropped her bomb about us having to work together."

"Okay. That works for me." Piper crossed her fingers. "Let's hope everyone buys it."

Coop pulled open the door to the diner. The place was still packed, even this late in the afternoon. He peered around. "There's an empty booth in the back, on the right."

"I see it." Piper walked in the direction of the vacant table.

She slid into the bench seat on the right and he sat next to her.

Piper grabbed two of the laminated menus and passed one to him. "How's the burger here?" she asked.

"Pretty good, but not as good as Layla's, if you ask me."

Their server appeared a moment later and set two glasses of water on the table. "What'll you have?"

"A cheeseburger, medium rare, with fries, and a Diet Coke." Piper slotted her menu back in the holder behind the salt and pepper.

Coop nodded. "Make it two." When their server departed, he asked Piper, "When do you want to tell the rest of the family about us?"

Piper's cell rang. "Let me see who this is. I'm expecting a call from another artist I interviewed."

"Sure. No problem."

Her gaze widened. "It's my mother. I wouldn't have expected her to call me so soon after that act she pulled today with Donny. She usually avoids me like the plague after one of her matchmaking stunts."

"Maybe Shane told her about finding us together this morning?"

She shook her head. "I don't think so. As far as I know, he was heading to work after he dropped off the stove at the donation center." Piper connected the call. "Hi, Mom. What's up?"

Coop could hear Jane's excited voice emanating out of Piper's phone, but he couldn't make out what she was saying.

Piper gawked at him and whispered, "Oh my God." To her mother, she said, "As a matter of fact, yes."

"What's going on?" he whispered.

She shook her head and he heard Jane start talking again.

She let out a lighthearted laugh. "Yes, Mom." Piper looked at him and grinned like a Cheshire cat.

He heard more of Jane's indistinct chatter.

Piper glanced at him and rolled her eyes. "Unbelievable," she murmured to him. To Jane, she said, "It's not like you gave me the opportunity when I saw you this morning. You were too busy trying to set me up with Donny."

Did Jane know he'd made Donny believe he was Piper's boyfriend? *Crap.* Had Donny said something to her?

"Wait. *What?*" Piper shook her head. "You're joking, right?" She smacked her hand to her head. "No. Absolutely not. That's the craziest thing I've ever heard." Her gaze widened. "No, she was… Mom? Are you still there?" She lowered the phone and stared at it.

The color drained from Piper's face.

Holy shit. He wrapped an arm around her. "What's wrong?"

"She hung up on me." Piper stared at him, a dazed expression on her face. "I forgot how the rumor mill works in this town."

His brows furrowed and he eased away from her. She seemed more confused now than upset. "What are you talking about?"

"Hellen Francis." Piper shook her head. "We can add notorious gossip to her nosy neighbor description. She couldn't wait to call my mother and tell her how she saw the two of us together."

"You're kidding." He let loose a hearty chuckle.

"Nope." Piper blew out a breath. "She watched us walk into the diner together."

"Man, you had me worried for a minute. From the look on your face, I thought something was seriously wrong."

"We were holding hands."

Why did she still look as if they were in a heap of trouble? "So what?" He waved off her concern. "Don't worry about blabbermouth Hellen. Actually, we should thank her. She did us a huge favor. She's solved our problem for us."

"I don't think so." She shook her head.

"Jane knows we're a couple now. She's probably on the phone with my mom right now." He'd get a call any minute from her asking if what Jane had told her about him and Piper was true. Problem solved as far as he could see.

Piper looked him in the eye. "You'd better hope not. Because you don't want her to tell Debby what she said to me."

"Why not?" This was the perfect solution as far as he was concerned. "What did she say?"

"She thinks we're about to become engaged."

He gawked at her. "Come again?"

"Betrothed. Affianced. Promised to each other." She cradled her face in her palms and shook her head.

Coop couldn't believe it. "How the hell did Hellen come up with that?"

"Remember when I said we were window shopping?"

Coop nodded. "Yes. What of it?"

"Apparently Hellen thought we were shopping for an engagement ring."

His jaw just about hit the floor. What the hell were they going to do now?

Chapter Eleven

How the hell had this happened? One minute Mom was asking if it was true that she was having lunch with Cooper and the next...

Piper replayed her conversation with Hellen in her mind again. Not once had she indicated anything about being engaged to Cooper. Heck, she hadn't even referred to him as her boyfriend.

Okay, yes. There were some diamond rings in the window display. A lot of them, in fact, but there'd been other pieces on display, too. How the woman had come up with her and Cooper shopping for rings was beyond her. She only knew she needed to nip this in the bud now before Mom went off on a rampage and told everyone in town. Assuming Hellen hadn't already done that.

Oh, dear Lord. Please no.

"Here you go." The server appeared holding two burger platters.

She'd get sick if she ate anything now.

"Change in plan," Cooper said. "We need these to go. And the check, too, please."

"No problem. I'll be right back." The server picked up the dishes and disappeared a moment later.

Coop clasped her hands in his. "It's going to be all right. We'll go and talk to your mother and straighten everything out."

"I tried doing that when I spoke to her just now. She wouldn't listen. She just gets something in her head and she just runs with it. She even denied trying to set me up with Donny this morning." Piper gritted her teeth. "'I have no idea what you're talking about, dear,'" Piper mimicked. "Good grief. She wants to go friggin' *wedding dress* shopping tomorrow. Not that I agreed to that. I gave Mom a hard no. Do you think she listened?" Piper didn't wait for Cooper to respond before she continued. "No sirree. She just kept chattering away as if I hadn't spoken a word." She shook her head. "I don't even have a diamond on my hand and she's planning the wedding already." Her stomach jumped and jittered.

"Piper." Coop lifted her chin and waited for her gaze to settle on his. "Is it possible that this is just your mom trying to set you up again?"

Piper threw her hands in the air. "That makes no sense."

He grasped her hands in his again. The gentle squeeze gave her comfort and she relaxed.

"I'm sorry. I didn't mean to snap at you. This whole thing has me rattled."

"It's all right." He offered a reassuring smile.

The server approached. She set a bag with the to-go boxes on the table and handed Cooper the check. He placed several bills in the holder. Handing it to the server, he said, "It's all set." To Piper, he said, "Come on, let's get out of here."

Grabbing the bag with one hand, he guided her to the exit.

She thought about what he'd said right before she'd lost it. "What did you mean about Mom setting me up again?"

"Think about it. As far as everyone knows, you just returned to New Suffolk a few days ago. I know we came up with a story to make our relationship plausible, but no one else knows that. There's no way anyone would even think we were engaged after just a few days."

Piper stopped walking midstride. "You're right."

"So why would your mother?" he asked. "What, exactly, did she say to you?"

Piper pursed her lips as she tried to remember the conversation. "First, she told me that she'd just gotten off a call with Hellen Francis and that she'd seen us together."

"Blabbermouth," Coop quipped.

Piper chuckled. "Yes, indeed. Then, Mom wanted to know if the two of us were having a late lunch together. After that she mentioned something about Hellen seeing us holding hands and did that mean what she thought it meant and why hadn't we told her."

"To be fair, you wouldn't have had anything to tell her about you and me. That all happened post Donny setup."

Piper scowled up at him. "Whose side are you on?"

"Ours." He grinned. "Now, how did she go from lunch and us being a couple to planning the wedding?"

"She said, and I quote, 'What Hellen told me is true then?'"

"And you answered yes."

"Of course." Piper agreed. "I thought Hellen had told her we were a couple, but apparently, she told her we were shopping for engagement rings. Unless…do you think my mom made that part up?"

"I think Hellen embellished her story and now Jane is trying to make sure it sticks. I mean, we did just hear both our moms confess to trying to set us up."

"Oh. My. God." Piper's eyes widened as comprehension dawned. "She's up to her old tricks again."

"So what do you want to do?" he asked.

She wanted to stop this once and for all. A plan hatched in her brain. She looked at him and grinned.

Grasping his hand in hers, she said, "Cooper Turner, will you fake marry me?"

"Have you lost your mind?" he asked.

Her smile lit up the sky that had turned dark with storm clouds. "No. I'm just trying to use the current situation to our advantage."

He shook his head. "You're going to have to explain, because I have no idea what's going on in that pretty head of yours."

"You think I'm pretty?" Her surprised expression made him chuckle.

He'd have thought that much was obvious from the way he'd been kissing her earlier today. "Don't play coy with me."

"I wasn't—" She shook her head.

Was that hurt in her gaze? Could she really not know how attractive he found her?

She straightened her shoulders. "What I was talking about was using what Hellen said about us window shopping for an engagement ring to our advantage."

They began walking again.

"Let's go to my place and we can warm up those burgers we ordered. They're probably cold by now, and I'm feeling hungry again." Piper turned and headed back the way they came.

He shook his head and followed. "Where are you going?"

"To my place. I live above the Coffee Palace. It's only a few blocks away and it's toasty warm inside." She rubbed her hands over her arms. "Now that the sun has disappeared behind the clouds, it's cold for this California girl."

"You're a New Suffolk native." He grinned. "Don't worry, you'll get used to the New England winters again soon."

"I hope so. Now let me explain what I'm thinking." She grabbed his hand. "You know, you're right about this walking thing. It helps me to think better, too."

"I daresay it's another thing we have in common." He winked at her.

She grinned. "I do believe you're correct in your assumption, my dear."

Her dear. He liked the sound of that. "All right. Let's hear it."

Piper told him her plan.

"Let me get this straight. You're going to pretend to be crazy about me over the next five weeks and not so subtly drop hints that you're expecting an engagement ring for Valentine's Day."

"You've got it." Piper nodded. "It fits in well with what you said earlier, that we've been dating since last summer when you came to LA. We might have to spend a little more time together than we initially planned." She shot him a speculative glance. "I can manage that, if you can."

Spending time with Piper was turning out to be much more pleasant than he'd ever imagined. "Sure. No problem."

"You'll end things right after the gallery opens, and tell everyone you're not ready for that kind of commitment. It's too soon."

He and Rachel had dated almost two years before he was ready to pop the question. He couldn't imagine proposing in such a short time frame. "That's the only part of all this that's true."

Her expression turned curious, but he wasn't going to elaborate.

"This plan gives both of us what we want and no one is the bad guy." She patted him on the arm. "Don't worry. I'll realize you dumping me was all for the best. Everything will be back to normal for the two of us in a couple of months."

"You don't think Jane will try her matchmaking again?" he asked.

"I don't think so. I'm banking on her not wanting to see me hurt again anytime soon. What about you? Will Debby interfere in your love life after this?" she asked.

"I don't see how she could. We'll prove to her once and for all that we don't belong together. Lord only knows why she thinks we do."

"I know." Piper's brows furrowed. "I was wondering the same thing when I heard her say that. She's obviously mistaken."

No doubt about it.

"Hey, Cooper." Fiona Carter, a fellow Humanity volunteer, came toward them.

"Hi, Fee." He smiled.

"It's great to see you. We missed you yesterday." Fiona gave him a quick hug.

Coop's brows furrowed. He never volunteered at Humanity on Sundays. Fiona knew that.

"Honey…are you going to introduce me to your friend?" Piper asked.

He couldn't help noticing how she emphasized the word *honey*, like she was trying to prove a point.

Fiona jerked away from him.

"I was just about to do that. Piper, this is Fiona Carter."

Piper extended her hand to Fiona. "Hi. I'm Cooper's girlfriend."

Fiona flicked a quick glance to him and back to Piper. "I didn't realize Cooper was seeing anyone. It's…ah… nice to meet you." She shook Piper's outstretched hand.

"You, too." Piper grabbed his hand with her free one and squeezed tight enough to cause some pain.

He flinched. What was with her?

Piper flashed an overbright smile. "So, how do you know Cooper?" she asked.

"We volunteer at Homes for Humanity," he said.

"Oh, how nice." Piper sounded none too pleased about that. "It was nice meeting you." She tugged on his hand. "We should get going." She pointed to the bag he carried containing their meals. "Our lunch is probably getting cold."

"Take care," he called as Piper practically dragged him away.

"See you on Saturday," Fiona called.

He waited a couple of minutes, until they were out of earshot of any passersby, and said, "You know, there's no need to be jealous of Fiona. There's nothing going on between us."

She looked up at him. Color invaded her face.

Coop grinned. He couldn't help it.

Piper looked him in the eye. "I'm not jealous."

He laughed and the heat on her face kicked up a notch. Could this situation get any more embarrassing?

"You could have fooled me," Coop said. "You made it damned clear that Fiona needed to keep her hands off me."

He was right, but she'd never admit that to him. "I reacted the same way any female would when a gorgeous woman she doesn't know comes up to her man on the street and plasters herself against him."

"I'm your man?" Cooper flashed a smug smirk.

Piper pulled a face. "You are for now, if this plan is going to work."

"She gave me a friendly hug," he protested. "That's all."

Piper grinned. "The way Jax hugged me this morning?" She'd almost forgotten about that. Jax's flirting was harmless. She didn't believe he was actually interested in her. He mostly flirted with her and Mia to annoy Shane. "I guess that makes you jealous, too."

It was Cooper's turn to blush profusely. "That was different. Jax was all over you. I had to make it believable. He and Shane would have known the truth if I hadn't said anything."

Piper nodded. "Exactly. Which is why I did the same thing."

"Fiona and I are just friends," Cooper grumbled.

"So are Jax and me. And you're kidding yourself if you don't think that girl is interested in you. Either that or you're blind as a bat. Did you not notice her reaction when I called you *honey*? She un-plastered herself pronto." Which was why she'd done it.

"Okay, fine. We're both just playing our parts," he said.

"Exactly," she agreed. Cooper was just as jealous as her.

The thought made her grin.

Chapter Twelve

"I've got to get going. Mia is waiting for me. We're going to Donahue's to watch Monday Night Football." Piper rose from the club chair in her mother's living room.

"I'm so happy for you and Cooper. I have to say, you two really know how to keep a secret." Jane kissed her cheek.

Piper straightened her shoulders. "Given how close the families are, we wanted to see how things went before we said anything." It was sort of the truth. Her stomach plummeted. Good grief. There wasn't an ounce of truth in any of those words. Lying to her mother was proving to be much more difficult than she'd expected. *Think of Donny and Blake*, she told herself. Piper sucked in a slow, deep breath and relaxed. Mom wouldn't stop her matchmaking. She'd made that perfectly clear. Piper was doing what she had to do.

"And things are good between you?" Mom asked.

Piper grinned. "They're the best they've ever been." That was the God's honest truth.

"I couldn't be happier for you." Mom looked as if a heavy weight had been lifted from her shoulders.

"Thanks." She couldn't help smiling. "I'm happy, too." Because Mom would finally stop interfering in her love life. Yes. That was why she was happy. It had nothing to do with Cooper. And the excitement swirling around her stomach at the thought of seeing him later tonight at Donahue's… She was playing the part of besotted girlfriend. *That's all.*

"You know, I'm free this weekend. It wouldn't hurt to look at wedding dresses. Just to see what's out there." Jane walked her to the front door.

Piper pulled a face. "Mom! I told you. Cooper and I are not engaged."

"But you're hoping that will change in the near future," Mom insisted. "You were looking at rings."

Piper chuckled. Hellen Francis was such a busybody. "Well, I did see something I liked in the window display and I did mention to Cooper that I liked it." Now, that was 100 percent the truth.

"I guess we'll have to wait and see." Mom crossed her fingers.

Piper laughed. She couldn't help it. "I'll see you later."

Mom flicked on the front porch light and opened the door. Gesturing for Piper to step through the opening, she said, "Love you, darling."

"I love you, too."

She hurried down the front steps and strode to where she'd parked her car in Mom's driveway.

Her phone pinged as she started the engine. She glanced at the text from her sister.

Front door open. Come in when you get here. I'm hopping in the shower now.

Piper sent a quick note back. Will do. On my way.

A few minutes later, she pulled her car into the driveway of the colonial blue, Cape Cod–style house where Mia and her daughters lived.

Exiting her car, she walked along the gray paver

stone walkway to the front door and stepped inside. "Hey, Mia. I'm here."

"I'm upstairs," Mia shouted. "Come on up."

Piper climbed the stairs two at a time. She reached the small landing at the same time her sister raced out of the hall bathroom with towels wrapped around her body and hair.

"Come in." Mia jerked her head toward the master bedroom. "Have a seat on the bed."

Piper sat. She peered around the space. "This looks different than the last time I saw it."

"It is. I started remodeling about a month ago." Mia grabbed clothes from her dresser. "This is my current project." She pointed toward the master bath. "I pulled out the tub, which is why I was showering in the girls' bathroom. Not ideal sharing a bathroom with the kids." She shrugged. "Should have waited because I don't have much time to work on it until my February break. Be right back." She walked into the bathroom.

Piper spotted a stack of photo albums sitting on Mia's dresser. "Hey, are these mom's pictures?"

"Yeah. She dropped them off yesterday. Aurora's class is doing an ancestry project. We're going to go through the old pictures and put a collage together so she can tell everyone about her family."

"Sounds like a lot of work for a third grader," Piper said.

"She's just doing immediate family and grandparents," Mia responded.

The sound of a hair dryer made it impossible to continue their conversation.

Piper wandered over to the dresser and opened the first book. Images from their family vacation to Disney World right before her thirteenth birthday filled several pages and Piper grinned as she looked through the photos.

Pictures of Christmas of that same year came next. The one of Dad dressed as Santa brought a somewhat sad smile to her face. Who would have guessed that would be his last holiday with them? Not his three kids, who'd made gentle fun of him for dressing up like he'd done every year since Mia was born. He always insisted he was the real deal and told them only kids that believed would get presents.

Piper flipped the page. She found an image of her standing with her friend Ilana. They were both dressed in party dresses. She laughed. Ilana's bat mitzvah had been the first major party she'd been allowed to attend without her parents. Of course they didn't need to be there. The Kepelmanns had invited the entire Turner family since they were friends and Ron and Debby made sure she didn't get into any trouble. Not that it had even been an issue.

Several more images from Ilana's party followed. The last one had her doing a double take. Was that her *slow dancing* with Cooper?

No. It couldn't be. Piper removed the image from the protective cover and walked with it into the hall, which had brighter light. She scrutinized the image and…yes, that was her with her arms around thirteen-year-old Cooper's neck.

Piper gawked at the image. She couldn't remember dancing with him. Okay, yes, it was fifteen years ago, but you'd think she'd remember that.

Why would she be dancing with him? They didn't like each other.

She peered at the photo again. They were both grinning ear to ear. Good grief, not only were they wrapped in each other's arms, they seemed happy about it.

"Oh, here you are." Mia walked into the hall. "I was wondering where you'd gone. So, what do you think?" She did a little twirl.

Piper shoved the picture in the back pocket of her jeans and focused on her sister. "You straightened your hair. It's so much longer this way. Oh, and I love the highlights. When did you do this?" Piper picked up a lock of Mia's brown, highlighted hair. "It wasn't this way when I saw you the other day."

"This afternoon," Mia answered.

Piper's brows furrowed. "Didn't you have school?"

"I had to take some personal time. We met with the judge this morning. As of eleven a.m., I'm officially a single woman again." Mia smiled an overbright smile.

Piper hugged her sister. "Are you all right?" She couldn't imagine what Mia had gone through this last year.

Mia gave a nervous smile and eased away. "To be honest, I'm not sure how I feel. We spent eight years together. Well, ten, if you count the two years we dated in college before we got married. That's almost a third of my life."

Mia straightened her shoulders and looked Piper in the eyes. "But, yes. I'm all right. I'm looking forward to the next chapter of my life. Whatever that might bring. Now, do these clothes say thirty and flirty or frumpy mom? I'm outta practice."

Piper grinned. "You look great. You're gonna knock 'em dead, sis."

Mia didn't look convinced.

"You're a knockout. Trust me," Piper said. "Let's get going. Layla, Abby and Elle are probably already there."

Mia glanced at her watch. "You're right. We need

to get there soon if we want a table. The place is usually packed for Monday Night Football. Let's do this."

Piper crooked her elbow and linked her arm with her sister's. "I'll drive. You have fun."

Mia snorted. "I can't drink that much. I still have to face a classroom full of first graders tomorrow."

They arrived at Donahue's pub fifteen minutes later. As they walked into the bar, Mia said, "Hey, you said you wanted to tell me something when we hopped in the car, but I never gave you a chance to say what it was. I've pretty much monopolized the conversation since you arrived."

"Yeah, there is something." She opened the door to the bar and gestured for Mia to proceed her.

Mia walked inside. "What is it?" she asked.

"It's about Cooper and me," she started.

Mia rolled her gaze skyward. "Don't tell me you guys got into another fight again."

"No-oo." She dragged out the word. "I wouldn't say that."

Hand on hip, Mia turned to face her. "Then what would you say? Hey, is that Jax Rawlins coming toward us?"

"Yes. He's in town for a couple of days. He and Shane stopped by the gallery earlier." That reminded her. She needed to nail down the details for Jax's show. She couldn't believe he'd volunteered to allow her to feature his pictures. People came from all over the world to view his work. This one show could skyrocket her gallery to elite status in no time flat. Talk about a stroke of good luck.

"Hello, ladies." Jax gave her a quick hug and released her. He turned his attention to Mia. "It's great to see you again."

Mia flashed a nervous smile. "Yeah, you, too."

"How long has it been?" Jax asked Mia. He couldn't take his gaze off her.

"Almost ten years," Mia admitted.

"Too long." Jax's tone held a hint of longing.

Piper's brows furrowed. Was there something between her sister and Jax? They both looked…wistful.

"Hey, Mia." Cooper came over and gave her sister a hug. "It's good to see you." He turned his attention to Piper. His gaze smoldered with heat.

Piper's pulse kicked up a notch.

"Piper, honey." Cooper pulled her into his arms and planted his lips on hers.

His hungry mouth devoured hers. Tasting, teasing, until every inch of her was on fire.

"What the heck!" Mia sputtered.

He released her and she swayed. Good Lord, the man could kiss.

"You can't seem to keep your hands off each other." Jax smirked. "You really need to get a room."

"*What* is going on?" Mia gasped.

Cooper threw his arm around her waist and steadied her. "You didn't tell your sister about us?"

"I was, ah, just about to." She sucked in a breath. Lord, she couldn't think straight when he was this close.

"Well…" Mia pointed back and forth a couple of times between her and Cooper. "This is an interesting development."

"I'll say," Jax snorted.

Cooper looked at her, his gaze filled with heat.

Her pulse soared into overdrive. Oh, this was quite an interesting development all right.

How the hell had this happened?

Chapter Thirteen

On Wednesday evening, Piper pulled her car into Mia's driveway. Elle and Abby waved as they exited the car next to hers.

She grabbed from the front passenger seat the big bowl of salad she'd prepared for their dinner.

"Hey, Piper. How's Cooper doing?" Elle flashed a smug smirk.

She wasn't sure. She hadn't seen much of him since he'd planted that smoldering kiss on her at Donahue's.

A shiver raced down her spine. The skill and talent that man possessed.

"Piper?" Elle nudged her.

"Cooper is fine." At least she assumed he was. She'd done her best to avoid him by scheduling artist interviews over most of the last two days.

What was she supposed to say to him?

Hey, Cooper, that was one hell of a performance the other night. You certainly convinced everyone we're a couple with that kiss.

Feel free to indulge anytime you like.

No, no, no. What was she thinking? This thing they'd started was complicated enough. They didn't need to add sex into the mix.

Anticipation hummed and buzzed inside her.

She needed to change the subject. Fast. "So, what are

we celebrating?" Mia had told her Elle had big news to share.

"I've been accepted to Boston University. I'm going to finish my business administration degree." Elle brandished the bottle of champagne in her hand.

"We're so proud of you." Abby slung an arm around her cousin's shoulder.

Elle's cheeks flushed crimson. "It's not that big a deal."

"It is, given everything you've gone through over the last few years." Layla walked up behind them carrying two platters of food. "And that's why we're celebrating tonight."

Elle gazed from Abby to Piper and to Mia's house. "I can't think of anyone else I'd love to celebrate with more."

Piper marveled at the bond these women shared. She'd never experienced anything resembling this closeness, this loving support, with her friends in LA, nor here in New Suffolk, when she was younger.

Or maybe you've never been open to the concept before. Maybe you pushed people away. Kept them at arm's distance so you couldn't get hurt the way Mom was hurt when Dad died.

She shook off the uncomfortable, unwelcome thoughts. "Let's break open that bubbly."

Piper knocked on her sister's front door. It opened and three giggling girls appeared. "Hello, ladies."

"Hi, Auntie Piper," Aurora greeted.

Brooke waved.

"Are you gonna come in?" Kiera asked.

Piper chuckled. "You guys have to move out of the way first. You're blocking the doorway."

"Come on in." Mia's voice came from somewhere inside the house.

Aurora, Brooke and Kiera ran into the living room and the adults stepped inside.

"Why don't you set the food on the island." Mia walked in from the kitchen that was open to the living room and dining area. A renovation Mia had done right after she and her ex had bought the place.

Mia and her brother, Shane, had inherited their father's creativity when it came to home makeovers and construction. Piper had inherited Dad's love of painting and sculpting, although Dad had liked to work with metals and she preferred clay.

"Hey, I love your necklace." Elle walked over and touched the antique silver, chunky, Bohemian bib choker fastened around Piper's neck. "Is it from the shop in town?"

Piper nodded. "I saw it in the window display the other day." She'd gone back to buy it yesterday afternoon.

"That's not all you were looking at." Mia winked. "I do believe you spotted a ring you might like." She held up her left hand and waggled her third finger.

"Wait. What?" Layla gasped.

Mia smirked and started humming Mendelssohn's *Wedding March.*

Heat crept up Piper's neck and flooded her cheeks. "Gossipmonger."

"Did Cooper give you a ring?" Abby grabbed Piper's left hand and held it up for inspection.

"Daddy gave Oriana a ring but she didn't like it." Kiera pointed to Piper's bare fingers.

Piper gasped. Oriana was the woman Kyle had left Mia for.

The room went silent and everyone stared at her sister.

"Okay, girls." Mia straightened her shoulders. "Time for you to go into the den and watch your movie."

"We want to stay out here with you guys." Brooke pointed to Piper and the others.

"That's not an option." Mia gestured toward the den, which sat to the right of where she was standing. "It's either a movie or bed."

The girls scurried away.

Mia followed and returned to the others a moment later.

"Your ex got engaged?" Layla asked.

"Are you okay?" Piper moved to Mia's side.

"I'm fine, and no, Kyle and Oriana are not engaged. He asked her on Monday. Right after he signed our divorce papers."

Elle pulled a face. "Oh, that's just poor form."

Piper agreed. "You knew he was going to ask her?"

Mia nodded. "He told me at the courthouse."

Piper slung her arm around Mia's shoulder and gave her a firm squeeze. No wonder her sister had gone out and gotten a makeover.

Abby snorted. "What a jerk."

"Yep," Elle agreed.

"Yes." Mia nodded. "That was a crappy thing to do, but I'm glad he told me so that I could reassure the girls that everything was okay."

"You're a really good mom." Piper pressed a kiss to Mia's cheek.

"So, what happened?" Elle asked.

"She turned him down." Mia held up a hand. She disappeared into the hall for a moment and returned. "I just wanted to make sure the door was still closed." In a hushed voice she added, "Apparently Oriana isn't ready to take on the responsibility of three kids, even part-time."

"Did Kyle tell you that?" Abby asked.

Mia nodded. "Yesterday morning." A hint of pink touched her cheeks. "He came over after he dropped the kids off at school."

Mia's cheeks went from pink to scarlet.

"What happened?" Piper asked. "Something must have, because you're bright red."

"Did you and your ex…" Abby made a funny motion with her hand.

Mia's brows furrowed. "Did we what?"

"She's asking if you and Kyle did the horizontal tango?" Elle smirked.

Piper smacked her hand to her head. "Please tell me you didn't sleep with him."

"Oh God no," Mia denied.

"Then why are your cheeks on fire?" Layla laughed.

"Oh my God!" Elle covered her mouth with her palm. "You were with Jax Rawlins. Ms. I-have-to-get-up-early-for-work-tomorrow-so-I-need-to-leave-now."

Mia's eyes went wide. "How did you know?"

"I'm not blind. You two couldn't keep your eyes off each other." Elle looked at Piper. "It was the same with you and Cooper. And I was right." Elle flashed a smug smile. "Even though you denied it."

"About you and Cooper," Mia began.

Piper shook her head. "Oh no. This time you don't get to change the subject. So, you and Jax?" Elle wasn't the only one who'd seen the sparks the other night, but she'd dismissed them because it was Jax. As Shane's best friend since childhood, he'd been around for as long as Piper could remember.

Mia held up a hand. "There is no me and Jax. It was one night only."

"But," Piper protested.

"No buts." Mia smiled. "I don't want a relationship.

I just ended my marriage. The last thing I want is something serious. And I would appreciate it if we could keep this between the five of us." She turned her attention to Layla. "Please don't say anything to Shane. He can be a little overprotective at times."

"Yes, he can," Piper agreed. She remembered all too well his reaction when he'd found her and Cooper. Heat pooled low in her belly just remembering the feel of Cooper's hands as they stroked along her spine and over her shoulders. And his scent. Fresh and clean with something more. Something she couldn't identify, but it drove her wild.

Stop it, stop it, stop it right now. She gave herself a mental shake.

"I know he means well, and I love my brother dearly, but this isn't any of his business," Mia said.

Layla lifted a finger to her lips. "Mum's the word."

Elle rubbed her hands together. "Now, I want to hear all the deets about you and Cooper."

"Um…" Piper's breathing quickened.

Abby chuckled. "Oh yeah. Check out that expression. She's got it bad for the hot construction guy."

Piper opened her mouth to deny the claim, but stopped before the words came out. This was what she'd hoped for. They believed she and Cooper were a couple.

Mia crossed her arms in front of her chest and smirked. "You, little sis, have a lot of explaining to do. Come on. Confession time. Is it true what Mom said? Are you hoping for a ring by Valentine's Day?"

"Yes." A little thrill raced through her. Because everything was going according to plan. *Not* because the thought of her and Cooper together sent shivers racing down her spine.

Nope. Nope. Nope.

* * *

The next morning, Coop zipped into a parking space at the mansion and booked it upstairs to Piper's gallery. He found her sitting at the kitchen island reviewing a large portfolio.

"Hey, Piper. Sorry I'm late. I slept through my alarm."

She peered up at him. "You must have been pretty tired."

Not exactly. Coop had tossed and turned until almost two thirty, and it was all Piper's fault. His imagination had gone into hyperdrive the last couple of days, conjuring pictures of their naked bodies entwined together, her long blond hair fanned over his pillow. He swallowed hard.

The cold shower he'd taken hadn't done anything to cool his libido. Even when he'd slept, he'd dreamed of her.

"It's no wonder you're tired. That client of yours has got you working six days a week with no time off for good behavior. She must be a real taskmaster."

Images of her dressed in tight black leather, holding a whip, flooded his brain.

Son of a... Coop yanked off his coat and casually held it in front of him to hide the sudden bulge in his pants.

What the hell was wrong with him? He wasn't even into BDSM. Although, with her... He shook his head.

"She's not that bad," he said.

"Seriously, you've been working hard since we started this renovation and I really appreciate it, but I don't want you to burn out. Between the work you're doing here and the time you volunteer at Homes for Humanity, you're working seven days a week. We've gotten a lot done. You deserve a day of rest. Take tomorrow off."

He shook his head. "No need. I'm fine."

"Cooper." Piper walked over to where he stood near

the entrance to the gallery and squeezed his arm. "You deserve some time off."

He couldn't miss the care in her gaze.

"Okay. I'll take tomorrow off, but only if you do, too. You've been working just as hard as I have." He gestured about the space with his free hand. "You stay long after noon most days to tackle the painting. That's why we're ahead of schedule."

"It's my place," she reasoned.

"Take the deal, Piper. We can do something fun together." The words came out of his mouth before his brain could stop them.

Piper blinked. "Are you asking me out on a date?"

Oh crap. Yes. No. Coop dragged a hand through his hair. He studied Piper. She looked…okay, maybe horrified was too harsh a description, but she didn't seem thrilled either.

Awkward. What was he supposed to say now?

"You mean we'll go on one of the 'dates' we talked about having? So that people believe we're a real couple?" she clarified.

"Right." If he nodded any faster, she might think he was a bobblehead. "Of course I did." Coop stopped nodding and released the breath he'd been holding. "What else would I mean?"

"Nothing." Relief flooded her features. "Good thinking. We need to keep up appearances."

Thank you, Universe, for small favors.

"Coffee's ready if you want some. The one on the left is yours." She pointed to the two pots resting side by side on one end of the island. "There's a breakfast sandwich from the Coffee Palace in the bag for you, too. It should still be hot. I just picked it up a few minutes ago."

He smiled. "Hey, thank you. I didn't get a chance to eat anything and I am starving."

"You're welcome." Piper grinned.

Cooper strode toward the island. "Hey, these are new." He gestured to the two bar-height chairs lined up in front of the counter.

"Layla is letting me borrow them until the ones I ordered arrive."

She'd been sitting in one when he first arrived, but his brain hadn't registered the fact. He was definitely sleep-deprived today.

Coop pulled out the chair Piper hadn't been sitting in. Something went flying off the seat and thudded on the ground. He glanced down. The contents of Piper's purse lay scattered on the floor.

"I'm so sorry," he said.

Piper rushed over. "No. It's my fault. I shouldn't have left my purse on the chair."

He started picking up the items and handed them to her. "Hey, what's this?"

"A picture of you and me when we were kids. I've been meaning to ask you about it." She handed the photo back to him. "Do you remember where it was taken?"

He studied the image and smiled. "At Ilana Kepelmann's bat mitzvah."

"That's what I thought." She looked him in the eye. "I don't remember dancing with you at that party."

He couldn't possibly forget. Some of the other boys at the party had dared him to ask her to dance, but the truth was, he'd wanted to.

Sometime between the end of seventh grade and the beginning of eighth, Piper went from annoying as all get-out to intriguing. His stomach would flip-flop every time she came near him.

Not that he would have admitted as much to anyone. His brothers would have teased the crap out of him if they'd known. His friends would have, too.

Still, he'd done his best to get her to notice him in the only way he knew how. Too bad his thirteen-year-old self didn't know pranks and dares were not the way to go. All he'd succeeded in doing was to make her even more aggravated with him than ever.

Until that night. When she smiled at him on the dance floor...

"Hey, Piper." Cooper stopped in front of Piper and Ilana on the edge of the dance floor in the ballroom of the New Suffolk Bay Beach Club, New Suffolk's version of a country club.

Piper's nostrils flared as she stared at him.

His stomach turned a loop the loop. Lord, why was he so nervous? All he had to do was ask her. It shouldn't be hard. So why did he feel like he might puke up the food they'd just eaten?

"Hi, Cooper," Ilana said, smirking at him.

"Hey," he said. "Nice party." His parents would be pissed if he wasn't polite. "Thanks for inviting me."

"You're welcome," Ilana said.

He returned his attention to Piper. She looked so pretty in the long coral dress she wore.

Ilana waved a hand in front of his face. "Did you want something, or are you just going to stand there staring?"

Coop swallowed hard. His stomach jumped and jittered. "You wanna dance, Piper?" His words came out in a rush.

She stared at him as if he'd grown another head, but said nothing.

Coop held his breath as what seemed like hours passed with no response from her.

"Piper." Ilana nudged her with her elbow.

She opened her mouth but no words came out.

"She'd love to." Ilana shoved her forward.

That was good enough for him. He rubbed his sweaty palm against his trousers and grasped her hand.

Coop led her to the dance floor, stopping when he found an empty space. He started moving, praying he wasn't making a complete fool of himself.

The hint of a smile crossed her face as she did the same.

That had to be a good sign. Maybe he wasn't as bad at this as Nick and Levi claimed he was. Coop breathed a sigh of relief.

The rock song ended and another started, a slow song.

His pulse soared. He'd never slow danced before. What the heck was he supposed to do?

Piper stood stock-still. She stared at him. Panic etched her bright blue gaze.

He peered around the room and stared at Dad and Mom. Dad had one hand on Mom's hip. His other held her hand. Coop grabbed Piper's hand with what was clearly too much force, because she bounced against his chest.

He didn't fall, thank God, but he did stumble back a couple of steps.

"Sorry," she mumbled.

"It's okay." He placed his hand on Piper's hip. Glancing at Dad, he noticed he swayed from side to side. Cooper tried to do the same but his movements weren't as smooth as Dad's.

Piper slanted a couple of worried looks in his direction as they moved.

Was he doing it all wrong? Cooper started to sweat.

He jerked his gaze toward the other couples on the dance floor. No. He'd copied them the best he could.

The song ended too soon as far as he was concerned. He would have liked to keep dancing with her like this.

Piper looked up at him. A brilliant smile crossed her face. "Thanks. That was fun."

She'd liked dancing with him.

He grinned.

"Cooper?" Piper nudged him.

He blinked. "What?"

She repeated her statement. "I don't remember dancing with you."

He nodded. "It was a long time ago."

"Fifteen years. It looks like we were having a good time together." It was more of a question than a statement.

He peered at the image again. *A great time.* Dancing with her had been the best part of that party.

Who would have guessed that three days later her world would come crumbling down and that nothing would ever be the same between them again?

Not the boy who blamed himself for not saving her father, and not the girl who would never forgive him.

Coop gave himself a mental shake. He needed to stop thinking about the past. He couldn't change it.

"I'm sorry I don't remember." Piper rested her hand on his arm.

It was time to lighten the mood. His lips curved into a smile. "I wasn't a great dancer back then. You probably blocked it out because I stepped on your feet all night."

Her sweet chuckle sent a flood of warmth rushing through him.

"I'm serious. I didn't have the mad skills I do today." He mimicked a few waltz steps in the area where they stood.

She laughed harder. "Sorry, I'm just not seeing it."

"Is that a challenge, Ms. Kavanaugh?"

"I believe it is, Mr. Turner."

He grinned. "Oh, it's on." Coop grabbed his phone. He opened his music app and typed in "slow dance music." He set the phone on the countertop when the melody started.

Extending his hand to her, he said, "May I have this dance?"

Surprise flickered across her face as she extended her hand to his.

Coop set his right hand on Piper's hip and grasped her right hand with his left. "What do you think of this?" He spun her out and back in again.

She smiled up at him. "Not too shabby."

He moved them about the space for a few minutes, adding more twirls and spins as they made their way across the room. When the song ended, he dipped her.

"Oh my." Her startled gaze landed on his. "That was pretty good."

The next song started to play.

Like all those years ago, he wasn't ready to end this yet. He liked holding her in his arms. Coop wrapped his arms around her waist, and enjoyed the press of her body against his. "How am I doing so far?" he murmured.

"Shh." Piper twined her arms around his neck and laid her head on his shoulder.

They moved together to the slow, sensual beat.

"Cooper. Piper." His mother appeared in the entry.

He froze at the sudden intrusion. So did Piper. They jerked away from each other as if they'd been caught doing something wrong.

"Mom." Coop ran a hand through his hair. "What are you doing here?"

Chapter Fourteen

"Debby." *Crap, crap, crap.* Heat scorched Piper's cheeks and flooded her face. She peered around the room, looking everywhere but at Cooper.

"I hope I'm not interrupting anything." Debby cast a knowing look in her direction.

Piper was pretty sure her cheeks flamed even brighter. Could she be any more embarrassed? She shoved her hands in her pockets and rocked back and forth on her heels. Lord, she felt like a teenager who just got caught making out with her boyfriend, which was totally ridiculous.

Get a grip. Piper sucked in a steadying breath and blew it out slowly. *You're a grown woman.* It wasn't as if she and Cooper had done anything wrong. They were just dancing, for goodness' sake. A frisson of pleasure trickled down her spine.

She shuddered. *So not the time to be thinking about that.*

"Of course not." Piper waved off Debby's concern. "This is a pleasant surprise." She needed to start locking the door on the lower level so people couldn't walk in unannounced.

"I'm so glad." Debby grinned.

"What are you doing here?" Cooper asked again.

"I wanted to see if you two were free for dinner on

Saturday evening." She turned her attention to Piper. "Ron and I would love it if you could join us."

"You could have just called," Cooper grumbled. "You didn't have to drop by." He turned and strode to the island. Grabbing a mug, he filled it with coffee. He moved to the side opposite the coffeemaker, hiding the lower half of his body from view. Setting his cup down, he propped his elbows on the granite surface.

Unfortunately, the island wouldn't hide her arousal. She grabbed her cardigan off the chair back and tugged it on.

"So, what do you say?" Debby flashed a hopeful smile.

Piper understood why Debby had stopped by in person to issue the invitation. It was a lot harder to say no to her face.

Cooper shot a sidelong glance at her and she nodded.

"I can't, Mom. I've already got plans."

"Me, too," Piper said.

"How about sometime next week?" Cooper suggested.

"What about next Friday?" Debby asked.

Cooper's birthday.

"That works for me." Cooper sent her an enquiring glance. "How about you?"

"Yes," she agreed. "I'm available, too."

"Six o'clock?" Debby asked.

"Sounds good," Piper said.

Cooper nodded. "That will give me time to shower and change after I get home from working on the Humanity houses."

An image of the stunningly gorgeous Fiona flashed into her mind. Piper gritted her teeth. Oh, she was jealous all right. Which made absolutely no sense. She and Cooper... There *was* no Piper and Cooper. Their relationship was a farce. A means to an end.

Okay, so she was attracted to him. Piper sucked in a deep, steadying breath. She could deny it all she wanted, but that didn't make it untrue.

How had this happened? A week ago, they couldn't stand to be in the same room with each other. Now... She glanced at him. He still stood on the other side of the island. Piper shivered. He wanted her as much as she wanted him. He'd proven that a few minutes ago when he'd held her close.

What did she want? The truth was she wasn't sure. She liked Cooper. She couldn't deny *that* any longer either.

Lord, just admitting that fact sent her head spinning.

"I'll make a reservation at the Italian place in Plymouth." Debby turned to Piper. "Ron and I love it there. The food is excellent."

"Great." She pasted a bright smile in place, grateful for the diversion from her musings. "I can't wait."

Debby hugged her. "I'm just so happy you two finally got together."

Piper swallowed hard. A pang of guilt swept through her for the deception they were playing.

"Mom," Cooper warned. He sent her an annoyed glance. "We talked about this."

"I'm just saying." Debby let go of Piper and crossed to her son. "See you later." She kissed him on the cheek.

Waving at Piper, she walked to the doors and exited the room.

"I'm sorry about that." Cooper came over to where she stood.

Piper laughed. "Which part? The dinner invitation we couldn't say no to, or your mom walking in on us?" At least she hadn't caught them in a compromising position the way her brother had.

"Both, but mainly the walking in on us." He flashed a heart-stopping smile. "Her timing is lousy."

Everything inside her went soft and mushy.

Heaven help her. She was in big trouble now.

Piper hummed along to the song blasting from the speaker as she painted. She frowned when the music stopped. Walking into the main part of the gallery, she jumped when she saw Cooper. "Oh my god, you scared me! I didn't hear you come in."

"I'm sorry! Didn't mean to startle you. I saw the windows open and wondered what you were doing here," he said. "I thought we agreed to take today off. We're supposed to go on a date. You're not standing me up, are you?"

Not a snowball's chance in hell. Oh, good grief. Get a hold of yourself. "No. Of course not." Piper tapped her watch. "It's only eleven o'clock. I figured we wouldn't head out until later. In the meantime, I thought I'd get a little painting done."

Cooper shook his head. "The date starts now."

She blinked. "Oh, okay. Where are we going?" Piper stared at her old jeans, sweatshirt and work boots. "I need to go home and change."

"You're fine as is." Heat flickered in his gaze as he eyed her from head to toe.

She laughed as she shook her head. "I'm not going out dressed like this."

"Okay. You'll need to wear something warm. And winter boots, too." Cooper grinned.

"We're going someplace outdoors?" She sent him a wary glance.

"The artist in you is going to love it." He grinned.

Okay. He'd piqued her interest. "All right. Let me finish up what I was doing and we can go."

Cooper nodded. "I'll meet you at your place."

Fifteen minutes later, she pulled her vehicle into her designated spot in the parking lot behind the Coffee Palace.

Exiting her car, she walked to the back door of the building.

Cooper jumped out of a silver F-150 and joined her.

"You have a truck, too?" she asked.

He nodded. "I don't usually drive the Camaro in the winter, especially when there's snow on the ground. I had to recently because my truck was in the shop."

She nodded. "Makes sense."

Piper opened the external door and stepped into the back hall. She climbed the stairs and unlocked the door to her apartment when they reached the landing on the second floor.

Walking inside, she turned to Cooper, and said, "I'll be right back. Make yourself at home."

She hurried into her bedroom and changed into a pair of skinny jeans and her light blue V-neck cashmere sweater. Releasing her ponytail, she ran a brush through her hair and added lip gloss.

Glancing at her reflection in the mirror, she nodded and exited her bedroom.

Cooper stood when she walked into the living room. "This is a cute place."

Piper peered around. "It's good for now, but eventually I'd like to find a house."

"Oh yeah? What are you looking for? A place on the beach?"

She nodded. "Probably. I had a place near the ocean when I lived in Los Angeles. I loved living by the water. You can't beat a fresh sea breeze and your toes in the sand. What about you?"

"The beach is okay, but I prefer a little more soli-tude. A place where my next-door neighbor isn't on top of me."

Piper chuckled. "What, no Hellen Francis types stop-ping by with cookies?"

Cooper grinned. "Exactly."

"There is something to be said for privacy." Piper walked to the closet. She grabbed her winter boots.

"Bring shoes for later. We won't stay outside for too long."

She grinned. "Now you're talking." Piper slid her feet inside the plush fake fur lining.

"Let me get your coat for you. You'll need something to keep warm, seeing as you're used to much milder temperatures." He winked.

"That's an understatement. The average temperature in LA at this time of year is in the high sixties. We'll be lucky if it gets above freezing here today."

"You're an outdoor girl at heart. You'll be fine."

He remembered that about her? A rush of warmth flooded through her.

Grabbing her long, down parka from the hanger, Cooper held it open for her.

Sure, she could put the coat on all by herself, but his kind gesture made her feel…special. Her heart gave a little kick. "Thank you, kind sir."

"You're welcome. Ready to go?" he asked.

"I am." She grasped a pair of high-heeled suede boo-ties and her purse, slinging the strap over her shoulder as she made her way to the door.

They exited the building and strode to Cooper's truck. Once inside, she asked, "Are you going to give me a hint as to where we're going? Other than some place outside followed by a place inside where I'll need shoes."

He pursed his lips as he started the engine. "We're going to stay in New Suffolk."

Piper let loose a chuckle. "So we're not going skiing or tubing at one of the nearby mountains?"

"Nope. Definitely staying more local." Cooper pulled out of the parking lot and turned onto Main Street. "Oh, and we'll have lunch, too."

She couldn't imagine where he was taking her. What local attraction had outdoor activities and a restaurant? "You've got me stumped."

Cooper flashed a mile-wide grin. "Don't worry. You won't have to wait long to see where we're going. But first, I need to make a quick stop. It's on the way." He turned on the road that led to the outskirts of town. "We'll be there in less than ten minutes."

The downtown hustle and bustle faded to a more rural landscape as they drove.

Piper stared out the passenger window. She marveled at how the sunlight dappled through the pine trees and evergreens, glinting on the fresh coating of snow that covered the ground. "This part of town is really beautiful. I don't think I ever appreciated that as a kid."

"It's peaceful," Cooper said.

"Yes." The landscape filled her with a sense of calmness and tranquility. "I can see why your parents love living out this way."

"Actually, they sold their place last May and moved closer to town."

She jerked her gaze to his. "Really? I would never have guessed your dad would want to do such a thing."

"Dad and Mom want to start traveling more. The upkeep on the house and all that land was a huge time suck. They didn't want that anymore."

Piper nodded. "I can understand that."

"While not immediate, retirement is sooner rather than someday in the distant future for them."

It made sense. Her mother was in the same boat. She'd started talking about wanting more time to pursue interests outside of TK Construction. Piper looked at it as a good sign. For so long now, her mother's life seemed to have revolved around work and home, with no social life to speak of. *Those first few years after Dad's death...* She'd trudged, zombie-like, through her days.

Piper gave herself a mental shake. Mom had her book club friends now. Maybe she'd finally start moving on with her life.

"We had some fun times there when we were kids," she said. Flag football games at Thanksgiving, barbecues and pool parties on hot summer days, and ice-skating on the rink Ron had built when the weather turned cold.

"You've got a huge smile on your face," Cooper said, grinning. "What are you remembering?"

She trained her focus on him. "I just had this flashback to when we were like six years old. We were all out in your parents' backyard and had a snowman building contest. Mia and Levi teamed up, and Shane and Nick, which left you and me.

"My dad decided the others had an unfair advantage, so he helped us and, of course, we won."

"You and me on the same team?" He snorted.

She laughed a deep belly laugh. "I know, right?"

"I don't remember that specific event, but you're still smiling, so it must be a good memory."

There went that crazy heart of hers again, beating a rapid tattoo. "Yes. It is." It was nice to finally be able to remember times spent with her father without being overwhelmed by sadness and despair. For too long, she'd suppressed all her memories in order to stop the bad ones. No emotions had been preferrable to grief.

"I'm glad," he said. His grin warmed her better than any fire could.

Piper sighed. "It must have been sad to see the place go. You spent your childhood there. It must hold a lot of memories for you, too."

"I have to admit that I was upset when they first told me, Nick and Levi they were selling the place." Cooper brought the truck to a stop. "That's why I bought it." He gestured out the window.

Piper's mouth fell open. The house looked totally different than what she remembered. "I see you've made some changes." The vintage one-story farmhouse now boasted new, larger windows with slate blue shutters, and a covered, wraparound porch. Stone siding covered the two bumped-out areas on either side of the front door, and white, vertical boards covered the rest of the exterior. Dormers with windows added dimension and style to the old facade.

"I love it."

It felt like...home.

Chapter Fifteen

She liked what he'd done. Warmth radiated throughout his entire body. "Thanks." Cooper beamed. He couldn't wait to show her the rest. "Come on. I'll show you the inside."

"I can't wait to see everything." Piper opened her door and hopped out.

Cooper walked over to where she stood. "This way." He grasped her hand in his and they walked over the pavers to the front entrance. He probably looked like a big goofball with this stupid grin plastered on his face, but he didn't care.

"I love the double doors. And those tall glass panels are fabulous," she said.

"It was really dark when you first came in before, but now…" Cooper unlocked the door on the right and opened it. "Look how much sunlight shines in." He stepped aside to allow her entry.

Piper stepped inside. "Look at these floors. The wood actually gleams."

They'd better. He'd spent hours sanding and applying several coats of urethane to make them shine. "It's the original flooring. I just refinished them."

"They're gorgeous. You did a phenomenal job."

He grinned and, yes, his chest puffed out…just a little.

Piper looked to her left. "This used to be Nick's room, right?"

"Yes. I ripped out the carpet and painted. I'm using it as a study right now."

"I love the cool gray paint," Piper said. "It's very modern, but you need some artwork on the walls."

Coop chuckled. "I haven't gotten that far yet. You're the art expert. Do you have any suggestions?"

"I'll think about it and let you know."

"Sounds good." He pointed to his right. "I haven't tackled the other bedrooms and the bathrooms yet, but the kitchen, dining and family rooms are completed. We can head there now." He gestured for her to precede him down the short hall and into the main space.

"Oh. My. Goodness!" Piper rushed into the family room. "Look at this fireplace!"

Coop grinned. "You like it?" He'd covered the standard red brick with limestone that went from floor to ceiling.

"It's amazing." She looked up at the vaulted ceilings. "You added wood beams." Piper bounced up and down on the balls of her feet. "It looks so cool."

He loved her enthusiasm. "I'm glad you like it."

Piper glanced to her left. "Dear God." Her mouth fell open. "Look at this kitchen. You removed the wall and opened it to the family room." She rushed over and stroked her hand over the white marble covering the blue island. "Be honest. Did you hire someone to design this space?" She touched one of the white Shaker cabinets that lined the walls, and the stainless steel six-burner stove.

He shook his head. "I did it myself." He'd renovated enough kitchens in his career to know what he liked and what he didn't.

"You have excellent taste. This is exactly what I'd do if I were to design my dream kitchen." She jerked her gaze from one end of the room to the other. "It seems bigger, too."

"It is." He nodded. "I used part of the formal dining room." He'd traded the space required to house his mother's china and buffet cabinets for more kitchen storage.

Piper nodded. "You removed the wall that used to separate the two rooms, too. I didn't realize that when I first walked in.

"I love how the kitchen, dining room and family room are open to each other. It's great for entertaining."

"I haven't done any of that yet. I've spent the last six months renovating, but I'm hoping to have a party to show everyone soon."

"You haven't shown this to anyone? Not even your family?" Piper turned an astonished glance in his direction.

"You're the first."

"Thank you. That means a lot." She brushed her lips against his cheek.

Coop closed his eyes for a moment. The fleeting touch sent shivers down his spine. He reveled in the sensation. "You're welcome." Was that gruff voice his? He cleared his throat. "Do you want to see more?"

She placed some much-needed space between them. "Yes, please."

He swallowed hard and tried to get his raging hormones under control. "It means going outside."

Piper flashed the sweetest grin, and his heart beat a rapid tattoo. "I think we can do that."

Two eight-foot sliders flanked the fireplace on either side. Cooper strode to the right side and opened the door. He stepped onto the patio and Piper followed.

"This is the same." He gestured to the hot tub and covered pool. "I added a putting green." He pointed to his left. "And the outdoor kitchen." He gestured to the built-in grill and mini fridge on his right.

"The gazebo looks new." Piper opened the gate to the fence that surrounded the pool and moved toward the structure.

He followed her. "Newer," he corrected. "The old one rotted out and Dad replaced it a couple of years ago with this bigger one."

Piper broke into a run. "Look at the icicles on the roof. With all the fresh snow, it looks like an ice castle." She scooped up two armfuls of snow and threw it up in the air. "It's so pretty. Come on." Piper spread her arms wide and fell backward. She let out a loud "woo-hoo" as she hit the ground.

"What are you doing?" he called as he traversed the short distance.

"Making a snow angel." She motioned for him to join her.

"You know that won't last, right? The weather report said it's going to snow six to twelve inches later today."

Piper clasped her hands over her heart. "I'll always have the memory in here." She stood and admired her handywork. "Perfect," she announced. "I forgot how much fun playing in the snow can be."

The smile on her face warmed him inside and out. "I'm glad you're enjoying yourself." This wasn't what he had planned—a quick trip to see the frozen water-falls at Long Pond, to appeal to her artistic nature, and a trip to Layla's restaurant for one of the famous burgers he'd promised her the other day had topped his to-do list—but he'd go with it.

"Let's make a snowman." Excitement shone in her bright blue eyes. "I'll start on the base. Can you start rolling the ball for the middle section?" she asked.

She looked so happy. Coop's heart beat a rapid tat-too. "Yeah, sure. No problem." He'd do just about any-thing to keep that smile on her face.

They worked in silence for several minutes. She, kneeling on the ground and continuing to add to her base, as he accumulated a second sizable sphere. When he thought the ball was big enough, he called over to her. "Are you ready for me to add this on top of yours?" Coop pointed to the chunk of snow sitting at his feet.

"You betcha." She motioned with her arm. "Bring it on over."

He rolled the ball over to where she sat.

Piper stood. "Okay, we'll lift it together on three."

He bent over and she followed suit.

"One... Two... Three!" Her hands went up. The ball fell apart in the air. Piper went flying backward and landed on her back.

He chuckled. He couldn't help it. "Are you okay?" he asked.

"I'm fine." She was laughing so hard, tears leaked from her eyes. Piper reached out an arm. "Can you help me up, please?"

He grasped her hand and pulled. She pulled, too. He lost his footing and fell forward, almost landing on her.

"You did that on purpose." He scowled, but he wasn't angry.

Piper laughed even harder. "I didn't. Swear to God. It was an accident. I'm sorry," she said between gasps of breath and more rounds of laughter. "Now this..."

A handful of snow landed on his face.

"That was on purpose." Piper tried to roll away.

"Not so fast." He snaked out an arm and grabbed her. Rising to his knees, he scooped a handful of snow and held it over her face. "Hmm… What to do, what to do? Should I do the same to you as you did to me?"

She grinned up at him. "No. I don't think so."

Coop cocked his head to the side. "Why not?"

"Well…" She glanced at his hand poised above her head and then looked him in the eye. "This is our first date."

"That didn't stop you from taking the first shot," he reasoned.

Piper batted her eyelashes. "I'm having such a great time with you. You wouldn't want to ruin it, would you?"

He lowered his handful of snow. "Your arguments are not swaying me."

"I…" She shrugged. "Don't have a defense. I deserve payback." Piper closed her eyes and scrunched up her face. "Go ahead."

He chuckled and tossed the snow to the side. "I've decided to let you off the hook this one time. But this is a one-time deal. The next time I won't be this lenient." Rising, he brought both of them to a standing position.

"Thank you, kind sir, for your mercy." Piper flashed a saucy grin. "I am sorry for my…lapse in judgment."

"Huh." Coop let out a belly laugh. "You don't look sorry. Don't sound sorry either."

"Oh, but I am. I really am." She grabbed his hand and started walking toward the rear of the property. "So, what other changes have you made out here?" She pointed to a spot a short distance away. "No ice-skating rink this year?"

He shook his head. "We haven't had one in years. No one to use it anymore."

"I guess not. We're all adults now," she said.

They walked along in silence for a few minutes until they reached a clearing near the edge of the property.

"It's been a long time since I've been back here."

The happy-go-lucky woman of a few minutes ago disappeared. Tension radiated off Piper in waves.

Shit. She was probably remembering that last bonfire their senior year of high school. It was the last time she came here.

"Not much has changed in the last ten years." She pointed to the outbuilding to her right. "Do the skunks still insist on making their homes there in the winter?"

Oh, yes. She was remembering that night, all right. *I hate you, Cooper Turner.* Her words echoed in his head.

He should never have brought her here. They'd been having a great time together. Why had he walked in this direction? "We should head back to the house."

"Wait a minute. Please." She lifted her gaze to his. "I'm sorry for the way that I treated you all those years ago. I was so awful to you, especially that night."

Coop blinked. He hadn't expected those words to come out of her mouth. Ever. "You were pretty mad."

"I know," she said. "Everything went wrong that night. I blamed you and I shouldn't have. It wasn't your fault." Piper flashed a rueful smile. "Well, not *all* of it. Some of it was Tom Anderson's fault."

Coop cringed. It had irked him beyond measure when he'd learned Tom had asked Piper to the Sweetheart dance. He'd viewed it as a betrayal of the worst kind. Still did, if he were honest.

"I'd wanted to go with him that night." She turned away and started pacing back and forth in a small area. "He was always so nice to me. Waiting for me so he could walk me to class. Offering to carry my books."

His hands clenched into tight fists. Tom had told him it was the other way around. That Piper had ordered him to do those things.

It wasn't outside the realm of possibility. They were both pretty geeky back then. Always struggling to fit in. An endless challenge for him, especially with two older brothers who'd always run with the popular crowd. And Piper…was the Ice Queen.

So, yeah, he'd believed Tom.

Idiot, idiot, idiot.

"When he backed out of our date after the skunk…" She waved a hand in the air again. "I was devastated."

Devastated? He blew out a breath. She'd really liked Tom back then. He would never have guessed Piper harbored such feelings. His heart gave a painful thud.

"The way Tom acted…"

He couldn't miss the hurt in her gaze. *Ah, hell.* "I'm sorry." His foolish behavior had made her miss out.

She stopped in front of him and grasped his hands in hers.

Lord, he could stare into her beautiful eyes forever.

He gave himself a mental shake. Where had that thought come from?

"It's not your fault. You didn't make me run into the shed. I chose to do that. Everyone else ran in the opposite direction." She let out a derisive laugh. "You weren't even that close to us. And Tom is the one who acted like I had the plague, not you." She shook her head. "But I blamed you nonetheless. I shouldn't have."

Coop blew out a breath. "Thank you for saying that."

"About damned time, right?" She gave him a tentative smile.

He laughed. He couldn't help it.

A gust of wind blew and Piper shivered.

"We should definitely head back to the house now," he said. Snow was starting to fall and the temperature was dropping.

"Agreed. Now would be a great time for the indoor portion of this date." Piper wrapped her arms around herself and rubbed her gloved hands up and down the sleeves of her parka. "I'm cold and wet from playing in the snow."

"Don't worry." He slung an arm around her shoulder and tugged her close. "We can throw your jeans in the dryer. I'll loan you a pair of my sweats while they dry."

"Sounds like a plan." She draped her arm around his waist.

Coop marveled at the feel of her pressed close to him. He liked it. A lot.

Maybe more than he should.

They reached the house a few minutes later.

He opened the back slider and gestured for Piper to precede him in.

"It's nice and warm." Piper unzipped her parka and slid her arms from the sleeves.

"I'll take that for you." Coop grabbed her coat. Removing his boots, he walked into the front hall and hung their coats in the closet. He strode back to where Piper stood in the great room. "Now, let's get you warmed up. What do you need?"

"Pants and socks," she answered between chattering teeth.

He walked down the short hall to the main suite. Once inside, Coop searched through his drawers for a pair of sweats that might fit her. Everything he owned would fall from her petite frame. He found a pair made of navy fleece with a drawstring waist and elastic at the ankles. It was the best he could do. He laid out the pants and added the socks she'd requested. Returning to the great room, he said, "I left a change of clothes on the bed. You can change in there."

"Thanks." Piper disappeared.

Hot cocoa and a fire would warm her fast. He got busy making both. The fire was easy. He pushed a button on the remote and the flames burst to life. Hurrying into the kitchen, he prepared the hot cocoa. Not that it was difficult, although he used almond-coconut milk instead of water.

Piper reappeared as he poured the hot chocolate into two mugs. "What do you think?" She performed a pirouette. "Am I runway-ready or what?"

His pants billowed around her waist and ankles and the excess material of the socks flapped as she moved her feet. She looked utterly adorable. "Perfect," he said.

She chuckled and moved to the island. "Is one of these for me?" Piper pointed to the mugs.

He nodded. "I'm going to change." His jeans were damp as well. "Be right back." Cooper hurried back to his bedroom. Grabbing another pair of sweats, he changed and went back to the great room.

He found Piper sitting on the couch with one of his picture frames held in her hands.

Coop made his way over to her, noticing her hunched shoulders and downcast face as he approached. And were those tears in her eyes? He sucked in a breath.

Why was she crying?

Chapter Sixteen

"What's wrong?" Cooper rushed over and dropped down on the couch beside her.

"Nothing. I'm fine." She scrubbed the backs of her hands over her face. "Really." She gave him a watery smile.

"Why are you crying?" He tilted her chin up and waited for her gaze to settle on him.

Damn. Piper cringed. "This collage of pictures." She tilted the frame so he could see the images. "They caught me off guard."

Cooper stared at the images, a look of confusion on his face. "Yeah, they were taken when your dad took me to the arcade on the pier for my thirteenth birthday."

"I'd never seen them before." Piper shook her head. He probably thought she was one card short of a full deck. "It's like finding a treasure chest full of gold coins." She rubbed her thumb over a picture of her smiling father, remembering how soft the skin on his cheeks was and how he always smelled of Brut aftershave. "It doesn't bring him back, but for a second…" She kissed his cheek. "These brought him to life for me."

Cooper smiled. "I'm glad they made you happy. He was such a great guy. I was so fortunate that he was my godfather. He always made me feel so special."

Piper glanced at the photos again. "You loved him a lot." She couldn't deny it. The images didn't lie.

"I did. Do. I miss having him in my life," Cooper said.

"Oh, Cooper." She buried her face in her hands. "I'm so sorry. So, so sorry. I was awful to you." She more than deserved his Ice Queen title. She deserved his condemnation, too. "All those years…" She'd gotten it all wrong. The truth had been staring her in the face for years. She'd chosen not to see it. How could she have been so blind? Cooper was never the villain she'd made him out to be. She'd needed someone to blame for all the anger and misery she was feeling, and she'd made Cooper the fall guy.

Piper lifted her head and gazed into his eyes. "Can you ever forgive me?"

"Piper." The look of devastation in his glittering gaze tore at her heart.

"Please, let me explain." Not that any explanation would justify her behavior toward him, but still, she had to try. She couldn't bear it if their story ended here. Piper grasped his hands in hers. She needed the contact.

"After my father died…" she began.

"You don't have to do this. I know how much losing him hurt you."

His concern for her—even after the horrible way she'd treated him all these years—showed him for the caring, compassionate person he always was. Shame on her for believing otherwise.

"I need to say this to you. It's important." Piper drew in a deep breath and blew it out slowly. "I missed him so much. I was angry—"

"At me. I know. You had every right to be. I let you down." Cooper dragged a hand through his hair.

She frowned. "What are you talking about?"

"I tried, Piper. I really did." He looked away from her. "But nothing I did helped."

She shook her head. "I don't understand. You're not making any sense." Piper grasped his shaking hands in hers and squeezed them tight. "It's okay, Cooper. You didn't do anything wrong." Why would he believe otherwise?

"I couldn't save him. I wanted to, but I couldn't." His breaths came out in short gasps.

Piper froze. Cooper blamed himself for her father's death? "No, you're wrong. You're not responsible. It's not your fault." How could he believe such a thing when it wasn't true by any stretch of the imagination?

He shook his head.

Piper jumped up and sat down on the other side of him. Grasping his face in her palms, she looked him in the eye. "Never once have any of us blamed you for Dad's death. Not me, not Mom, not Mia and not Shane.

"Cooper, I want you to listen to me very carefully. My dad had a massive heart attack that day. He died instantly. *No one* could have saved him. Not you. Not the paramedics. Not anyone. You've got to believe me, and you've got to stop blaming yourself. It was never your fault."

He looked at her and for the first time since they'd started this conversation, there was hope in his gaze.

"I thought that's why you hated me so much," he said.

"No. No." She kissed his cheek. "I was furious with my father for leaving us. I understand that now, but at thirteen, all I wanted to do was lash out." Piper stood and started pacing back and forth. "All of the rage and grief I was feeling bubbled up inside and erupted. Unfortunately, it landed on you." She stopped and looked at him. "When I saw you skateboarding in the parking lot of the funeral parlor, I thought…" Piper drew in a deep breath and released it. "There you were gliding over the pavement like it was just another normal day." She swallowed hard. "Like nothing was wrong while my whole world had crumbled to pieces. I thought you didn't care. About Dad, who I know loved you so much, or any of us, but most of all about me."

Cooper flinched and the hurt expression on his face broke her heart.

"That probably doesn't even make sense to you, because we were never particularly close growing up." Although…looking back on it now, something had changed between them the summer between seventh and eighth grade. She'd started…noticing him. He made her laugh, and having him around wasn't so bad anymore.

Then everything went wrong.

Piper clasped a hand over her mouth and swallowed her groan. She'd screwed everything up, big-time. "I know now that none of what I believed back then is true." Piper wrung her hands together. "But at thirteen…"

Cooper stood and walked out of the room.

She was all alone.

Again.

Ho-ly hell. Cooper couldn't believe what he'd just heard. All this time, he'd told himself that Piper couldn't forgive him for not saving her father, but he'd been wrong. About so many things.

He couldn't blame her for the conclusions she'd come to. Looking back on it, he may have believed the same if he were in her shoes. At least his younger self would have.

Coop dragged a hand through his hair. She wasn't the only one who'd messed things up back then. He'd done a good job of that himself.

His younger self couldn't understand why someone

as vibrant and full of life as Victor would suddenly leave this earth. Someone should have been able to save him.

The idea that he hadn't done enough had lodged itself in his subconscious and had remained there ever since.

He'd failed, and the guilt he'd suffered as a result had driven every interaction with Piper since.

She'd never blamed him. He was the one who couldn't forgive himself.

Idiot, idiot, idiot.

Coop strode back into the great room.

Piper looked at him, devastation etched in her beautiful, delicate features.

A heavy weight settled in his chest. Yes, he'd messed up all right.

"I should go," she said, her voice void of all emotion.

"No. Please don't." Nausea roiled in his belly. "I don't want you to leave." He pulled her into his arms and held her tight. "I need you to stay."

She peered up at him, a wary expression on her face. "I assumed…"

Coop grasped her hands with his. He needed the contact. "We've both done a lot of that over the years." He shook his head. "I got it wrong, too. All of it. Let me explain."

Piper locked her gaze with his and nodded.

He told her everything. Pouring out his heart until there was nothing left unsaid between them.

When he finished it was like a heavy weight had been lifted from him.

She gazed at him, eyes glossy with unshed tears. "We're quite a pair, aren't we?"

He kissed their joined hands and smiled. "That we are."

"So…" Piper worried her bottom lip. "Where do we go from here?"

Before he could answer, his stomach gave a loud rumble.

Piper burst out laughing and all the tension he'd experienced earlier drained away.

"I'm thinking somewhere to eat." She rubbed her belly. "I'm a little hungry after this afternoon."

"I'm afraid you're going to have to settle for Chez Turner." Coop pointed toward the glass slider that led to the backyard. "The snow is really coming down now."

Piper walked toward the kitchen. "Works for me. My clothes are still wet and I'm not about to go out dressed like this. No offense." She gave a little smirk.

"None taken." His gaze traveled over her from head to toes. "But I think you look great." Although he'd never be able to wear those sweats again without thinking about how the material had caressed her soft skin. At least, he assumed it was soft.

His pulse soared. Oh yeah, he wanted to know for sure.

A happy grin crossed her face. "Good to know, Turner. Good to know. Now, what can we make?" She opened the fridge and stuck her head inside.

Coop liked the sound of *we*. He walked into the kitchen to join her.

Piper pulled out a Ziploc bag full of cooked chicken breasts he'd marinated in Italian dressing before grilling and veggies for a salad.

"These still good?" Piper held up the Ziploc bag.

He nodded. "Yep. Cooked them last night."

"Perfect. We can have a chicken salad." She handed him the head of lettuce and a cucumber. "You prep those and I'll take care of these."

"Bossy, aren't we?" He grinned.

"I'm a take-charge kind of girl. Got a problem with

that?" She shot him a deadpan glance that lasted all of five seconds before she burst out laughing.

They peeled and chopped vegetables for a few minutes in companionable silence, then Piper turned a concerned expression in his direction.

"Are we okay?" she asked.

"We're more than okay. We're great." He brushed his lips against hers because he wanted to. Because he needed to. Because it had been too damned long since he last tasted the sweetness of her kiss.

Her supple lips met his in the most achingly tender kiss he'd ever experienced.

Coop slid one hand around her head and the other around her back and drew her closer. He reveled in the feel of her warm body pressed against his.

Piper twined her arms around his neck and clung to him. "Cooper." She moaned his name and deepened the kiss. "So damn good."

"You don't know the half of it." The taste of her lips, honeyed with the thrill of anticipation, sent a flood of heat rushing through him.

He lifted her into his arms, and a startled "Oh!" escaped from her mouth.

"Where are we going?" Her eyes danced with delight and she gave a soft chuckle.

"In here." Coop nodded to the sofa in the great room as he walked. "Where it's more comfortable."

Piper grinned. "Sounds like a plan."

Coop dropped down on the sofa and set Piper on his lap. A big mistake because she wriggled her sexy little bottom against him. He groaned. "You're going to kill me if you keep that up."

"We can't have that." Her lips brushed against his as she spoke. "I'm enjoying this too much."

Coop gazed into her bright blue eyes. "Me, too,

sweetheart. Me, too." He brushed featherlight kisses along her jawline to the hollow beneath her ear.

He licked and nipped at the thrumming pulse and she shivered. "You like that." It was a statement, not a question.

"God, yes. I want to touch you."

At this moment, he wanted that more than he'd ever wanted anything in his life.

Her fingers grabbed at his shirt, fumbling with the buttons. She let out a cry of frustration. "Take off your shirt," she demanded.

"You *are* bossy." He grinned. With one swift movement, he set her on the cushion beside him and pulled his shirt over his head.

Piper grabbed the shirt from him and tossed it on the floor. "Like I said earlier, I'm a take-charge kind of girl."

Oh yes, she was, and he liked it.

Piper straddled him and laid her palms against his bare chest. She closed her eyes and slid her hands over his pecs and shoulders. "Your skin is as smooth as I imagined."

"Fantasizing about me, are you?" He sent her his best sexy grin.

Her lids opened and she looked him in the eye. "Since I saw you at Donahue's the evening Nick's band played."

All those weeks ago? Before they'd struck their deal? He couldn't believe it. Coop scrutinized her face. The stark vulnerability in her gaze touched him, soul-deep. Their relationship might be a farce, but this desire, no, this fierce attraction they held for one another was real. It was more tangible, more genuine than anything he'd experienced in a long time. "I haven't been able to get you off my mind either."

Piper tugged her sweater over her head. Her eyes glittered a deep sapphire blue as she gazed at him. "Touch me, Cooper. I need you to touch me."

She wouldn't have to ask him twice. Lord, she was beautiful. He skimmed his hands over the lacy cups of her bra and she moaned.

The sound sent all of his blood heading south. He unclasped her bra and slid the straps from her shoulders. He tossed the lacy garment toward the spot on the floor where his shirt lay in a heap. "Exquisite," he murmured. Perfect in every way.

Her smile sent a rush of heat coursing through his body. Cupping her breasts in his palms, he stroked his thumbs over the distended tips.

"Oh." Her head fell back and a long moan escaped her parted lips.

Coop savored her delightful cries of pleasure. He wanted, no, *needed* to hear more of them. He twisted the buds between his thumb and finger.

She cried out again and a sense of deep satisfaction rumbled through him.

She dragged his head to her and kissed him again. Slow and languid as she stroked her fingers over his chest and back.

Coop thought he might die from the sweet pleasure of her hands on him.

"I think we should take this into your room." She grinned against his lips. "There's a big bed and it will be much more comfortable than the couch."

"Your wish is my command." He gripped her bottom in his hands and stood in one swift motion.

Holding her tightly, he kissed her hard, and together they laughed as he stumbled towards the bedroom.

For the first time since he could remember, Coop never wanted to let her go.

Chapter Seventeen

Striding into the bedroom, Cooper stopped by the bed. He gazed at her as if she were the most precious, most important thing in the world to him.

No other lover—not that there'd been many over the years—had looked at her with such adoration, such passion.

What did that say about the choices she'd made thus far in her life? When it came to men, she'd opted for casual, easy, commitment-free. She'd never wanted anything more.

But now…

How could one look from Cooper turn her inside out and send her spinning out of control? Because that was how she felt right now.

He kissed her with such sweet tenderness. Everything went all soft and mushy inside her. How could she have lived without this warmth and genuine affection for so long?

He broke the kiss all too quickly, as far as she was concerned. She could stay here all night long just kissing him.

Coop flashed her the most heart-stopping grin and her heart melted.

"What?" she asked when he just kept smiling.

"I was such an idiot. You are kind, and gorgeous,

and…" He glanced down at his sweatpants, which she was still wearing.

"And the best-dressed girlfriend you've ever had?" she quipped.

He chuckled. "Why did we waste so many years at odds with each other when we could have had this?"

One thing was certain, she never would have been ready for whatever this thing was between them, and she couldn't deny there was definitely something between them, if she hadn't worked through her grief. It was a long hard road, nearly ten years in the making, but she was glad she'd persevered.

"Maybe we needed to go through everything else to have this now?"

"Maybe so." He tumbled them onto his bed. "I'm glad we're here now."

Her heart slammed in her chest, beating so hard she thought it might break her ribs. "Me, too." It was the truth.

Piper gazed into his gorgeous green eyes. God, she could get lost in those fathomless pools. "Kiss me." She needed to feel connected with him.

"Bossy." His sexy grin devastated her.

"Desperate," she corrected.

His gaze turned smoky and a longing, both physical and something more, flooded through her. "I need you." More truth. "So much I ache inside." Piper didn't want to think about what any of that meant right now. She only wanted to feel. "I can't wait any longer." She removed the remainder of her clothes with one quick tug and tossed them over the edge of the bed.

"Slow down. We have all day."

"I can't." Not with all of this frantic need coursing through her body. "Next time, I promise we'll take it slow, but now…" Piper pulled him close and stripped off the rest of his garments.

"I have to admit, this is much better." He explored the soft lines of her back, her waist, her hips.

Piper let out a blissful sigh. This was heaven on earth. "Do you have any idea how much I like it when you touch me?"

Cooper flashed a wolfish grin. "As much as I love doing the touching? Your skin is so soft. So smooth." His fingers skated over her breast and across her silken belly.

She cried out when his skilled fingers found the sensitive spot between her thighs.

Cooper lowered his lips to hers. His tongue tasted, teased, demanded, and she thought she might go insane from the sheer pleasure of it.

"Now. *Please*, Cooper." He'd reduced her to a mass of jangling nerves.

"Hold on a second." He reached inside the nightstand drawer and grabbed a foil packet. Tearing it open with his teeth, he removed the condom and sheathed himself.

Cooper slid into her in one swift move, filling her completely.

He moved slowly at first, then faster and harder, driving the ache inside her to a fever pitch.

"So damned good." Her breaths came in sharp pants.

With a shout, they tumbled over the edge and drifted down to earth together.

Piper wasn't sure how much time had passed when Cooper stirred.

"I'll be right back." He slid out of bed.

She propped herself up on her elbows and watched as his naked form strode toward the bathroom. The statue of David couldn't hold a candle to Cooper Turner. The man was sexy as all get-out. And he was all hers...*for now*. She planned to take full advantage of him.

Piper grinned. She couldn't remember the last time she felt this alive, this exhilarated. This...ecstatic, exultant, joyful. *Happy.*

Yes, being with Cooper made her happy.

It wasn't just the sex—a frisson of pleasure trickled down her spine when she thought about what his hands and mouth could do to her body. Yes, the sex was phenomenal, unparalleled, best she'd ever had, if she was honest.

But she liked spending time with him, too. Cooper was kind and sweet and caring. He made her laugh and she felt content when they were together.

Which meant what?

Piper shook her head. She didn't want to think about it. She wanted to enjoy the here and now.

"Come back to bed, Cooper."

"Bossy!" he growled from the bathroom.

She cracked a smile even though he wasn't there to witness it.

"Just a second," he called.

Piper gazed around the space while she waited. She hadn't really looked at the room earlier when she'd come in here to change. She'd been too focused on removing her wet clothes to notice the blue-gray feature wall with a wooden diamond pattern behind the bed, the art deco nightstands, and the... "Whoa. Is that...?"

Piper jumped out of bed and hurried to the wall where two photos hung.

The ginormous dragon and delicate swan stared back at her.

"What are you doing?" Cooper slid his arms around her waist.

Her bottom came into contact with his hard shaft and she groaned.

"I saw the same photos in the TK Construction lobby a few weeks ago."

"Oh," he said.

Piper turned so they stood face-to-face. "Is that all you have to say?"

He shrugged. "Those are from the ice art festival."

"Why do you have—" Her gaze widened. "Did you carve those?"

"Yes." He nuzzled the sensitive spot where her neck joined her shoulders.

She laughed. "Stop trying to distract me. Seriously, you made them?"

"I did."

"Cooper, they're amazing. The scales... Those alone must have taken hours to etch."

He nodded. "The dragon took me a week."

"It's incredible." She turned and studied the image. "You're very talented." Turning back to face him, she asked, "Why didn't I know this about you?" She shook her head. "Don't answer that." She already knew the answer. All those years when they could have been...

Not hating each other. What a complete waste of time.

"The past is the past. There's nothing we can do about it now." Cooper dropped a tender kiss on her lips. "It's where we go from here that counts."

He was right. Piper planned to learn everything she could about this handsome, sexy, sweet, funny, wonderful man. She smiled. "Did you enter again this year?"

"Uh-huh." Cooper pressed a soft kiss to the hollow beneath her ear.

She giggled because it tickled. "What are you going to make?"

"I thought you wanted me to come back to bed?"

"I did. *Do*," she corrected. She grinned. "But first, I want to hear what you're planning to sculpt. And—" she rubbed her belly "—I want you to feed me." She kissed his cheek.

"Honestly, I don't know what I'm going to make. The theme this year is love, since they're judging the sculptures on Valentine's Day. Got any ideas?"

"Not off the top of my head, but I'll think about it." She glanced around the room looking for her clothes. Damn. They'd never gotten around to tossing their wet items in the dryer. She walked over and picked up the pair of sweats Cooper had loaned her earlier.

"Hold on a second. I've got something more comfortable for you." Coop disappeared into the bathroom and returned a moment later with a huge white terry-cloth robe. He tossed it to her.

"Thank you." She slid her arms into the soft, fluffy material. Overlapping the edges, she tugged the belt tight around her waist and tied it in a knot. She laughed when she caught a glimpse of her reflection in the mirror. The garment was three times her size.

Piper followed Cooper into the kitchen. They finished preparing the salad and filled two bowls.

"Let's eat in the family room. We can watch TV." Cooper, now dressed in the sweatpants he'd worn earlier, strode to the couch. He patted the spot next to him and Piper sat.

He draped an arm around her shoulder and pulled her close. "Are you warm enough?"

Piper breathed a contented sigh. She could get used to this. "I'm perfect."

Cooper powered on the television. "How about a movie?"

"As long as it's something funny." She pursed her lips. "Or they blow stuff up."

Cooper let out a deep belly laugh. "What, no chick flicks?"

"I'm not into the whole happy-ever-after theme."

"Is that why Jane has made it her mission in life to find you a husband?"

"You got it." Piper smirked and gave his cheek a gentle pinch. "She thinks that if she finds me the perfect man, I'll change my mind."

"But you won't?" He shot her a curious glance.

"Nope." She shook her head. "No way. No how."

Cooper grasped her jaw and gently lifted her head to meet his gaze. "Can I ask why?"

The care and compassion in his gaze touched her to the core. Piper swallowed hard. "I'm scared. What if…" She closed her eyes and drew in a deep breath. "Love doesn't last. People fall out of love every day, or they leave you. Look at Mia and Shane. They both thought they were in love and they ended up divorced. And my mother…" She shook her head.

Cooper nodded. "It's hard to put yourself out there again after you've been hurt, regardless of who or what may have caused that wound."

Finally, someone understood her. "Exactly. You get it."

"Unfortunately, yes." He couldn't hide the pain and bitterness he'd experienced.

The sadness in his gaze tore at her heart. "Someone hurt you, didn't they?"

For a moment he said nothing. He stared straight ahead as if he were lost in his own thoughts, but then he nodded. "Her name was Rachel. I thought she was as in love with me as I was with her." Cooper let loose a derisive laugh. "I even bought her a ring."

Piper's gaze widened. "You were engaged?"

"No." He shook his head. "I planned to propose, but she broke it off before I could."

She pressed her lips to his cheek. "I'm so sorry."

"Me, too, but at least no one knew what I'd planned to do. I didn't make a huge fool of myself."

"You didn't tell anyone? Not even your family?" Her mouth dropped open. "You guys are so close."

"Honestly, I don't know why I didn't tell them." Cooper shrugged. "Maybe I knew subconsciously that it wouldn't work out and I didn't want them feeling sorry for me." He locked his gaze on her.

"I can understand that," she said. If she were in his shoes, she wouldn't want people to pity her either.

"I know you do." Cooper grasped her hand in his. "It used to drive you crazy when people pitied you after your father died."

Piper nodded. She'd appreciated the care and compassion people had offered, but the pity... She'd *hated* it.

Piper released his hand. Lifting his arm, she draped it over her shoulder and snuggled in close to him. "She's a fool, if you ask me."

"Huh?" Cooper's brows furrowed into a deep V.

"Raquel, or whatever her name is."

Cooper chuckled. "It's Rachel, and why do you think she's a fool?"

"Because you're a great guy, Cooper Turner. How could she possibly do better?"

He laughed.

The joyful, deep sound rumbled through her and she smiled. "I'm serious."

"You're pretty great yourself." He kissed her soundly, and took her breath away. "Now, finish your salad, and let's watch that movie." Cooper wiggled his brows.

He wanted to change the subject, and that was fine by her. "Yes, sir." She gave him a jaunty salute.

He selected a James Bond movie and they settled in. After she finished her meal, Cooper collected the plates and brought them to the kitchen. When he returned, he pulled her into the crook of his arm and she snuggled in close.

"This is nice." Cooper dropped a quick kiss on the top of her head.

"It is," she agreed. She'd never experienced the simple intimacy of being held like this before. Sure, she'd had other relationships, but they'd lacked any real closeness.

This thing with Cooper...*isn't real.* She needed to remember that. They'd struck a deal out of mutual need. She needed to get her mother off her back once and for all and he needed a date to a wedding.

They were both playing a part. End of story.

Still...her heart ached at the idea of this thing between them ending.

Stop psychoanalyzing everything when you promised you'd just enjoy this time together. Live in the moment.

Cooper traced lazy circles over her shoulder and upper arm.

Frissons of pleasure trickled down her spine.

"Are you cold?" Cooper asked. "Do you want me to crank up the heat?"

Enjoy this time together.

"No-oo." She drew out the word. "Not in the least."

Piper trailed a finger down Cooper's bare chest. "I'm plenty warm." She dipped her finger into the waistband of his sweatpants and withdrew it immediately. "In fact, one could say I'm hot." Piper licked her lips. "On fire, even."

"Maybe you should take some of your clothes off?" he suggested. The heat in his gaze contradicted the casual tone of his voice.

"You think it might cool me off?" Lord, she adored their banter, this playfulness. Another new experience with this sexy, kind man, and one she could definitely get used to.

"It's worth a try."

Piper nodded and stood. Releasing the belt, she shimmied out of the robe and let it pool on the floor around her feet.

"Better?" He arched a brow.

Piper sat on his lap, her legs straddling him. She grinned. "Oh, yes."

"Are you sure?" He nuzzled the crook of her neck.

A languid heat filled her. "Yes." This was what she wanted. What she needed... What was *real*. She couldn't deny it. This desire, or longing, or whatever name you called it, was tangible. And mutual.

When it came to pleasuring each other, neither of them was acting. She was damned sure of that.

It was the only thing she was sure of.

Her phone started to ring.

Oh, for crying out loud. "Ignore it," she commanded.

"Bossy," he growled but his lips continued skating over her skin.

The ringing stopped, thank God. Piper grasped his hands and placed them on her breasts. "Touch me. Please. I need your hands on me."

Her phone started ringing again.

Her head dropped forward. *You've got to be kidding.*

The ringing stopped but Mia's annoyed voice started yelling, "Your sister is calling, your sister is calling. What are you waiting for? Pick up the phone already."

Cooper chuckled. "That's an interesting ringtone."

She sighed as her phone repeated its demand. "Mia recorded it and downloaded the file to my phone so I wouldn't ignore her calls."

"You should probably get that."

"Right." Mia would keep calling until she answered. She wiggled off his lap. He groaned and she flashed him a very satisfied grin.

Yes, this thing between them was real, all right.

Standing, she reached for the robe lying in a pile on the floor. She yanked her phone from the pocket. "Hey, Mia, what's up?"

"The power is out in town. I'm checking in on my little sister to make sure she's doing okay in this storm," Mia said.

"I'm fine."

Cooper stood and shed his pants.

She sucked in a breath. He was all hard planes and corded muscles. Piper reveled in his glorious arousal and the knowledge that she'd done this to him.

In one swift motion, she found herself planted on the couch with her back pressed firmly against the plush material.

"Just fine?" Cooper whispered in her other ear. "I'll have to see if I can do better."

Mia started speaking again. "Abby and Elle said to tell you they're riding out the storm at Elle's place, if you want to join them."

"I'm not home," Piper squeaked as Cooper closed his

mouth over the tip of her breast. "I'm with Cooper." She didn't catch the rest of whatever her sister was saying because Cooper was doing delightful things with his hands as he skimmed them over her body.

"Ohhh," she moaned when he stroked his finger between her thighs. Her breaths came in short, sharp gasps.

"Enough talking," he growled. Grasping her phone with his free hand, he tossed it.

Piper heard Mia's startled gasp and her, "Are you and Cooper...? Oh, my God, you *are*!" as the phone hit the floor.

Cooper scooped her into his arms and strode toward his bedroom. "I can't get enough of you."

Piper looked into his eyes. Desire blazed from his emerald-gold gaze. And something more...

Something she couldn't—no, *wouldn't*—name.

Chapter Eighteen

The sun shone bright in the Saturday morning sky as Cooper pulled his truck into the parking lot behind the Coffee Palace.

Piper wanted to groan when she spotted the thick blanket of snow covering her car. She'd need to give herself an extra fifteen or twenty minutes to clean it off and warm the engine before she headed over to the gallery.

At least the parking lot is plowed already.

She turned to Cooper and dropped a kiss on his lips. "I'll see you tomorrow." They both had plans this evening. Poker night with the girls for her and watching the game at her brother's place with the guys for him.

Piper hopped out of the truck and headed toward the back door that led to her apartment. She touched the back pocket of her jeans, making sure her phone hadn't fallen out when she jumped out of Cooper's truck.

She couldn't forget to print out the pictures she'd snapped of the exterior of Cooper's house while he was clearing the snow earlier. She'd need to get started painting a portrait of the farmhouse today, if possible. Cooper's birthday was six days away and she wanted to have it done by then.

Opening the door to her place, she stepped inside. A shiver ran down her spine. Damn. No power all night meant no heat either. How long would it take for the apartment to come up to temperature? Probably long enough that she didn't want to sit here in the cold. She'd hop in the shower, and head to the Coffee Palace after.

Twenty minutes later, she exited the door that led out to the back parking lot.

"Ho-ly cow." Piper stopped dead in her tracks. She grinned at the sight of her car sans the snow last night's storm had deposited on it.

Cooper must be responsible. Who else would have cleaned away the snow for her?

She walked over to her vehicle. He'd even shoveled the two feet in front of her car that the plow hadn't removed.

Grabbing her phone, she found his number in her contacts and connected the call. "You sweet, sweet man," she said when he answered.

He gave a sexy little chuckle that turned her insides to mush. "Why, thank you. I see you found my little surprise."

"Yes, I did. You didn't have to clean my car off." She could have taken care of it. Was more than capable of removing a bit of snow. It came with the territory when you lived in New England in the winter. "But I really appreciate you doing it for me." She cleared her throat and murmured in her best sexy voice, "I'll have to give you a special thank-you next time I see you."

"Sounds promising. What did you have in mind?" he asked.

"You'll have to wait and see." Piper heard a groan as she cut the connection. She flashed a smug smile to no one in particular as she walked around the front of the building and entered the Coffee Palace. A blast of heat hit her and she smiled.

"Hey, Piper." Elle gave a little wave from behind the counter.

"Good morning. It's nice and warm in here."

"Thank goodness for the generator," Elle said. "It was freezing in my apartment when I got up. Needless to say, I was psyched when I got down here."

"It's still cold upstairs." Piper unzipped her parka. "That's why I'm here."

"Hey, Piper." Abby walked in from the back room. "We missed you last night."

"Yeah," Elle said. "We had a mini poker night."

She nodded. "Mia called to let me know."

"I would have called you myself, but I don't have your number," Abby said.

"Me either," Elle added.

"Let me give it to you now." Piper rattled off the digits and both Abby and Elle added her to their list of contacts. She did the same.

"How's Cooper?" Elle smirked. "Did you two have *fun* last night?"

Had Mia spilled the beans about what she and Cooper were doing when she'd called? Her cheeks burned. "He's, um…good." She needed to change the subject. "What's the coffee of the day?"

"There's a few." Elle laughed and pointed to the sign on the counter.

Piper eliminated the decaf flavors. She needed the caffeine. "I'll have a large chocolate raspberry with cream and two stevia."

"Anything else?" Elle asked.

Piper eyed the confections, looking for something yummy. She spotted a cupcake with loads of chocolate frosting and candy hearts on top.

Before she could order, a deep rumbly voice said, "She'll have one of those." And a finger pointed to her intended selection.

She whirled around and found Cooper standing behind her. A flood of warmth rushed through her, and she was pretty sure a goofy grin was plastered across her face. "Hey, stranger. Long time no see." Almost thirty whole minutes. She chuckled to herself.

The urge to launch herself into his arms was strong, but she resisted. Barely. Lord, what was it about seeing this man that made everything inside her go soft and gooey?

Cooper yanked her against him and crushed his mouth to hers. He kissed her as if she were all he could ever want. All he would ever need. Her heart filled to bursting point.

He released her a few moments later.

Breathless, she asked, "What are you doing here? I thought you needed to get over to the Humanity houses."

"I do, but I saw you walk in and wanted to see you again."

Piper flashed a mile-wide smile. "It's nice to see you again, too."

Elle cleared her throat.

Piper winced. "Oh, um… Sorry."

"Don't apologize." Elle flashed a wicked grin. To Cooper, she asked. "Anything for you?"

He pulled out his wallet and handed Elle his credit card. "Piper's order, two boxes of coffee and a couple dozen doughnuts. Gotta take care of the Humanity crew, too."

"Thank you." She kissed his cheek. He really was a sweet, sweet man.

Elle handed Piper her order. Turning her attention to Cooper, she said, "It'll be ten to fifteen minutes for the boxes. I need to brew the coffee."

Cooper nodded. "No trouble. I'll wait."

"Have a seat. Someone will bring you your order when it's ready," Abby said.

"Perfect." Cooper escorted Piper to the closest open table and pulled out her chair.

Piper sat. "So, how'd you know what I was going to order?" She gestured to the sugary sweetness sitting atop her plate.

Cooper moved the other chair to sit by her side instead of across from her. "For as long as I can remember, you've always had a sweet tooth."

"You remember that?" A little thrill raced down her spine.

"I do. You used to hoard your Halloween candy and have a piece every day, and you never shared it with anyone else."

Piper laughed. "It's true."

"As far as chocolate is concerned…" He dipped his finger into the frosting and scooped up a smidge. "That's a love we both share."

He licked the frosting from his finger. Piper sucked in a deep breath as a languid heat filled her belly. *So not the time or the place. So not the time or the place.* She repeated the mantra hoping it would cool her fevered body.

More in control now, Piper cut the cupcake and handed half to Cooper. "Today is your lucky day. I'm feeling generous." She winked.

He shook his head. "I got that for you."

Piper kissed his cheek. "And I want to share it with you." She began plucking the chalky candies from atop the frosting on her half and set them on her plate.

"You don't like conversation hearts?" Cooper snagged one from his half.

"Is that what they're called?" she asked. "I never

knew the proper name before. I've always called them the Valentine's candy with the sayings on them."

"That works, too." He popped a heart in his mouth. "I can't remember the last time I ate one of these."

"I haven't had them since I was a kid." She stuck a candy on her tongue and savored the sugary sweetness. "I'd forgotten how tasty they are."

Cooper handed her a heart that had XOXO on the face.

She grinned. "Aww, hugs and kisses. How sweet."

Cooper winked. "I'm a sweet guy. You said so yourself."

"Yes, I did, and I'd say it again." She plucked off more of the hearts and added them to the pile on the side of her plate.

"I thought you liked them." Cooper's brows furrowed.

"I do, but I'm a purist when it comes to chocolate." Grabbing another candy, she read the words etched on the surface. "Be Mine." The idea sent little thrills of excitement skating down her spine. "What do you say?" The words came out before she could stop them.

"Oh, man. Can I?" Batting his eyelashes in an exaggerated fashion, Cooper clasped his hand over his heart and sighed.

Piper shook her head, but she was smiling. "Ha, ha, ha."

"I know. You think I'm immature."

Not anymore. She understood now that he was just trying to fit in the best way he knew how. "Lighthearted," she corrected. "It's not a bad quality to have."

He let out a low, rumbly chuckle that sent her pulse skittering. Grasping the Be Mine candy from her hand, he set it aside. "I think we'll keep that one. Let's see what else we have here." Cooper picked up another candy from her plate. "Always and Forever." He scoffed. "I know that's not true."

"Agreed," she said.

"No use saving this one." He dropped the heart in his mouth and crunched it.

Piper laughed. She broke off a piece of her cupcake and lifted it to her mouth. "I'm totally with you on that score." *Always* and *forever* weren't words in her vocabulary when it came to relationships with the opposite sex.

He quirked his lips and grabbed another of her discarded candies. "Bossy." Cooper winked and gave her a sexy grin. "Now, *that* I'll agree with."

Piper arched a brow. "It does not say that."

"Yes, it does," Cooper insisted.

"I don't believe you." She gestured for him to hand over the heart. "Let me see."

"I don't think so." He popped it into his mouth.

"No fair." Piper shook her head.

He shrugged. "I guess you'll just have to take my word for it."

"Nope." She licked the chocolate frosting off the piece of cupcake she held in her hand.

"You did not just do that." He shot her a you-have-got-to-be-kidding look.

Piper chuckled. "I sure did." She flashed him an impish smile. "The frosting is the best part."

He laughed. A deep sound that rumbled through her.

God, she loved hearing that sound. It made her feel all warm and fuzzy inside. She grinned.

He grabbed another heart and read, "Marry Me." Snorting, he said, "For God's sake. Why would you include a statement like this in kids' candies?"

"I agree. We need to get rid of it." Grasping it from

him, Piper dropped it on the floor and crushed it with her boot.

"I love it." Cooper smirked. "You're as jaded as me."

"Absolutely." She winked at him.

Elle walked over and set Cooper's order on the table. "Two dozen doughnuts and two boxes of coffee to go."

"Thanks," Cooper said.

Elle disappeared and they were alone at the table again.

He gave a reluctant sigh. "I've gotta get going." He ate the last of his cupcake and stood.

"I should get going, too. I'll walk out with you."

Cooper dropped a tip on the table and grasped a box of coffee in each hand.

"I'll take these for you." She grabbed the box of doughnuts and followed him to the door.

A tall man with short, black hair came toward them from the opposite direction as they walked to Cooper's truck. He stopped in front of them.

"Is that you, Piper?" the man asked.

At first glance, she couldn't recognize him, then comprehension dawned. "Tom Anderson." Cooper's best friend.

Piper pinned a congenial smile in place. "It's nice to see you."

"It's great to see you, too, Piper," Tom said.

Son of a bitch. Coop's hands clenched around each box handle he was carrying. Of all the people he could run into, it was just his bad luck he'd bump into Tom.

"What's it been? Ten years?" Tom wrapped his arms around her and gave her a hug.

Coop was going to lose his shit if Tom didn't step away from Piper. He didn't want him touching her in any way, shape or form.

He and Piper were…

The truth was, he wasn't sure what he and Piper were anymore. Last night had changed things. At least it had for him. Yeah, they'd had sex. Great sex. Fantastic for sure, but that wasn't what had changed things. He and Piper had shared…something potent, and compelling and powerful.

Something he'd never experienced with any other woman before. Not even Rachel.

Which meant what?

Hell if he knew. How was he supposed to approach Piper and find out what was going on in her brain with all of this uncertainty roiling around inside his?

He couldn't.

The only thing he knew for sure was that he didn't want Tom anywhere near Piper. But he was going to look like a class A jerk if he went all caveman on her and threw her over his shoulder and walked away.

Even though that was exactly what he wanted to do.

"Yes. Can you believe it?" The smile Piper aimed at Tom sliced through his heart like a sharp knife. Which was crazy. She was just being polite.

He couldn't blame her. He hadn't told her about Tom and Rachel, because yeah, he still felt like a complete moron for not having figured out what was going on in front of his face.

Looking back on the situation, he should have figured it out sooner, but he'd been so caught up in the fantasy of what he believed was the perfect relationship, that he couldn't see the truth.

Or maybe he hadn't wanted to comprehend what was going on. The signs were there, but he chose to believe Rachel when she told him she was working late. And when he'd found Tom leaving her place one evening…

His gut plummeted. *Idiot, idiot, idiot.* Yeah, he'd wanted to believe Tom's story about helping Rachel plan a surprise birthday party for him.

He hadn't wanted to believe either of them were capable of such betrayal.

"Last I heard, you were living in Los Angeles and running a successful art gallery," Tom said.

It required every ounce of self-control Coop possessed not to reach over and slug Tom.

"I was, but I decided to come home and open my own place. The Kavanaugh gallery is opening in less than a month." Piper eased away from Tom and some of the tension inside him subsided.

Tom's grin broadened. "That's fantastic. We should get together soon and catch up."

Coop stiffened, every bone in his body going rigid. *No friggin' way.*

"Maybe in a few weeks," Piper said.

Wait. What? Coop jerked his attention to Piper. She wanted to get together with him? Did she still have a thing for him after all these years?

She moved to his side. "We're busy getting the space ready at the moment."

Coop pulled her close, so her shoulder and hip touched his. "We won't have any free time until after the gallery is up and running."

"You two are together?" Tom arched a brow.

"Yes." It gave him immense satisfaction to give Tom that news.

Chapter Nineteen

Piper pulled into Mia's driveway at seven o'clock sharp on Saturday night.

Her phone pinged. She pulled her cell from her pocket and glanced at the screen. Smiling, she read the text from Cooper.

How was your day?

A rush of heat radiated through her chest. Such a sweet guy to check in on her and see how she was doing.

She texted back. Been crazy busy since I left you this morning.

She still couldn't believe they'd run into Tom Anderson after leaving the Coffee Palace this morning. Although why she was surprised, she couldn't say. It was bound to happen, sooner or later. You couldn't hide in a small town.

Piper continued texting. Got a lot done at the gallery. She'd been able to do a good deal of work on the portrait she was painting of his house, too, but she couldn't tell him that. Wait until you see the progress I made with my art studio. It's really coming along. How was your day?

She snorted as she remembered the pole-axed expression on Tom's face when Cooper told him they were a couple. Like he couldn't believe it was possible. She wasn't sure whether he believed she was too good for Cooper, or the other way around. It was insulting either way.

Cooper's text came through. We worked on the interiors of the two houses that were enclosed. Just got home a few minutes ago. Grabbing a shower now and heading to Shane's to watch the game.

Have fun, she texted.

You, too. Save some chocolate for me.

Will do. Piper grinned as she shoved her phone back into her jeans pocket.

She hopped out of her car and noticed two others parked in the driveway. Elle and Layla must have arrived early.

The door opened before she reached the front stoop.

"Come on in," Layla said. "Mia is putting a movie on for the girls. She asked me to let you in."

Piper walked inside. "Am I the last to arrive?"

Layla closed the door. "Yes. Abby and Elle are already sitting at the table. They came together."

Piper laughed. "Here I was congratulating myself for being on time, and you all arrived early."

"Only by five minutes." Layla walked beside Piper as they moved toward the kitchen.

A woman Piper didn't recognize also sat with Elle and Abby at the table. "Hello." She walked over and held out her hand. "I'm Piper Kavanaugh."

"This is my sister, Zara," Layla said. "She's visiting from Manhattan. Piper is Shane's youngest sister," Layla said to Zara.

Zara grasped her hand. "It's nice to meet you."

Piper smiled. "You, too. How long are you in town for?"

Zara released Piper's hand. "A few days. I'll probably head home on Wednesday since I didn't end up arriving until today."

Layla sat in one of the empty chairs at the table. "She was supposed to arrive yesterday, but got delayed because of last night's storm."

"We did get hit with a lot of snow." She'd awoken to the sound of a snowblower and found Cooper outside clearing the eighteen inches they'd received. She'd put on a pot of coffee and made eggs and toast when he finished the driveway. Piper smiled to herself. It was all very domestic. The thing was, she'd enjoyed starting her day with him.

She walked around the table and grabbed another of the empty chairs.

"Hey, Piper." Abby waved.

"Hey, Abby." She gave a little wave. "Elle, I meant to ask you this morning when I saw you at the Coffee Palace, have you started classes yet?"

Elle shook her head. "The semester starts on Monday. I can't wait to get back into the swing of things. I've heard really good things about my Marketing professor. One of my friends took his class last year and loved it. She told me we're going to get some real-life experience."

"That's great," Piper said. "What's going on with you, Abby?"

"Yeah, Abby." Elle nudged her in the ribs with her elbow. "What's going on with you?"

Abby rolled her eyes and shook her head. "There's nothing going on."

Elle arched a brow. "You looked pretty cozy with Nick Turner this afternoon."

"He asked me if I could cater an event. We were going over the menu. That's all," Abby said.

"I don't know. You two looked pretty chummy," Elle insisted.

Layla poured herself a glass of red wine from the bottle that was on the table. "Nick's engaged."

"*Exactly*," Abby confirmed.

Elle picked up her glass of white wine and sipped. "I heard there's trouble in paradise."

Piper remembered their meeting a few weeks ago when she'd run into Isabelle and Nick at Donahue's pub. Isabelle had seemed ill at ease. Maybe there was some truth to what Elle had heard.

"Oh, come on, Abby. I know you have a thing for him," Elle said. "You have his order ready and waiting for him every morning so he doesn't have to wait."

"To be fair, she does the same for me," Layla said.

Abby nodded. "That's because you come in every day, and so does Nick." Abby shook her head. "Nick and I have been friends since kindergarten. Honestly, I can't imagine being anything more than that with him." She looked at Piper. "How are your renovations going?"

Elle grinned. "Way to dodge, Abs."

Piper laughed. She'd been thinking the same thing. "The place is really coming together. With any luck we'll wrap up everything in a couple of weeks."

"That's great." Mia strode into the room with a stemmed glass in each hand. She set one in front of Piper and another in front of the last empty chair. With a smug smirk on her face, she added, "It's nice to know you and Cooper are getting some actual work done."

Elle and Abby started laughing.

Heat crept up her neck and flooded her cheeks. Yep, Mia had definitely told them what Piper and Cooper were doing while she and her sister were on the phone last night. She leaned back in her chair and crossed her arms over her chest. "Ha ha. You're funny."

"Okay. What happened?" Layla asked. She looked from Mia to Piper. "It must have been good, because your face is beet red."

"Oh, it was *good* all right." Mia doubled over laughing.

"Come on. Spill," Layla demanded. "Elle and Abby obviously know. I'm feeling very left out of the loop on this." She pouted her lips.

"It's not that big a deal." Piper grabbed the bottle of red wine and poured a healthy glass. Turning to her sister, she said, "By the way, I'm staying here tonight."

"No problem," Mia said.

"If it's not that big a deal, then how come you're not sharing?" Zara asked.

Piper glared at her sister, and Mia laughed even harder. "Fine, I'll spill." She told the group what happened.

"That's hysterical," Zara said. Turning to Layla, she said. "Do us both a favor and don't answer my call if you and Shane are in the middle of getting busy."

"We weren't... I wouldn't have..." Piper's cheeks burned hotter.

Everyone laughed even harder.

Piper let out a resigned sigh. She was never going to live this down.

"You two were so cute at the Coffee Palace this morning," Abby said.

"Yeah," Elle agreed. "You were acting all lovey-dovey."

"What are you talking about?" Mia asked.

"Piper—" Abby pointed to her "—and Cooper were kissing and touching and whispering sweet nothings in each other's ears. At least that's what it looked like from where I was standing behind the counter."

"You were?" Mia stared at Piper, a look of confusion on her face. "I've never known you to be all touchy-feely with a guy before. You're usually more…cool and reserved."

That much was true. Piper usually preferred a less sentimental, less sappy approach to her relationships, but Cooper was different.

She liked him. More than she believed possible. Piper swallowed hard. Yeah, she couldn't deny it any longer. Somehow, he'd wormed his way past all her defenses and she'd fallen for him.

Holy. Friggin'. Crap.

Coop pulled his F-150 into the driveway of Shane's beachfront home. He could hear the soothing ebb and flow of the waves as they crashed on shore. A blanket of snow currently covered what would bloom into lush landscape come spring.

Was this the kind of house that Piper wanted to live in? He could see the appeal. Heck, the beach was Shane's backyard.

Still… She'd enjoyed frolicking in his large back-yard yesterday.

Coop shook his head. Why was he even thinking about where Piper would want to live? Okay, yes, he liked her, but they weren't at the point of moving in together.

Although… No. *Absolutely not.* He'd dated Rachel for two years before he'd even thought about moving in with her. Now he was thinking about living with Piper after spending less than a month with her?

They weren't even a real couple at this point.

Yeah, he was losing his mind, all right.

Opening his door, he jumped out of his truck and walked along the pathway that led to the front porch.

Shane opened the door, but blocked the entrance, his arms crossed over his chest.

Crap. They hadn't talked since he'd found him and Piper... Groping each other. Yes, that was pretty much what they'd been doing to each other that day. If Shane knew about last night... Coop pulled at the collar of his shirt. "You gonna let me in?"

Shane shook his head. "Not until you tell me what your intentions are toward my sister."

Seriously? He scraped a hand through his hair. Okay, yes. Shane was overprotective when it came to his family. Coop should have seen this coming, especially after the way he'd reacted when he'd learned they were together. "I, ah, want to date your sister." That was the truth. What would Piper say if he told her as much? "Do I have your permission?"

Levi appeared in the open door frame beside Shane. The two of them doubled over with laughter.

Shane stepped aside and gestured for Coop to enter. "I'm just giving you shit."

Levi smirked. "You should have seen the look on your face."

"Priceless." Shane high-fived Levi.

Coop shook his head and stepped inside. "You guys are a barrelful of laughs tonight."

"Yep," Levi agreed.

Coop followed his brother and Shane across the hall.

"You remember Duncan, don't you?" Shane asked. He pointed to his fellow Emergency Medical Services responder.

Coop nodded and extended a hand. "It's been a while."

"Months," Duncan confirmed.

Shane slapped Duncan on the back. "Lover boy was seeing someone and she wouldn't allow Cruz here to come out and play, but now he's a single guy again."

Duncan rolled his eyes. "Yeah, yeah, yeah. Laugh it up, Wall Street. Not all of us are as lucky as you when it comes to finding the right match."

"I told you, I'm an EMT now, Cruz, just like you. My Wall Street days are over, but you're right about the lucky part. Layla is a treasure."

Levi made the sound of a whip cracking and they all laughed.

Coop scanned the room. "Where's Nick?"

Levi pointed in the general direction of Shane's kitchen. "Mr. Doom and Gloom is on the phone with Isabelle."

Coop's brows furrowed. "Is something wrong?"

Shane shrugged. "Not sure. He was pretty quiet when he arrived, then he got a call from Isabelle and he's been on the phone with her for thirty minutes now."

Nick walked into the room looking as if someone had smacked him upside the head.

"Hey, man. You okay?" Coop asked.

Nick sank onto the couch and dropped his head in his hands. "Isabelle wants to postpone the wedding."

"What?" Levi looked at Coop, a stunned expression on his face. "How come?"

Nick lifted his gaze. "She got an offer for a new job. In Tokyo."

"Japan?" Shane asked.

Coop sucked in a deep breath. That was a long way away from New Suffolk.

Nick nodded. "Her company offered her the job today. It's a one-year assignment. Apparently, it's a

pretty big deal that they've selected her." His face fell.
"We're supposed to get married next month and my fiancée and I won't even be on the same continent."

"Can you move the wedding up?" he asked.

Nick looked as if Coop had grown two heads. "First
off, the wedding venue is booked solid for the next year
and a half, and even if that weren't the case, we couldn't
pull everything together before she has to leave."

Levi eyed Nick curiously. "When is that?"

"In a few days." Nick threw his hands in the air.
"Talk about little to no notice." He jumped up from
the couch and started pacing back and forth. "How is
someone supposed to uproot their lives in a week? It's
not enough time, damn it." Nick continued ranting as
if no one else was there.

Coop couldn't understand most of what Nick was
saying, but his last words came through loud and clear.
You think you know someone.

An image of Rachel flashed in his brain. Nausea
roiled around in his gut and burned a path up his throat.

He'd thought he'd known Rachel. Look how that
turned out.

And Piper... He'd known her since birth, but this
thing with her was pretend. A deal they'd made.

He liked the Piper he'd gotten to know over the last
few weeks, but how could he say for sure what she was
really like?

Chapter Twenty

Piper headed back to the gallery at eleven o'clock on Wednesday morning. Flakes of snow drifted down from the gray sky.

Her phone rang as she reached the outskirts of town. She pressed the button on her steering wheel that connected the call.

"Hello."

"Hey, Piper. It's me." Cooper's voice boomed over her car speakers. "Were you able to get the things you needed at the hardware store for the bathrooms?"

She smiled. "Yes, although I had to drive to Plymouth because our local store was out of the fixtures I wanted. I'm on my way back now. I should be there in a few minutes."

"Actually, I won't be here when you arrive. I have to take off a little early today. I'm heading out now."

Her brows furrowed. He hadn't mentioned needing to leave early this morning. Usually, he gave her a heads-up when they started the day. "Everything all right?"

"Everything's fine," he answered. "I'll see you later, right?" he asked.

"Yes. I was planning to come to your place around dinnertime, if that's okay." She needed to spend the afternoon working on the portrait she was painting of his house. Cooper's birthday was only two days away.

"That works. I'll see you soon."

"Bye," she said and disconnected the call.

Her phone dinged a few minutes later, indicating she'd received a text. Piper wouldn't check it while she was driving. She'd wait until she arrived at the gallery. She'd be there soon.

Five minutes later, she pulled into a spot by the side entrance of the mansion and hopped out. Grabbing the bag with the boxes of fixtures from the passenger seat, she strode to the building. Piper entered the mansion and hurried up the stairs.

"Mom, Debby. What are you doing here?"

Her mother walked over and kissed her cheek. "We were wondering if we could convince you to have lunch with us today."

"How did you get in?" she asked. "The side door was locked." She'd needed to punch in the code in order to gain access. "Did Layla let you in?"

"No." Debby came over and gave her a big hug. "Cooper was walking out when we arrived." She chuckled. "He was very mysterious as to where he was going. All he said was he had something important to do."

"Yes." Mom flashed a mile-wide grin. "Very, very important."

"Maybe, just maybe…" Debby trailed off, but she raised her ring finger and waved it. "Valentine's Day *is* less than three weeks away."

Piper grinned. She couldn't help it. Everything was going according to plan. Time to play the part. "Do you really think it's true?"

Cooper always tells me where he's going, but this time he didn't.

What if… A lick of excitement swept through her.

No, no, no, no, no. He wasn't… They weren't…

Piper gave herself a mental shake. She was one card short of a full deck for even considering the idea.

Debby nodded. "I've always thought that you two belong together."

Why did Debby keep insisting that was true?

"I guess we'll just have to wait and see." Mom grinned.

"In the meantime, how about lunch?" Debby asked.

Piper blew out a breath, thankful for the subject change.

"Yes, I haven't seen you in forever," Mom said.

Piper rolled her gaze skyward. "Nothing like guilting me into it, Mom."

Mom just smiled. "I'll take that as a yes."

"A short lunch. I've got things to do here," she said.

"The place is really coming along." Debby circled her hand in a gesture that was meant to include the entire space. "I can't wait to see what it will look like with all the art in it."

Me either. A little thrill ran through her. "You'll have to come to my grand opening."

Debby gave her another hug. "Ron and I wouldn't miss it for the world. We're so proud of you."

"Me, too." Mom swiped at the corner of her eye.

"Aww, Mom. Don't cry." Piper wrapped her arms around her.

"I'm not." Mom held her tight. "I just wish your father could be here to see what you've done. He would love this."

He really would. Piper sucked in a deep breath and released it. *I wish he was here, too.*

She eased away from her mom. "Did you have some place in mind for lunch?" She walked to the bar and set the bag containing the bathroom fixtures on top.

"How about Layla's place? It's quick and convenient."

"Sounds good to me." She still wanted to taste the burger Cooper had told her about.

"Perfect," Debby agreed.

She pinned a smile in place. "Let's go."

They rode the elevator to the first floor and exited the building.

Walking into the restaurant, they requested a table in the main dining room. A hostess showed them to a table by the windows that overlooked the ocean.

There was no gentle ebb and flow of the water today. The icy water churned and the waves sounded like an explosion as they crashed on shore.

Piper gazed out the window, mesmerized. "It's beautiful, even at this time of year."

"It is," Debby agreed. "I can't think of a venue that has more spectacular views."

"Speaking of venues, did you know that Layla is doing weddings here now?" Mom's casual tone didn't fool Piper.

Debby shook her head. "I didn't know that. Did you, Piper?"

She leaned back in her chair and crossed her arms over her chest. "Did you two rehearse that?"

"I don't know what you're talking about, darling," her mother said.

Piper made a tsking sound. "You never do, Mom. You never do."

"Hello, Jane," their server greeted as she approached the table. "Layla is working on your tasting menu now and the first course should be out in a few minutes."

Jane nodded. "Thank you, Susan."

Piper gawked at her mother. "Don't know what I'm talking about, my ass," she mumbled under her breath.

So much for getting to taste the burger I've heard so much about.

"What was that?" Mom shot her an annoyed look.

She flashed a bright grin. "I asked what we'd be eating today."

"The chef has prepared selections of beef, chicken and fish for the three of you this afternoon," their server said. "Along with a medley of starters. Would you care for anything to drink?"

A glass or three of wine would make sitting through Mom's pitch about having her nonexistent wedding here much more palatable, but alcohol in the afternoon made her sleepy. And let's face it. She needed to keep her wits about her. *More caffeine it is.* "I'll have a Diet Coke, please."

Mom and Debby each ordered a glass of chardonnay.

When their server left, Debby made a show of looking around the restaurant. "I just love all of the fairy lights woven through the potted plants."

"Yes," Mom agreed. "They were such a big hit for the EMT fundraiser Layla held last spring that she decided to keep them."

Debby nodded. "I remember that. All of the gold glitz and glamour. It's too bad you weren't here to see it, Piper. It really was quite lovely."

She wasn't into glitz and glamour. Piper preferred understated and classy to in-your-face.

Susan returned and set the drinks down in front of each of them. They thanked her, and she moved to another table.

Mom smiled. "All of the women wore elegant gowns. Just like they would for a wedding."

"Can't you just see it?" Debby asked.

And here we go...

Debby continued, "A ceremony on the beach, when the weather turns warmer, of course. At sunset, so the sky is streaked with vibrant shades of orange and purple."

"With only family and close friends," her mother added.

Actually, that sounded nice. Right up her alley, if she were to get married. Which she wasn't.

Their server placed small dishes of canapés, olives and cheeses on the table.

Piper served herself a canapé. Lifting the mini sandwich to her mouth, she bit into the savory goodness. "This is delicious."

Mom looked at Debby and winked. Piper tried but failed to hide a smile.

"Can you imagine eating hors d'oeuvres on the patio?" Debby pointed out the window to the massive space below, covered with sand-colored pavers and a bronze two-tier Greco Roman–style fountain in the center.

Piper nodded. She may as well make it worth their while. They were going to a lot of trouble to make her see the light. "Fresh urns of flowers mixed with the warm sea breeze. Wrought iron tables and chairs with linen tablecloths. Servers decked out in black pants and white shirts with bow ties mingling discreetly among the guests, serving trays of appetizers and champagne."

"Yes, yes." Mom's voice shook with excitement.

"When the bride and groom finished their photos, everyone would move back into the restaurant to dine on Layla's delicious food. While we gaze out at the stars twinkling in the evening sky." Piper slanted a glance at Mom and Debby. They hung on every word she said.

"Instead of a wedding cake, Abby would provide an

assortment of cupcakes from the Coffee Palace." Because Abby's cupcakes had more frosting than cake, which was what she preferred. "The dessert would be served with her special blend coffee." For Cooper, of course.

"We could have a live band set up at the bar," Mom proposed.

"A DJ would be more fun," Piper insisted. After all this was supposed to be all about her and her groom.

Debby glowed with happiness. "It all sounds perfect."

Piper exhaled a wistful sigh. It really did. *What if...*

She looked at her mother. Images of her from right after Dad's death flooded her mind. She couldn't get out of bed most days. And the zombie-like person who greeted her when she did... She wasn't going to end up like her. *Nope. Never going to happen.*

She laid her palms on the white tablecloth and leaned forward. Locking her gaze on the two women sitting across from her, she said, "Too bad we don't have a bride and groom."

"Well, maybe not at this precise moment," Debby agreed. "But I'm sure we will soon."

Piper burst out laughing. They were persistent, if nothing else. "I surrender." She raised her hands in the air. It wasn't as if they could force her and Cooper to do something neither of them was interested in.

Except... If she were to get married... Piper gazed around the room. Layla's restaurant was a beautiful venue and she could picture this room filled with the people she loved most...

What was wrong with her today? *Love doesn't last. It devastates and destroys the one left behind.* How could she have forgotten that? All she had to do was look at her mother for the constant reminder.

Piper glanced across the table, and really looked at her, for once. The all-consuming sadness permanently etched on Mom's features was gone. And the heavy burden Mom used to carry seemed to have disappeared.

Before her sat a vibrant, vivacious, loving woman. The complete opposite of the mother Piper remembered from her childhood.

Why had she never noticed that before? When had this change happened?

"Here we are." Their server's voice pulled her from her musings.

Piper blinked and focused on the here and now.

"Everything looks so good, Susan," Mom said.

She set a large serving tray with three small platters sitting atop on a stand beside their table. "Beef tenderloin." She placed the first dish on the table in the center. "Pan seared salmon, and chicken in a red wine sauce." She positioned the two dishes next to the first.

"I can't wait to taste everything," Debby said.

"Is there anything else I can get you?" their server asked.

"Not right now, thanks," the three of them said at the same time.

"Okay. Enjoy your meals." Susan picked up her tray and headed back to the kitchen.

"Dig in," Mom said.

Thirty minutes later, Piper hugged her mother and Debby and waved goodbye as they strode out of the restaurant. She grabbed her purse and was heading to the main exit when Tom waved her over.

"Hi, Piper." Tom stood. Wrapping his arms around her, he gave her a big bear hug. "It's so good to see you again." He loosened his grip, but didn't let her go. "How are you?"

"I'm good." She stepped away from him and put some much-needed space between them. "Are you having lunch with someone?" Piper gestured to the empty plate opposite Tom, with a knife and fork laid across it.

"Yes." He nodded. "They had to leave. I was just finishing up. Care to join me?" Tom offered a winsome smile and reached for her hand. "I hate eating alone."

"Sorry, she can't." Cooper appeared by her side, a thunderous expression on his face. He wrapped a possessive arm around her and pulled her against him.

Piper gawked at Cooper. What had gotten into him?

"Hi, baby." Cooper planted a hard, demanding kiss on her mouth. "Sorry I left you alone."

What the hell? Piper felt like she'd just fallen down the rabbit hole.

"We need to get back to the gallery." Without letting go of her, Cooper marched them toward the exit.

"Bye, Piper. It was great seeing you again," Tom said. "Let's get together soon."

She tried to wave, but Cooper kept going.

Once outside, she stopped and stared at him. "What was that all about? Why did you frog-march me out of there?"

Something was up with Cooper, and she needed to know what.

Shit. What was he supposed to tell her? The truth was, he wasn't sure why he'd acted the way he had. He'd spotted her the minute he'd walked into the restaurant. He was on his way over to her when Tom stopped her.

His brain started screaming *danger, danger, danger.*

His body took over, and the next thing he realized they were standing here in the parking lot.

"What are you talking about?" The words popped out of his mouth before he could stop them.

Piper slammed her hands on her hips and glared at him. "Now you sound like my mother."

Great. He wasn't sure which was worse, being lumped in with her mother or telling her the truth about Tom and Rachel.

What kind of moron doesn't realize his girlfriend and best friend are screwing around right under his nose?

Coop winced. Yeah, he'd take being lumped in with her mother.

"What is going on with you? You went all caveman on me in there."

A hint of a smile formed on his face. "I didn't throw you over my shoulder and drag you out of there." Even though he'd wanted to.

She rolled her eyes. "No. Thank goodness. I might have clobbered you if you had."

"Noted." He dragged a hand through his hair. "I'm sorry." What else could he say? Seeing Tom with Piper... Bile swirled in his gut and burned a path up his throat.

He didn't want Piper anywhere near Tom, or any other guy for that matter.

He didn't want to think about what that meant.

Chapter Twenty-One

Coop pulled his F-150 into the parking lot of the old colonial mansion at 5:00 a.m. sharp on Friday morning. Another two weeks and these early starts would end.

That was a good thing—because he hated waking up at dark o'clock. He wasn't an early-morning kind of guy—so why was his stomach churning at the idea of them ending?

Who was he kidding? He knew why. When this project ended, he wouldn't see Piper every day.

He treasured this comradery, this rapport they'd developed, since he started her gallery renovations. He liked having her around. Liked working with her all day and sharing a glass of wine in front of his roaring fireplace in the evenings. He enjoyed cooking a meal together. He adored sharing it while they watched a movie and tumbling into bed after.

And yeah, he liked the lovemaking. *Loved*, he mentally corrected. Coop grinned. That part of their relationship was spectacular.

He would miss it. All of it.

He'd miss *her*. More than he would have ever guessed possible. A few weeks ago, he couldn't imagine how he was going to get through five weeks with her. It had felt like a long prison sentence with no time off for good behavior. Now… He couldn't imagine not seeing her smiling face every day.

The million-dollar question was, what was he going to do about it?

Coop rubbed the back of his neck. Could he convince her to turn their fake relationship into something real? Sweat beaded on his brows and his hands turned clammy.

He rubbed his hands on his jeans-covered thighs. Sucking in a deep, slow breath, he blew it out slowly.

It wasn't like he was proposing marriage. *No friggin' way.* The idea of putting his heart out there again, of opening himself to that kind of pain… *Not gonna happen.* But…he'd be interested in extending this thing between them for longer than the time frame they'd originally agreed on.

Piper's grand opening was in fifteen days. He wanted more time with her.

Now he just needed to convince her she wanted the same.

Coop slugged down a gulp of coffee and hopped out of the truck. He strode across the empty parking lot to the gallery entrance and punched in the numbers on the keypad lock.

He rode the elevator to the second floor and stepped into the hall when the doors opened.

The lights were on. "Piper? Are you here?" She'd said something about needing to pick up a few things at her place before she headed to the gallery when she left his place this morning.

No answer came.

"Hello?" he called.

The scent of fresh-brewed coffee filled the room. Piper must be here. She was the only other person besides him with the entrance codes for both the external door and the one they'd erected on the first floor to separate her space from Layla's restaurant.

He walked into the main room, setting his phone next to the speaker on the island as he walked by.

The snap and pop of something sizzling filled his ears. Oh my gosh, was that bacon he smelled? He inhaled again. Yes indeed, it was. Coop grinned. "Come out, come out, wherever you are."

"I'm in the kitchenette," she called. "Come on back."

Coop ducked around the wall that now separated the kitchenette from the island that would be turned into a bar area as soon as he finished the construction. That was on today's agenda, along with a few other small projects, like adding baseboards to the newly installed walls that separated the main room into three smaller sections, and removing the carpet and the odd pieces of furniture stored in what was originally the third bedroom when Layla's grandparents had used this space as an apartment.

Piper was standing at the counter in front of an electric griddle. With her hair piled on her head in a haphazard bun and a large apron that read *Kiss the Cook* draped over the front of her, she looked adorable.

He snaked his arms around her waist and pulled her against him so they stood chest to chest. He crushed his lips to hers.

"What was that for?" she asked, breathless, a few minutes later.

"Just doing what you asked." He grinned and pointed to her apron.

"Ah." She chuckled. "I see."

"What's all this?" he asked.

Piper beamed at him. She removed her apron and set

it on the counter. Opening the microwave that sat adjacent to the griddle, she pulled out a serving plate laden with food. "Chocolate chip pancakes with real maple syrup and bacon."

His favorite breakfast of all time. "Wow. What's the occasion?"

"Why, your birthday, of course." She kissed him again.

His eyes widened. "You remembered?" She hadn't said a word before leaving the house this morning. In fact, she hadn't said anything during all the time they'd spent together over the last five days.

"Of course, I did. I made all your favorites." She piled utensils on top of two empty plates that she grabbed with the other hand. "Would you mind getting the orange juice from the fridge?"

His favorite morning beverage—okay, his second favorite after coffee. He couldn't believe she'd gone to all this trouble for him.

It was, hands down, the nicest birthday gift he'd ever received from a woman, and the most thoughtful by far.

"No problem. Do you need me to bring anything else?" he asked.

"The glasses." She jerked her head toward the counter. "I already set out the coffee mugs on the island. We'll eat out there."

Coop got the juice and glasses and followed her out.

Piper set everything atop the marble surface. "Well, what are you waiting for? Dig in."

He frowned. "What about you? Aren't you joining me?"

"I will. I just need to grab one more thing. I'll be right back." She hurried down the hall toward her art studio and disappeared a moment later.

Coop stabbed his fork into the stack of pancakes

and placed three on his plate. He added several slices of bacon. Setting his dish down in front of him, he reached for the jug of syrup, made on a farm just over the state line in Vermont.

"Close your eyes," Piper called. "I have a surprise for you."

"What is it?" he asked.

"If I told you, it wouldn't be a surprise, now would it?" She had a point.

"Are your eyes closed?" she asked.

He laid down his utensils and lowered his eyelids. "Yes." He grinned, feeling like a little kid again. "They are. You can come out now."

Her shoes echoed down the hall as she approached. "Keep them closed while I get this set up," she said.

"Bossy." He chuckled.

"Damned straight." Piper snorted. "And no peeking."

"I'm not." Coop crossed his heart. "My eyes are closed. I swear."

"Make sure you keep them that way. I need to go back to my studio and grab one more thing. Be right back."

Coop's brows knit together. He couldn't imagine what she was doing. "Come on, you've got me really curious. Can't you give me just a little hint?"

"No. You'll find out soon enough." Her footsteps retreated. A moment later she returned. "Okay, I'm back. I need one more minute."

Something thudded against the wood floor and she let out a muffled curse.

Coop chuckled. "Everything okay?"

"I dropped something on my foot, but I'm fine." Piper mumbled something else he couldn't make out. "All right. I'm ready. You can open your eyes now."

He raised his eyelids. A large, framed picture sat propped against a black, shoulder-height easel.

Not a picture. A painting. Of his house. His jaw dropped. "Did you paint this?"

"Yes. You can put it in your study, or in a different room, if you want. I wouldn't want to tell you what to do with it." She flashed a cheeky grin.

Coop jumped off his chair and came closer to get a better view. He scrutinized the image. "The detail is amazing. It looks just like the front of my house. Landscape and all." He stared at her. "This is incredible. Thank you so much. I love it."

"Happy birthday." Her smile sent a flood of warmth rushing through him.

Coop just stared at her, awed that she'd given him such an extraordinary gift. She'd created something personal. No woman had ever done such a thing for him.

Such a loving, giving woman. And he thought he didn't know her. How ironic was that? "Thank you." He grasped her jaw and brushed his lips over hers. "I'll treasure it always."

Piper twined her arms around his neck. "I'm so glad you like it."

"Love it. I absolutely *love* it." He kissed her again.

Piper grinned and eased away from him. "We should probably eat before breakfast gets too cold."

"You're right." He clutched her hand and they walked back to the bar together. Sitting on the bar stool, he cut into the pancakes and he brought a bite to his mouth. Coop savored the buttery, sweet goodness. "Oh, man. These are delicious."

His phone buzzed.

Piper reached out and slid the phone over to where he sat.

He would have ignored it, but his father's number flashed across the screen. Coop connected the call. "Hey, Dad."

"Good morning, son. Happy birthday."

"Thanks."

"So, I know we stopped exchanging birthday gifts with each other years ago, but I've got a little something for you today."

Coop laughed. His parents said that every year, and every year they gave him something. "Thanks, Dad. You can give me my present tonight."

"I won't see you tonight," Dad said.

His brows furrowed. "We're having dinner together. Mom set it up with me and Piper a couple of weeks ago."

Piper chuckled and winked at him.

"We're not getting together tonight," Dad insisted. "That's my gift to you. We can get together another time."

"But Mom—" he started.

"I'll talk to her. Go have fun with Piper."

Coop grinned. "I will. Thanks, Dad."

Dad laughed. "You're welcome. I'll have your mom touch base with you next week."

"You're giving me the entire weekend, not just today? That's a hell of a present. I love it," he said and smirked, even though his father couldn't see his face.

Piper chuckled.

"Wiseass," Dad grumbled. "Have a good day. Love you, Cooper."

"Love you, too, Dad."

"Bye, son. See you soon." Dad ended the call.

He turned to Piper. "We're off the hook for tonight."

"Are you sure? Debby won't be happy. And I don't want to piss her off."

"Don't worry. Dad said he'd smooth things over with

her." He stabbed his fork into another chunk of pancake. "So, tell me. How did you know all of my favorites?" he asked.

Piper plucked up a piece of bacon from the serving dish and munched on it. "We may not have been the best of friends growing up, but we did spend a lot of time together. Your dad used to make thin, almost crepe-like pancakes with chocolate chips for breakfast every Sunday." Piper gestured to his plate. "And you loved them." She served herself a pancake. "You used to hog the bacon, too." She winked and added three more slices to her plate.

He laughed. "What about the OJ? I never drank that as a kid."

"No," she agreed. "But I noticed you've consumed a glass every morning over the last five days while you waited for your first cup of coffee to finish brewing." Piper grinned and pointed her index finger to her head. "I used my mad deductive skills and figured you'd grown to like it."

"Brilliant, my dear. Simply brilliant." He gave her a quick peck on the lips. "But seriously. Thank you." He kissed her again because he wanted to. "You didn't have to do this."

Piper leaned close and wrapped her arms around his neck. She looked him in the eyes. "I know, but I wanted to."

Her smile filled his heart to bursting point.

"Now would you like to hear what else I have planned for your birthday celebration?" she asked.

His gaze widened. "There's more?"

"Yes sirree. We do have to work this morning, but I thought we could head to Boston this afternoon. Since you love to walk, I thought we could check out one of the Freedom Trails. Now that we have the evening free, how about a nice dinner in the city when we're done?"

"Sounds perfect." He leaned close, intending to kiss her once again, because yeah, kissing her was one of life's great pleasures, but his phone started to ring. Coop blew out a breath. Now who was calling him?

"You should probably get that," she said with a reluctant sigh. "It's probably someone calling to wish you a happy birthday."

He grabbed his phone and glanced at the caller ID. His brows furrowed. "Hey, Everett. It's pretty early for you to be calling. What's up?"

"Happy birthday, my friend."

He chuckled. "Thanks, man. I'm impressed you're up and cognizant at—" Coop glanced at his watch "—six a.m. to make this call."

"You should be. I don't have to head to the office for another three hours, but I know you start your day early, so I made the effort."

"Ha ha. Heading to the gym?"

Everett laughed. "Can't fool you, can I? Yeah. I'm on my way now. Figured I'd kill two birds with one stone."

"Huh?" Coop's brows drew together in a deep V. "What do you mean?"

"I haven't heard from you in a few weeks, and Annalise and I are still waiting to meet your new woman."

Damn. Coop pinched the bridge of his nose. He'd hoped Ev would have forgotten about that by now.

"Everything okay?" Piper asked.

"Is she with you right now?" Everett asked.

Piper must have heard Ev's question, because she answered. "Yes. I'm here with Cooper."

"Put the call on speakerphone," Everett demanded. "I want to talk to her."

He shook his head. "Not a chance."

In a surprise move, Piper grabbed his phone and pressed the speaker button. She danced away from him when he reached for the phone. "Hello, this is Piper. Who am I speaking with?" She grinned at him.

"I'm Everett, Coop's fraternity brother. I'm the one getting married next week. I take it you're Coop's new girlfriend and the person he's bringing to the wedding?"

"I am," she confirmed. "It's nice to meet you, Everett. So, what's up? Why do you want to talk to me?"

Coop let out a loud snort.

"I've been asking Coop to introduce you to us for a while now, but he refused," Everett said.

Coop shook his head. "Hey, that's not true. Piper and I have been busy. That's all."

"That is true," Piper said. "He's been working hard these past few weeks. I hear his client is very demanding."

"Bossy," Coop muttered.

Piper's smile lit up the whole room. God, he loved her smile.

"Sounds like he needs a break. How about dinner tonight? You can help us taste-test the food for the rehearsal dinner next Friday."

How could he have forgotten Everett's wedding was a week from tomorrow?

"That sounds fun," Piper said. "I'll let you two work out the details." She turned off the speaker and handed his phone back to him.

"Are you sure?" he asked Piper.

She nodded and kissed his cheek. "It's no problem."

"Okay, Ev. What time?" he asked.

Piper smirked and leaned in close. She whispered in his other ear, "Payback's a bitch."

He flashed a what-are-you-talking-about-woman look at her.

She tilted her head and nibbled his earlobe.

Coop swallowed hard. "What was that, Everett?"

Piper trailed her fingers over his chest.

He shuddered. Now he understood. She was getting even with him for doing the same thing to her when she was on the phone with her sister the other night.

Everett started speaking, but Coop couldn't make out what he was saying because Piper was doing delightful things to the pulse slamming at the base of his throat with her tongue.

Piper grabbed the phone from him again. "Text him the information." She disconnected the call and shoved his phone in his back pocket. "You were doing too much talking."

He sent her a wolfish grin. Lifting her, he placed her on top of the island.

"Touch me." She grabbed his hands and placed them on her breasts.

"Bossy." He skimmed his fingers under her sweater and pulled it over her head.

"You love it."

Yeah, he did. He loved everything about this beguiling, bewitching woman.

He *loved* her.

His heart thundered loud enough to wake the dead.

Chapter Twenty-Two

The smell of tasty treats filled the air as Piper walked hand in hand with Cooper around the food colonnade at Faneuil Hall in downtown Boston on Friday afternoon.

"How about some ice cream?" Cooper asked over the background noise of chatting passersby as they continued on their way.

It had been years since she'd last visited and she'd forgotten how massive the historical structure was and how many retailers occupied the enormous space.

"You do know that it's the middle of winter, right? We came in here to get out of the cold." She pointed to the mass of humanity surrounding them. "Do you see anyone else eating a frozen dessert on this cold, blustery day?"

He laughed. "No. That doesn't mean I can't have any. It's never the wrong season for ice cream, as far as I'm concerned."

"We just had a chocolate chip cookie. Are you planning on eating your way from one end of this place to the other?" she asked.

He linked her arm with his. "Now, that would be quite a feat. How many kiosks do you think there are?"

"Twenty-nine, according to this." Piper waved her folded marketplace map.

Coop nodded. "Impressive, but I'm not interested in

trying something from all of them, just the sweets. So, is that a yes to the ice cream?"

She shook her head. "No, thanks. I'm going to pass on any more sugar before dinner."

"You're such a spoilsport. A little more sugar won't hurt you. We walked for hours on the Freedom Trail. Certainly that entitles us to a cupcake?" he asked as they passed the North End Bakery.

She chuckled. "Good try, Turner, but the Freedom Trail is only two and a half miles long. We spent almost three hours on it because we kept stopping at each of the historical spots. A half hour at the Paul Revere House, twenty minutes at the Old North Church, and I can't remember how long we meandered around the Massachusetts State House. Not to mention the rest of the sites on the tour. Besides, I don't see any cupcakes." Piper pointed to the display case as they strolled by the bakery. "But don't let me stop you if you want something else." She kissed his cheek. "You *are* the birthday boy, after all."

He flashed her the sweetest grin and her heart turned over. The man was absolutely adorable.

"Yes, I am. I've decided I want a cannoli." He turned them back the way they came and they stepped up to the counter together. "I'll have one of those, please." He pointed to the rack on the top shelf of the case. Looking at her, he asked, "Are you sure I can't interest you in one? They're really good."

Piper gazed at the tray. With all of the creamy filling stuffed in the sweet, crispy shell, they did look delicious. "Maybe we can split one?"

"That's my girl." He pulled her close and draped his arm around her shoulder.

His girl. She liked the sound of that. She'd decided

not to beat herself up about what was or wasn't developing between them. She liked spending time with Cooper, and she was pretty sure he enjoyed spending time with her, too. She'd go with the flow for now.

Coop broke the shell in half. At least he tried to, but the pieces came out uneven.

"I'll take the smaller piece, please." She extended her palm to him. "I need to save at least a little room for dinner tonight."

He handed her the treat and they continued on their way.

Piper bit into the sugary confection. "You're right. It's fantastic."

"It is." Cooper cocked his head toward the exit. "We should head back to the hotel. We need to change before we meet up with my friends."

"Agreed. It was a good idea to stay here overnight tonight." They exited Faneuil Hall and headed toward the waterfront area. "That way we can relax and have a drink without having to worry about driving the forty minutes back to New Suffolk. I especially like the idea of staying in the same place we're having dinner." Piper grinned. "No car or bulky winter coat needed. We'll just take the elevator down to the main level and walk into the restaurant."

"That's why I suggested it," Cooper agreed.

The wind picked up the closer they got to the water and Piper shivered. Without saying a word, Cooper pulled her into the crook of his arm. He slanted his body to shield her.

Sweet, sweet man.

"So, tell me more about these friends we're having dinner with," she invited. He hadn't told her anything, and she had to admit she was quite curious. "How do you know them?" Why had Everett pestered Cooper to have dinner?

"Everett is one of my fraternity brothers. We met freshman year of college. He was my roommate. He's become my best friend."

"Really?" She'd assumed Tom still held that status. They'd been friends since preschool.

Cooper nodded. "We've had this connection since the first day we met. I know he'd go to the ends of the earth for me, and I'd do the same for him. Do you know what I mean?"

Piper had never experienced a relationship like that outside of her siblings. She'd never allowed anyone close enough to make such a friend. She realized it was why she hadn't exchanged phone numbers with Elle and Abby until they'd pressed the point. She'd kept all of these kind, supportive women at arm's length for the same reason she ran like hell from relationships with the opposite sex. She didn't want to get hurt.

The thing was, she liked Layla, Abby, Elle and even Zara. They had each other's backs and they'd have hers, too, if she allowed it. All she needed to do was take down the walls she'd erected around her heart and let them in.

Piper slanted her gaze to Cooper. Could she let him in, too?

"Annalise is Ev's fiancée. They met at work about three years ago. She's a great person. Kind, supportive, and a heart of gold." He smiled at her. "She's a lot like you."

Her heart turned over. Yes, this man was the sweetest.

"She's become a close friend, too," he said.

"They both sound like great people."

Cooper nodded. "They are. I think you'll like them a lot. I know I do."

Piper shot him a curious glance. "Can I ask you a question?"

"Sure. What is it?"

"Why are we having dinner with them? I'm not complaining. I'm just curious as to why."

A hesitant expression crossed his handsome face. He stayed silent for a moment as if deciding what to say.

"Do you remember the other night when I told you about Rachel?" he asked.

She nodded. "Your ex, right?" The woman he'd wanted to marry. Piper swallowed past the painful lump in her throat. Lord, what was wrong with her tonight? Who cared if he'd loved the woman enough to want to marry her? Not her.

Liar.

"Yes. That's her. Rachel and I met through Annalise. She's Annalise's cousin." Cooper shook his head. "I don't want either her or Everett feeling sorry for me."

Piper nodded. "So we're having dinner with them to show them that you've moved on."

"Exactly. I also don't want them worrying about any awkwardness at the wedding. Rachel and I are both in the wedding party."

No wonder Cooper had wanted a date for the wedding. She couldn't imagine having to face someone you loved, especially at a wedding, if that person chose someone else over you. "Don't worry. I've got you covered. We'll make her sorry she ever dumped you."

Piper wasn't sure why he turned silent again. His stony expression sent a wave of unease coursing through her. What was going on with him? What wasn't he telling her?

They reached the hotel a few minutes later. The stunning lobby with its shining marble and glittering vintage chandeliers awed her as they crossed to the elevator bank. "This really is a spectacular place for a wedding, if grand opulence is your thing."

Cooper peered over at her. "But it's not your thing." It was a statement, not a question. "You're more of an intimate gathering of family and close friends at a small but classy venue person."

She looked at him. He knew her well. Not that she would be getting married any time soon. But if she was...

They rode the elevator to the second floor. When they reached their room, Coop opened the door and gestured for her to precede him in.

Piper gazed around the space. She hadn't had the opportunity to check out the room earlier. When they'd checked in, they'd dropped their luggage and headed out right away. She walked to the floor-to-ceiling windows that offered spectacular sweeping views of the city skyline.

Cooper came up behind her. He wrapped his arms around her waist and pressed her against him. "I had a great day today. It means a lot to me that you went out of your way to make my birthday special."

He turned her to face him. His tender gaze sent a rush of warmth flooding through her system. Her heart beat a rapid tattoo. "I'm glad you had fun."

"I did because I was with you." He grasped her chin with his fingers and brushed his lips over hers and... there it was again. That warmth that rushed through her and made her feel all tingly inside when he came near.

Cooper tucked a loose strand of her hair behind her ear. "Thank you. I can't remember the last time I enjoyed myself this much."

Piper smiled. "You're welcome."

He released her, reluctantly, if the look on his face was anything to go by. "We should get ready." Glancing at his watch, he added, "We need to be downstairs in twenty minutes."

"It won't take me long. I just have to change my clothes and throw my hair up."

He eyed her skeptically.

Piper burst out laughing. "Don't worry. I promise I'll be ready on time." She walked to the closet and grabbed her suitcase.

Cooper's brows furrowed. "Where are you going?"

She dropped a quick kiss on his lips as she passed by him. "To the bathroom. To get changed."

"You could get changed out here, with me." He sent her a wolfish smile.

Piper grinned and made a tsking sound. "Not if you want to be on time. Don't worry, I won't be long."

She hurried into the spacious bathroom and shut the door. Stripping out of her clothes, she shimmied into her short, black knit dress with a drop shoulder and loose, long sleeves. Gathering up her long hair, she twisted it into a haphazard bun and secured it with an elastic band.

She added a touch of blush and raspberry-colored lipstick. Stepping into her strappy heels, she surveyed herself in the mirror. "Not bad," she murmured.

Piper closed up her suitcase, opened the bathroom door and wheeled it out. Cooper stood in front of the bedroom mirror straightening his collar. Dressed in a pair of navy dress pants and matching jacket with a white button-down shirt, the man looked sexy as all get-out.

She let out a wolf whistle. "You clean up nice, Mr. Turner."

He looked at her. His eyes turned smoky, and a little

thrill of excitement ran through her. "So do you, Ms. Kavanaugh." He snaked his arm around her, pulled her against him and kissed her senseless. "So do you."

Piper sucked in some much-needed air when he released her. "Let's go meet your friends." She eyed the massive king-size bed with its plush comforter. "Now. Before I change my mind."

"By all means." He let out a deep, rumbly chuckle and crooked his arm.

She looped her arm through his and grabbed her purse on the way to the door.

They rode the elevator down to the ground floor and crossed the lobby to the restaurant's etched-glass double doors with gold metal frames.

"After you." Cooper pulled the right door open and gestured for her to precede him.

Piper peered around. "I love the ambience of this place." The low lighting and floor-to-ceiling windows gave diners an unobstructed view of the Boston harbor while they ate. "The long tables make it a great venue for a large gathering."

Cooper nodded. "There are a lot of people coming to the rehearsal dinner. We have twelve people in the wedding party alone, and that doesn't include the bride and groom. Oh, there's Ev and Annalise." He pointed to a couple seated at a table in front of the windows sipping a glass of wine.

"Are you ready?" Cooper gave a nervous chuckle.

She nodded. "I told you. I've got your back." He was counting on her, and she wouldn't let him down. She clasped his hand in hers.

He walked with purpose to where the couple sat. "Hi, guys."

Everett stood and clapped Cooper on the shoulder. "Hey, man. It's good to see you. Happy birthday, buddy."

Annalise rose. "I'm so glad you could join us this evening." She hugged Cooper and kissed his cheek.

Cooper put his arm around her. "Everett, Annalise, I'd like you to meet Piper. Honey, these are my friends, Everett and Annalise."

"It's so nice to meet you." Annalise grinned and shook Piper's outstretched hand.

"You, too," she agreed.

Annalise and Everett returned to their chairs.

"Have we met before? You look familiar." Everett scrutinized her face.

Cooper pulled out her chair for her and she sat. "I don't think so," she said. "I've been living in Los Angeles for the last ten years."

"Then how did you two meet?" Annalise asked.

Cooper sat in the empty chair beside her. He grasped her hand in his and gave it a gentle squeeze. "Actually, Piper and I have known each other pretty much since birth."

She nodded. "Our fathers opened a construction firm together about thirty-five years ago."

"That's it." Everett snapped his fingers. "I knew your last name sounded familiar when we spoke on the phone this morning. I do know you, er, your family," he corrected. "I've met your brother. Shane, right? You also have a sister, but I can't remember her name."

"Mia," Piper said.

Everett nodded. "You look like her. That's why I thought we'd met before."

"You know my sister?" Piper's brows drew together.

Everett grinned. "I spent a lot of time at Coop's house during the summer when we were in college.

Your brother used to hang out with us. Sometimes your sister would join us, too."

"I forgot about that," Cooper said.

"Wait a minute. You live in LA?" Everett asked her.

"I did until a few weeks ago. I moved back to New Suffolk in early January."

"So you just started seeing each other?" Annalise asked.

She shook her head. "We started dating last summer." That was the cover story they'd agreed on when they'd made their deal.

Was that only a couple of weeks ago? So much had changed between them in such a short amount of time. She was happy they'd cleared up the misunderstandings between them, because the man sitting beside her was an incredible person and she was lucky to have him in her life.

"You old devil, you. You never said a word. Here I was thinking you'd spent the last ten months pining over Rach—" Everett yelped. He glared at Annalise. "Why'd you kick me?"

She gave him a do-you-have-to-ask look and then gestured to Piper.

"Oh, ah…sorry." Everett flashed her a contrite expression.

"It's okay," she said. "Cooper is just fine now."

"That's right." Cooper snaked an arm around her and pulled her close. He beamed a happy smile. "As a matter of fact, Rachel did me a favor. If she hadn't left me, I would never have reconnected with Piper." He lowered his lips to hers.

His sweet, tender kiss was almost her undoing. She blinked and drew in a deep, steadying breath.

If she wasn't careful, she might start believing that

this thing between them was real. It felt genuine, true. It felt…right.

"Aww," Annalise cooed.

Piper jerked her head away from Cooper and faced the couple sitting across from her. Heat scorched her cheeks. Once again, she'd lost sight of everything and everyone else when Cooper came near.

"That's so cute." Annalise went all dreamy-eyed. "You guys make such a great couple."

Real, or not. Annalise was convinced. That was what mattered tonight.

"I know." She flashed a 1000-watt smile. "Isn't he great?" Piper gave Cooper a peck on his cheek. "I've never been happier." *That's the truth.*

Everett grinned and nodded. "I'm happy for you, buddy." To Piper, he said, "You're a lucky woman."

She leaned her head against Cooper's shoulder. "I know I am."

Later in the evening, Cooper laid his fork and knife across his empty plate and leaned against the chairback. "That was a fantastic meal."

Piper nodded. "Annalise, your guests at the rehearsal dinner are going to love the choices you've selected."

"I hope so. I can't believe the wedding is a week from tomorrow." Annalise turned to Everett. Glancing at her watch, she said, "Eight days from now, we'll be married."

"I can't wait, my love." Everett kissed Annalise.

Cooper cleared his throat. "I think that's our cue to leave."

Everett and Annalise jerked apart.

"Sorry." Annalise wiped her lipstick off Everett's

mouth. "Sometimes I forget…" Her whole face turned fire-engine red.

Trust me, I know the feeling. Piper grinned. "It's not a problem."

"Don't leave yet." Everett straightened in his chair. "Stick around for a while. The night is young, and it's your birthday. Let's celebrate with a drink in the bar. You two are staying here at the hotel tonight, right?"

"We are," she agreed.

"Us, too," Everett said. "We don't live that far away, but I didn't want to have to drive after a couple of glasses of wine."

Cooper nodded. "Same goes for us."

"This way we can relax and enjoy ourselves. There's supposed to be a live musician in the bar tonight. Do you like jazz?" Annalise asked.

Piper smiled. "I love it."

"Let's grab a table now," Cooper said.

Piper gestured toward the restaurant exit. "I'll meet you over there. I need to make a stop in the ladies' room first."

Annalise giggled and stood. "That makes two of us. You guys go ahead."

Piper walked with Annalise toward the restaurant exit and into the hotel lobby.

"The restrooms are around the corner." Annalise pointed to her right.

They started walking.

Annalise turned her head toward Piper. "I'm really happy for you and Cooper. He's such a great guy."

She nodded. "He is." Cooper was one of the best guys she knew.

Annalise flashed a brilliant smile. "I'm just thrilled that Cooper has found someone." She turned serious.

"I was worried about him and so was Everett. It's been almost a year since...well, you know." She gave a little twirl of her wrist.

"Since Rachel ended things," Piper supplied.

Annalise's brows furrowed. "Um...yes."

Something in Annalise's expression told Piper there was more to the story than she was letting on.

Piper arched a brow. "You don't sound convinced."

Annalise let out a soft chuckle and waved away Piper's concern. "It all worked out. Cooper has you, and Rachel has Tom."

Tom? No. It couldn't be. Piper stared at Annalise. "Cooper's friend Tom?"

Annalise gasped. "You didn't know?"

"I didn't." *Cooper forgot to mention that little detail.*

"I assumed Cooper had told you." Annalise shook her head.

Nope again. Why hadn't he?

An image of his face floated into her mind from earlier when they were walking back to the hotel. His stony expression when she'd told him she'd make Rachel regret dumping him. It didn't make any sense unless... Could Cooper still want Rachel?

Piper's stomach plummeted.

Chapter Twenty-Three

Piper peered around the partitioned section of the ballroom at the hotel in Boston. Everett and Annalise's guests milled about the space, noshing on oysters and littleneck clams on the half shell, jumbo shrimp cocktail, short rib dumplings and a whole lot more while they sipped wine and mixed drinks. They all waited with bated breath for the wedding party to finish the picture-taking portion of the evening so they could move on to the main event. Dinner and dancing.

With its ornate columns and elegant chandeliers, she supposed the space was nice enough, although this space did not offer spectacular views of the harbor. That was reserved for the dining room, which they'd move to as soon as the photographer completed his mission.

Still, Piper couldn't help but remember Layla's restaurant and the gorgeous patio that overlooked the Atlantic Ocean.

Now that she'd envisioned that fantasy, nothing else compared. Damn Mom and Debby for making her think about weddings and receptions.

Tom waved at her from across the room as he made his way to where she stood.

She still couldn't believe he and Cooper's ex were a thing.

Why hadn't Cooper told her? She was obviously

going to find it out today. It wasn't like she couldn't put two and two together when she saw them.

Her mind kept circling round and round the events of the last couple of weeks. Cooper's caveman actions when he saw her talking with Tom in Layla's restaurant. His stony expression the night they had dinner with Annalise and Everett, when she promised to make Rachel pay for dumping him. Not to mention the look on Annalise's face when she'd mentioned Rachel leaving Cooper.

None of it made any sense.

Could Cooper still have a thing for Rachel?

Her stomach churned at the idea. Which meant what? *You care about him. A lot.*

"Hi, Piper." Tom pulled her into his arms and gave her a big bear hug. "How are you?"

Okay, the touchy-feely thing from him was driving her a little crazy. He acted like they were long-lost friends. The truth was, they were casual acquaintances at best. "I'm fine." She stepped back when he released her. "And you?"

"Doing okay. Hey, would you like to grab a drink?" He gave her a winsome smile. "We can finally catch up with each other."

Why? They'd never truly been friends. Not even when she'd had that crush on him in high school—for all of five minutes—and certainly not after the way he treated her after the skunk incident.

"Thanks, but—" She was about to turn him down when her phone started broadcasting, "Your sister is calling, your sister is calling. What are you waiting for? Pick up the phone already."

Son of a gun. She thought she'd turned her phone off before Everett and Annalise had exchanged vows, but she'd only turned the volume down. Good thing Mia hadn't called during the ceremony.

"Please excuse me," she said.

"Rain check?" he called to her retreating form.

Piper shook her head as she headed toward the exit.

"Hello." She stepped into the large hall that connected the banquet rooms to the main lobby.

Throngs of people milled about out here as well.

"Hey, got any plans for tonight? Elle and Abby are coming over," Mia said.

"I can't. I won't be home until sometime tomorrow afternoon." She and Cooper planned on having a leisurely breakfast in the morning and indulging in a couples massage at the hotel spa before heading back to New Suffolk.

"Where are you? I can hardly hear you. There's a lot of background noise."

She laughed. "That's because there's a lot of people here." Over two hundred guests were attending this event. "I'm in Boston at a wedding with Cooper. One of his fraternity brothers just got married."

"Interesting." Mia snickered. "Maybe you can get some ideas for your own wedding. I hear Cooper's been looking at rings. According to Mom, a proposal is imminent."

Piper snorted. "Didn't Mom already tell you? She and Debby already have the whole wedding planned."

"Yeah, I heard about that. I almost feel sorry for you." Mia chuckled.

"You don't sound it." Piper spotted Tom heading her way. *The man won't take no for an answer.*

"Who won't take no for an answer?" Mia asked.

She hadn't meant to say that out loud. "Tom Anderson. He wants to have a drink and catch up."

"I can't believe it." Mia huffed out a breath. "He's got a lot of nerve after what he did to Cooper."

Piper knew there was more to the story than Annalise had let on. "What happened?"

"He slept with Rachel. While Rachel was still going out with Cooper. For like a couple of months."

Piper's jaw dropped. She couldn't believe what she was hearing.

Tom strode toward her like a heat-seeking missile flying toward its target. Her hands clenched into fists.

"Piper? You still there?" Mia asked.

"Yeah, but I've got to go. I'll call you tomorrow." She disconnected the call.

"Here you are." Tom waved at her as he approached.

Piper gritted her teeth. *Damn it.* She didn't want to talk to him. Not after what he'd done. The guy was a class A jerk.

She opened her mouth to tell him as much and closed it without uttering a word. She wouldn't cause a scene. Not on Annalise and Everett's wedding day. They didn't deserve that.

"Hey, we need to be getting back inside." Tom draped his arm around her shoulder and propelled them forward. "They're about to introduce the wedding party."

Piper stopped short. "I'm capable of walking to my table alone. You don't have to escort me there."

Tom held up his hands as if he were surrendering. "I was just trying to be nice, that's all." He gave her an affable smile. "What kind of friend would I be if I left you alone with over two hundred people you don't even know?"

"Friend?" Piper rolled her eyes. "Do you even know what that word means?"

"Of course I do." Tom stared at her as if she'd sprouted another head.

"Oh, so you were being a *friend* when you started seeing Rachel behind Cooper's back?"

Tom shook his head. "Okay, I didn't mean for that to happen."

She gawked at him. How could he say such a thing? "And yet it did, because you did nothing to stop it."

Tom crossed his arms over his chest. "Don't go all judgmental on me. You have no idea what was going on at the time. I was going through a really tough time and Rachel was there for me. We didn't mean to hurt anyone."

Piper shook her head. "Yeah, but you did."

"You think Cooper's such a great guy? Well, let me tell you…"

"No." Piper held up her hand to stop Tom from saying anything further. "Let *me* tell you. Cooper is the kindest, sweetest, most loving man I know." He made her laugh, and she was happier when he was around. Her life would be empty without him in it.

"Oh, please. You're not fooling me." Tom's features twisted into a sneer. "You and Cooper hate each other. Everyone knows that."

"You're wrong." Piper shook her head. "We—"

"*Love* each other?" Tom gave a disparaging laugh. "You've got to be kidding me. I'm not buying that you're in love with Cooper for a single second."

Of course, she wasn't, but she liked him. A lot. *A lot, a lot.*

Piper caught a glimpse of Cooper standing with the other groomsmen. Her heart turned over and everything went all soft and mushy inside.

Oh dear Lord in heaven. It was true.

Piper's jaw nearly hit the ground. Somehow, some way, she'd fallen head over heels for Cooper Turner.

No, no, no. That wasn't the plan. Love didn't last. She knew that.

He smiled and waved at her, and her chest filled to bursting point.

She *loved* Cooper Turner. With all her heart and soul. What the hell was she supposed to do now?

Coop stood by the door to the groomsmen's suite, people-watching while he waited for the photographer to finish photographing the bride and groom.

Piper walked out into the hall with her cell glued to her ear. God, she looked amazing in her long navy gown that clung to her in all the right places. He couldn't wait to dance with her later and touch all of the smooth, creamy skin on display.

She grinned a mischievous smile and he wondered who she was talking to.

"Checking out the scenery?" His fraternity brother and fellow groomsman, Jack, handed him a glass of Scotch on the rocks. "Mind if I check out the scenery, too?" He winked and stood beside him.

They stood in silence for a few moments.

"Hey, guys." Everett clapped both men on the shoulder. "The DJ just asked our guests to take their seats. Five minutes and then we head in."

Coop nodded but he never moved his gaze from Piper. What was he going to do about her? Was he ready for something more? Things were pretty good right now. Why mess up what they had by getting feelings involved? Then again, things were slated to end between them sooner rather than later. Piper's grand opening was a week away, and he still hadn't asked her if she'd be interested in extending their deal indefinitely. The words got stuck in his throat every time he started to bring it up.

"Now, there's a sight to behold." Jack gestured to where Piper stood.

"Hands off," he growled. "She's taken."

"Ah…" Jack gave a sage nod. "So that's how it is. Another one bites the dust."

He jerked his gaze to the man standing beside him. "What are you talking about?"

"You. You're a goner for the short, blonde chick standing by the door. I was wondering when I saw you with her before the ceremony started. I can understand why. She's gorgeous." Jack snorted and shook his head. "Won't be long until we're all gathered together again for another walk down the aisle."

"Speak for yourself." Coop wouldn't be getting married anytime soon.

"You're funny." Jack chuckled.

Tom appeared by Piper's side.

Every muscle inside him stiffened. What the hell was he doing? Why wouldn't he just leave Piper alone? He started into the hall, ready to put a stop to Tom's meddling once and for all but froze when she smiled at him. His stomach jumped and jittered.

Coop loved her smile. It made him feel like he was everything she could ever want. Everything she'd ever need. All was right with his world again.

Except…

She wasn't smiling at him. She was smiling at Tom. His stomach plummeted.

"Hey, loverboy," Jack called. "There'll be time for her later. Right now, we gotta go. It's showtime."

He turned to see the bridal party lining up.

"Come on, Cooper." Rachel gestured for him to join her. It was the last thing on earth he wanted to do, but he had no choice. He trudged over to where she stood at the back of the line.

The announcements began. Coop gritted his teeth.

"We're up next." Rachel extended her hand to him.

Coop fastened his palm to hers, albeit reluctantly.

"Would it kill you to smile? I don't want to do this anymore than you do, but I'm at least making a show of it for Annalise and Everett."

He wanted to bare his teeth and growl, but she was right. He needed to pretend for a little while longer. For Everett and Annalise.

"And the maid of honor and best man—" the DJ shouted "—Rachel McCarthy and Cooper Turner."

Upbeat music started playing and he and Rachel entered the room. They joined the rest of the wedding party and waited as Annalise and Everett made their entrance.

Coop slanted his gaze toward Piper's table. He spotted Tom seated next to her.

Son of a bitch. The two of them were laughing together and having a grand old time.

His hands clenched into tight fists.

Coop wasn't sure how much time had passed by the time the waitstaff cleared the dishes. Most of the evening was a blur.

"Hey, man." Everett clapped him on the shoulder. "Your duties as best man are done." His expression turned serious. "Thanks for everything. I know the past few hours with Rachel have been less than pleasurable for you, and I—*we*," he corrected, "because I need to include Annalise, too—appreciate you toughing it out for us. You're a true friend."

The sound that came from his mouth was a cross between a snort and a laugh. "I'm just glad I'm done."

"Obligation fulfilled." Ev gave him a thumbs-up. "Time for you to have some fun. Go find Piper and get her out on the dance floor."

"I'll do that." He needed to talk to Piper. He'd overreacted earlier when he'd seen her and Tom together. Not that she knew that—thank God for small miracles. Seeing her with Tom… Bile churned in his gut.

No, damnit. Piper wasn't Rachel. She wouldn't do to him what Rachel had. She'd been nothing but honest with him since the beginning. So why was he creating trouble where none existed?

Coop walked over to her table. "Excuse me," he said because one of the other women sitting with her was talking. "I was hoping I could steal you away for a dance?"

She looked at him, uncertainty in her gaze.

Had she picked up on the bad vibes he'd been putting out lately?

She gave him a hesitant smile and nodded. Standing, she joined her hand with his.

Coop guided them through the maze of couples to an empty spot on the dance floor.

The DJ announced they were going to slow things down and a romantic ballad came through the speakers.

Coop drew her in close and she melted against him. He blew out the breath he'd been holding.

They danced together to the slow, sensual beat, and he couldn't help remembering the day they'd danced together in her gallery. Coop grinned. He'd wanted to show her how much better the adult version of him was compared to his thirteen-year-old self.

"This is nice." He liked holding her close like this.

She didn't respond.

"Are you having a good time?" he asked.

She nodded, but never uttered a word.

"You're awfully quiet. Is everything okay?"

"Yes. Sorry. Just thinking." Her voice held an odd tone that set his nerves on edge.

He eased away from her to see her face. She looked… "Are you sure you're all right? You're white as a ghost."

Her face turned stricken. "I need some air." Piper bolted from the room.

He raced after her and found her in the hall, pacing back and forth. Color had returned to her features. At least that was a good thing. "Hey, what's going on?"

She peered up at him. "Nothing. I'm tired, that's all. Plus, I've got a splitting headache. I'm going to call it a night." She started to walk away from him.

A muscle in his neck jerked. "Oh, sure. You were fine earlier when you were with Tom. All smiles and full of energy, but now you have a headache. Is there something going on with you two I should know about?"

Piper rounded on him. "You've *got* to be kidding me."

He crossed his hands over his chest. "I call it like I see it."

She stared at him as if he'd lost his mind. Maybe he had. "You're one to talk. You think I didn't notice how chummy you've been with your ex all night? Well, I did. And so did everyone at our table, including Tom."

"You can't be serious." Although he couldn't deny that a tiny part of him was cheering because Tom was pissed. "Come on, Piper. What's really going on here?"

Her whole face turned beet red. "You know what? I'm done with this whole charade. It's over. Our deal is done."

"Fine by me," he spat.

She turned and started to leave.

Stop her. Don't let her go.

Coop couldn't move. His stomach churned as he watched her walk away.

Chapter Twenty-Four

Piper rubbed her bleary eyes and snuggled up under her favorite blanket, a gift from her father for her tenth birthday. She ignored the knocking on her apartment door. Maybe they'd go away if she stayed silent. No one knew she was here.

"I know you're home." Mia's voice was muffled. "I can hear your TV."

Damn it. That's what she got for binge-watching... wait for it...*romance* movies all night long.

Piper shook her head. She'd started channel surfing and stopped on the channel playing *Falling for My Brother's Best Friend*. Out of curiosity, of course.

That was five movies ago. And yes, she'd liked each and every one of them.

"You might as well let us in, because we're not going away," Elle called.

Piper heaved out a sigh. Grabbing the remote, she flicked off the television and tossed the blanket aside. She rose from the couch. "Hold your horses. I'm coming."

She trudged to the door and opened it. Mia, Layla, Abby and Elle stood in the hall.

"Why did you dodge all my calls?" Mia asked.

She'd turned off her cell after leaving the wedding reception last night. She didn't want to speak to anyone. Still didn't, but it appeared she didn't have much choice in the matter.

Not true. She could ask them to leave, but she didn't want to. She wanted the love and support these wonderful, funny women had offered from the start. "Come in, ladies. I hope you brought chocolate." Piper yawned. "And coffee. Lots and lots of coffee."

Piper tried, but failed to stifle another yawn. She hadn't slept. Too many things running through her mind. Like how she'd gone from enjoying being held in Cooper's arms as they moved to the slow beat of the music to, "I can't do this anymore," five minutes later.

Okay, yes. She was being quiet. She'd needed to come to terms with the fact that she'd fallen in love with him—her insides were still jumping all over the place at that revelation—because that was the last thing she'd ever wanted. One way or another, love didn't last. Mom. Mia. Even Shane because he'd gotten divorced, too. He might have Layla now, but who knew if it would last?

And Cooper… Why was he acting all kinds of crazy? He'd practically accused her of cheating on him.

Piper mentally smacked the palm of her hand on her forehead. Of course it was because Rachel had cheated on Cooper with Tom. Which meant what, exactly? He didn't trust her not to do the same?

A heavy weight settled in her chest.

Doesn't matter. Their deal was done. They'd ended their charade.

Her heart gave a painful thud. Not because they'd ended it. It was the fact that Cooper couldn't trust her. She'd thought they'd become friends. It was the one good thing that had come out of all this.

The idea of going back to the way they used to be… Her stomach twisted. She couldn't bear that.

Piper closed the door when the last of her friends walked in.

"Coffee. The way you like it." Abby handed her a large to-go cup.

"Chocolate." Elle handed her a cupcake. "With extra frosting, because I have a feeling you need it."

Her chest filled to bursting point. How lucky was she to have such compassionate friends? Fortunate was an understatement.

"Thank you so much." She glanced at the sugary treat. *No conversation hearts.* Why moisture pricked at the corners of her eyes, she couldn't say. She didn't even like the candies that much.

Oh, who was she trying to fool? Not the sisterhood, if the expressions on Abby's, Elle's, Layla's and Mia's faces were anything to go by. That just left herself.

"What's wrong?" Mia draped an arm around her shoulder and guided her to the couch and sat beside her.

"Nothing. Everything's fine," Piper insisted. She tried to smile. She really did.

"Then why are there tears streaming down your face?" Layla sat on the other side of Piper.

"Did you and Cooper have a fight?" Abby grabbed one of the club chairs in the living room.

"Is that why you changed your plans and came home last night?" Elle plopped down in the other chair.

"We broke up." Piper scraped the back of her hand across her face. Lord, why was she crying? She never shed tears when a relationship ended. She never moped around lamenting what might have been.

"Oh, honey. What happened?" Mia hugged her tight.

"He said stupid stuff. I said stupid stuff." Why had she done that? *I was jealous, that's why.* She should have explained. Instead, she'd lashed out. She couldn't stand to see Cooper with Rachel. Not for one minute.

Every smile he flashed at Rachel was like a dagger through her heart.

Piper blinked because, damn it, more tears were starting to fall.

"It's okay." Layla patted her arm. "You can fix this. Talk to him. He's probably thinking the same thing."

Apologizing wouldn't solve anything. It was not like they were a real couple and could get back together.

A loud wail escaped from her parted lips. It sounded like a wounded animal. What was wrong with her? Tears wouldn't solve anything.

"It won't help," Piper insisted. "You don't understand."

"You had a silly fight." Abby acted as if it were no big deal. "You can kiss and make up. It's allowed."

"You've never done that before." Mia gave a sage nod of her head. "You end things and it's over. It's okay to care enough to want to fix things between you and Cooper. I'm sure he wants that, too. You two are great together. He loves you. I know how much that scares you, but it's a good thing." She smiled. "Trust me."

She shook her head. "It's not like that between us." *Ah, hell.* The waterworks were in full force again.

"What do you mean?" Elle asked. "Anyone can see you two are crazy for each other."

She swiped a hand across her face. "It was all for show."

Layla's brows drew together in a deep V. "Come again?"

Piper slumped back against the couch. "We were acting." She explained about the deal she and Cooper made.

Elle burst out laughing. "I wasn't serious when I told you to do that."

"Maybe not, but I was desperate." Piper's lips quirked

into a small smile. "My mother wouldn't stop fixing me up. And Cooper…" She wasn't going to explain further. "Let's just say he had his own reasons for making the deal.

"Everything was perfect until…" Piper heaved out a sigh.

"Until you fell in love with him," Mia finished.

She nodded. "That wasn't supposed to happen." She still didn't want a serious relationship. This thing… Cooper… It was hard enough.

"Does Mom know about any of this?" Mia asked.

Piper shook her head. "She certainly doesn't know about our deal, and I don't want her to know about the breakup until after the gallery opens. I have too much on my plate to deal with right now. The last thing I need is for her to go into fix-up mode again."

The idea of dating anyone other than Cooper… Piper shuddered.

An image of Cooper holding his gorgeous ex in his arms as they whirled around the dance floor last night slammed into her head. No, damn it. She wasn't going to think about him with her.

She straightened her shoulders and lifted her chin. Enough was enough. It was time to move on. She wouldn't spend the rest of her life pining over a man because he was gone.

Mom's face appeared in her mind.

The loneliness… The devastation etched in her beautiful features after Dad's death…

No way. She wouldn't end up like her.

She couldn't go through that. Wouldn't.

"You're still here." Levi propped his tall frame against the open door of Coop's office at TK Construction. "It's after eight p.m."

"I'm working." Coop kept staring at the computer monitor sitting on his desk.

"You said the same thing every night this week."

Coop glared at his brother. So what if he'd worked late the last four days? "I've got things to do."

"Ah." His brother gave a sage nod. "That must be why you've locked yourself in this office for more than sixteen hours a day since you came back from Everett and Annalise's wedding."

He nodded. "That's right. I need to catch up after being out of the office for five weeks."

"While you renovated Piper's gallery," Levi stated.

Coop stiffened. Leave it to his brother to bring her up. Not that he'd been able to get her off his mind. The truth was, she'd consumed his thoughts 24/7 since she walked out on him during the reception.

Coop gritted his teeth. She'd acted as if everything they'd shared during the last few weeks meant nothing to her.

He wouldn't think about her anymore. "Is there a reason why you're here?"

"Yes. Are you still participating in the ice art competition on Friday?" Levi asked. "You haven't told the committee what you're planning to sculpt yet."

"I don't know what I'm going to do yet."

"Remember it's a love theme this year, since the festival lands on Valentine's Day."

Coop groaned. Talk about a kick in the teeth. This was going to be the worst Valentine's Day ever. "I've changed my mind. I'm going to pass this year."

"You're not entering?" Levi's brows knit together.

Coop blew out a breath. "That's what I said."

"But you enter every year," his brother insisted.

"I don't have time this year. These quotes need to go

out in the next two days." Coop gestured to the stack of paperwork piled on the right corner of his desk.

Levi sauntered in and dropped into the chair in front of Coop's desk. He grabbed a handful of the quotes and thumbed through them. "These have already been reviewed. By me." He pointed to his signature at the bottom of each page.

Okay. Fine. Levi was right. He'd already reviewed all the quotes that needed to go out. Coop just…needed to keep busy.

He didn't want to go home.

Everything there reminded him of Piper. Which was crazy. It was his house. He'd lived there all his life.

Without her.

So why did he wake each morning and reach for her, and why was he disappointed to find her side of the bed empty? Why did he set out two plates for dinner before realizing he'd dine alone? And why couldn't he bear to look at his favorite comfy T shirt, the one Piper had commandeered to sleep in?

Coop scrubbed his hands over his face. He knew why. He missed her smile. Her laugh. He missed the way she snuggled against him while they sat on the couch in front of a roaring fire, or when they watched TV. He missed the way her body fit with his.

He missed…her.

His brother crossed his arms over his chest and narrowed his gaze. "Okay. What's going on?"

"Nothing. Why would you think something is going on?" He hadn't told anyone he and Piper were no more. They'd agreed to break up after her gallery opened and he was going to stick to the plan, even if she hadn't.

She must not have said anything either. Otherwise, Shane would have paid him a visit. Coop remembered

Shane's reaction when he'd first found them together. He could only imagine what would happen when he learned about the breakup.

"You won't enter the love-themed ice art competition." Levi's voice boomed in the otherwise silent room. "And you're making excuses to work late, like you did when you and Rachel split.

"Did something happen between you and Piper?" Levi asked.

"I don't know what you're talking about." Coop lowered his gaze to the quote sitting in front of him.

Levi let loose a loud snort. "What'd you do to make her dump your sorry ass?"

His lips tightened into a thin line. "Oh, sure, take her side."

Levi rolled his gaze skyward. "What happened?"

Coop looked his brother in the eye. "It's none of your business."

"Hate to break it to you, but I'm the least of your troubles. When Mom finds out…"

His shoulders slumped. She was going to be on his case for sure. Mom adored Piper. Mia, too. "It's none of her business either. Piper and I broke up. End of story."

"You really think that's going to fly, given how close our families are?" his brother asked.

Neither of them had thought about that little complication when they'd come up with this deal. How could they have believed for a second that a fake relationship would work?

"Why don't you tell me what happened. Maybe there's a way to fix this before Mom finds out."

Was that even possible at this point? Lord, he wanted that more than he could say, but he couldn't see how it was possible. "Okay." Coop slumped back against the back of his leather chair. He told his brother everything.

Levi doubled over with laughter. "A fake relationship. Now, that's one for the books."

"I needed to save face at the wedding," he insisted.

Levi laughed even harder. "You actually believe that, don't you?"

Coop scowled. "It's the truth."

"You could have chosen anyone to take to the wedding. Hell, Fiona from the Homes for Humanity crew would have jumped at the chance. She's had the hots for you for months now. But you chose Piper. Why do you think that is?"

Coop closed his eyes and prayed for patience. "I told you. She needed this as much as I did."

Levi grinned. "You still won't admit it, will you?"

"Admit what?" he growled.

"You've had a thing for her since you were in the eighth grade. Ask Mom, she's been saying you belong together for years."

Damn it. He wished Mom would keep her thoughts to herself when it came to Piper and him. "Mom has no idea what she's talking about. Piper and I didn't even like each other until recently."

Levi's smile widened. "That doesn't mean you haven't been crushing on her all this time. Now why don't you tell me why Piper ended your deal early? It doesn't make sense."

"I don't know." He knew he sounded like an obstinate child, but he couldn't help it.

Levi burst out laughing again. "Man, you really have it bad."

He had it bad for her all right. Too bad his feelings weren't reciprocated.

An image of her standing with Tom at the wedding burst into his head. The smile on her face... *His* smile. That was how he thought of it, because she only flashed it for him. He told his brother what happened with Tom.

Levi shook his head. "Boy, you really are a moron."

"What?" he cried. "Did you even listen to me?"

"You saw her talking with Tom," Levi stated.

"Yes." He nodded.

"And she was smiling."

"Yes," he repeated.

"I understand that Tom's a sore spot with you."

Sore spot was an understatement. The guy was supposed to be his friend and he'd turned around and slept with *his girlfriend*. Coop didn't trust Tom, or Rachel, for that matter.

"The whole thing sounds pretty innocent to me," his brother said. "Did you ask her about it?"

"No," he admitted. He'd...reacted without any thought. Which was pretty damned stupid when he thought about it now.

Coop exhaled a heavy sigh. He couldn't trust Tom, but Piper... *Ah, hell*. She'd never lied to him. Not once in all the years they'd known each other.

"Please tell me you didn't accuse her of cheating—" Levi broke off and shook his head. "*No*. You wouldn't be that stupid."

Coop looked away. He couldn't meet his brother's gaze. He might not have said the words, but yes, that was exactly what he'd done.

"What is wrong with you?" His brother jumped up from his seat and thwacked him in the head, like he used to do when they were kids.

Coop recoiled. "What the *hell*?"

"This is Piper we're talking about, not Rachel," Levi

said. "Piper would never do anything like that to you. Or anyone else, for that matter. You should damned well know that."

His brother was right. He'd allowed his anger, his fear of losing her and his insecurities—because that was what it really boiled down to—to get the better of him.

He loved Piper. He wanted her to love him, too, but he'd never plucked up the courage to ask her to turn their fake relationship into something real. Something that would last.

Stupid, stupid, stupid. "I know. I know. I screwed up. Big-time." He couldn't have made a bigger mess of things if he'd tried. "The question is, how do I fix things?"

Levi arched a brow. "Is that what you want?"

"Yes." He wanted a life with Piper. More than anything else in the world.

Chapter Twenty-Five

Piper stood in the middle of her gallery on Saturday morning and peered around the space. The wood floors gleamed. LED lights highlighted Jax Rawlins's wildlife photos that hung on her freshly painted white walls.

In less than six hours, the rooms would be filled with patrons milling about the space, commenting on the displayed pieces. Servers would discreetly serve trays of delicious hors d'oeuvres provided by Layla. A bartender would serve beer and wine in fluted glasses from behind the beautiful new bar.

In less than six hours, her lifelong dream would become a reality.

She should be beyond excited. She should be floating on cloud nine. She should be doing a happy dance.

So why was she standing here with a heavy weight in her chest?

Tears gathered in the corners of her eyes. Cooper wouldn't be here to share this with her, that was why.

She swallowed hard. How could she miss someone so much it physically hurt? Instead of getting better each day, the pain in her chest grew worse and worse. How was that even possible after such a short time together?

Piper dragged the back of her hand over each eye to stop the tears from falling.

It wasn't supposed to be this way. She wasn't supposed to fall in love. Love wouldn't last, and when it ended…

She couldn't handle the despair. Couldn't relive the all-consuming grief she'd experienced when her father died.

Piper drew in a deep, steadying breath. Life without Cooper…

She rubbed at the center of her chest. She couldn't think about that reality.

"Piper, honey?" Mom's muffled voice came from the first floor. "Are you here? The door is open."

Right. She'd propped it open when she'd arrived because she needed to unload the contents of her car. Toilet paper for the restrooms, paper towels for the kitchen. Cleaning supplies, coffee from the Coffee Palace, boxes of tea she'd ordered online. Piper had forgotten to close it behind her after the last trip.

She opened the doors to the gallery and stepped out on the landing. "I'm up here."

Mom hurried up the stairs and presented a beautifully wrapped box to her.

"What's this?" Piper asked.

"It's something for good luck on your new adventure." Mom kissed her cheek. "I'm so proud of you, sweetie."

A rush of warmth filled her and she smiled. "That's so nice. Thank you. Do you want to see inside?"

Mom grinned. "Are you kidding me? I thought you'd never ask, but first, I want you to open the gift."

Her brows drew together. She'd planned to wait until they walked inside but now was as good a time as any. "Okay." Piper removed the wrapping paper and lid. Inside lay three-inch tall, baby-pink-colored wood letters that spelled out her first and last name.

"Do you remember those?" Mom asked.

"Yes. They used to hang on my bedroom wall when I was little." Piper had removed them when she'd entered middle school and Mom had remodeled her room.

"Your father carved them for you the day you were born. I know you already have a sign on the wall that says Kavanaugh Art Gallery." Mom pointed to the block letters that stood to the right of the gallery door. "But I thought you might like to have those—" she gestured to the letters in the box "—to hang in your studio."

"Dad made these?" She touched the letters reverently. "I never knew that." Piper swallowed hard. She wasn't going to cry, damn it, but the tears started falling nonetheless. Happy tears. To receive such an unexpected treasure made her day. "I'm so glad you saved them." She hugged her mother hard. "These are perfect for my studio."

"I'm so glad you like them," Mom said.

Piper wiped her eyes and grinned. "I love them. It's such a thoughtful gift." One of the most thoughtful gifts she'd ever received. "Come on." Piper opened the door to her gallery and gestured for Mom to precede her. "I can't wait to see what you think."

Mom stepped inside. "Oh, Piper." Her gaze darted around the room. "This is fantastic. The space looks amazing. I love the mix of old and new," Mom said, gesturing from the wood floors and ornately carved crown molding that surrounded the ceilings to the industrial metal shelves behind the bar.

Piper beamed a mile-wide smile. "I'm so glad you like it."

"Where's Cooper?" Mom peered around the room. "I saw his truck in the parking lot and assumed he was up here helping you."

"Cooper's here?" She raced to the windows. Yes. His truck was indeed parked in the parking lot.

Piper spotted him. Happiness bubbled up inside her.

He walked toward the building and…into Layla's restaurant.

He wasn't here to see her.

Her heart clenched. The painful thud making it hard to breathe.

She turned away from the window.

"What's wrong, honey?" Mom rushed to her side.

"Nothing." Piper couldn't look her mother in the eye.

Her mom draped an arm around her shoulder. "You look like you've lost your best friend. What's going on with you and Cooper?"

"Don't worry about Cooper and me." Piper marched over to the bar and grabbed her coat from where she'd draped it over the chair back. The last thing she wanted was to tell her mother she and Cooper were finished. "I need to head out. I have a few more errands to do before the grand opening this afternoon."

"You broke things off with him, didn't you?" She couldn't miss the accusation in Mom's voice.

Piper stiffened. Of course her mother thought Piper had ended the relationship. Why had she ever believed she could fool her?

Idiot, idiot, idiot. Her plan would never have worked, because Mom knew her too well.

Piper turned and faced her mother. "Yes. I ended things with Cooper."

"But why? I don't understand. You seemed so happy together."

She was happy with him. Happier than she'd been in years. Piper drew in a deep breath and released it. "It didn't work out, so I ended things."

"You didn't give it a chance," Mom countered. "You've never given any relationship a chance."

Piper folded her arms over her chest. It appeared that they were going to have this out once and for all. "I don't want a relationship. I keep telling you that, but you never seem to listen. You keep setting me up with guy after guy."

"I want you to find love, sweetheart."

"Why? So I can end up like you? Distraught and devastated for the rest of my life? Or divorced like Mia and Shane? That's a hard no. I'll skip the heartbreak, thank you very much."

Her mother gawked at her. "Is that really what you think?"

Piper's eyes bugged out. Why would she think otherwise? "Mom. It's been more than fifteen years since Dad passed and you haven't so much as *looked* at another man."

"Oh, Piper." Mom laid her head in her hands. "I thought I was protecting you all these years, but I've done you a huge disservice."

"What are you talking about?"

Her mother lifted her head and looked Piper in the eyes. "I thought you and Mia and Shane would be upset if you knew. You loved your father so much."

Piper rubbed at her temples. "I don't understand. What would we be upset about?"

"I've had other relationships," Mom said.

Piper blinked. She couldn't have heard her right. "Say that again."

Mom dragged her fingers through her hair. "I've dated other men over the years. I just haven't told you about them."

Piper shook her head. "Do you really expect me to believe that? Why wouldn't you tell any of us?"

"At first, you were young and I didn't want to expose

you to someone if things didn't work out, and then…" Her mother shrugged. "I thought you'd be mad. You loved your father so much."

There was some truth to what Mom believed. As a teen, Piper would have seen it as a betrayal against her father.

"There is someone I'd like you to meet if you'd be open to the idea." Mom gave her a tentative smile. "His name is Chris."

Piper's jaw dropped. "Book club Chris?" The person Mom had gone away with last summer?

Red color crept up Mom's neck and flooded her cheeks. "Yes. We hit it off when he joined our group last year."

"Oh my God. All this time I believed Chris was a female friend of yours."

Her butt-in-ski mother, who'd made it her life's mission to find Piper a husband, had a secret boyfriend. Talk about the hypocrisy of it…

Although… Given Mom's perceptions of how she thought Piper would react to that news, she understood why Mom never said anything.

"I'm so happy for you." She hugged her mother. "Are things serious between you?"

Her mother's smile broadened. "I think he's going to propose soon."

Piper gasped. "And you're going to accept if he does?"

"I will." Mom grasped Piper's hands in hers. "I loved your father with all my heart, and it's taken me a long time to find someone who I can love again. I can't… I won't allow this opportunity to slip away."

She'd been wrong about her mother. On so many levels. Mom might have been grief-stricken when Dad died, but she hadn't stopped living. She wasn't wasting away, pining for something that could no longer be.

She wasn't trying to live vicariously through Piper, or anyone else. Just the opposite. She'd found the courage to move on with her life, and had never given up on finding love again.

"Chris is a wonderful man," her mother continued. "He's kind and loving. He makes me laugh." Her mother glowed with happiness. "I can't wait for you and your brother and sister to meet him."

"I'm thrilled for you, Mom." Piper hugged her again. "You deserve to be happy and I can't wait to meet him. He's a lucky man to have you."

"You deserve to be happy, too." Her mother's words shook with conviction.

"Mom…" Piper began.

"Do you love Cooper?"

Piper closed her eyes. She couldn't lie anymore. Not to Mom, and not to herself. "With all of my heart."

Mom kissed her cheek. "Take a chance. Turn your fake relationship with Cooper into something real. Something lasting."

Piper stiffened. "You knew?"

"Of course I did." Mom planted her hands on her hips, but she was smiling. "Did you really think Debby and I would believe that story the two of you concocted?"

Yes. She'd 100 percent believed Mom had bought their tale hook, line and sinker. But once again, Mom was one step ahead of her. Piper snorted. "I can't believe both of you knew all this time and never said anything."

"It almost killed me. Debby too, but we went along with it. Actually, we did everything we could to encourage the idea.

"She's right you know. Debby," Mom added when Piper's brows knitted together. "You two belong together. We all saw your budding romance start that summer between seventh and eighth grade. Ron and Debby. Dad and me. Then your father died and whatever was starting to grow between you and Cooper died, too. Don't make that mistake twice."

"Oh, Mom." Piper sniffed and wiped the moisture gathering in the corners of her eyes.

Her mother winked. "Layla's place *would* make a great wedding venue."

"Mom!" Piper gasped. "I don't even know if Cooper feels the same way about me as I do about him." He'd been so angry with her at the wedding.

"There's only one way to find out." Mom flashed a wide grin. "Ask him."

Piper's mind spun faster than a Tilt-A-Whirl ride at an amusement park.

"Make peace with the past, Piper, and choose a life worth living.

"Choose love, darling. I'll see you later. And I'll bring Chris to the opening, if that's okay." Mom giggled like a schoolgirl.

Could she take the risk and open her heart? Could she be brave, like her mother?

"Yo, Coop." Levi stuck his head through the tarp that surrounded his ice sculpture on the front lawn of the colonial mansion. "You've got thirty minutes until the deadline."

Thank goodness he'd convinced Layla to sponsor his exhibit at the last minute. He would have been excluded from the contest if she hadn't.

"I'll be done. I'll be done." He chiseled a piece of ice away from his sculpture. No way could he not be. His entire future with Piper was riding on this.

Levi peered at Coop's work. His brows knitted into a deep V. "How is this supposed to win Piper back?"

"She'll understand." At least he hoped she would.

Levi shook his head. "Tell me again why you didn't just talk to her. Why couldn't you just apologize for being a butthead and beg for forgiveness?"

That was plan B, if this didn't work. He could and would grovel if the situation called for it. "Actions speak louder than words. I want to show her how I feel."

Levi shrugged. "If you say so."

"I do." Coop glanced at his brother. "How's it going in there?" He gestured to the second story of the old mansion that housed Piper's gallery. He wished he could be there with her. To support her and cheer her on. If he hadn't been such a… What had Levi called him? A butthead. He'd been called much worse by his brothers for less offensive behavior.

What if Piper couldn't forgive him? What was he going to do then? *No, damn it.* He couldn't think that way. He'd fix this. He had to.

"The place is packed. I'm pretty sure she sold every print."

Coop smiled. "That's great."

"Yeah. Her customers are crying for more. Jax says he can't wait to come back."

I'll just bet he can't. Coop's lips tightened.

"What was that?" Levi asked. "I didn't catch what you said."

Great, now he was grumbling out loud. "Nothing. You should get going. I need to finish this up and I need every second I have left."

"Good luck." His brother waved and stepped outside.

"Thanks." He was going to need it.

Chapter Twenty-Six

"Congratulations, little sister." Mia walked up and slung an arm around her shoulder. "You did it. Day one of your new business was a resounding success."

Piper peered around the now-empty room. A wide grin spread across her face. "Yes, it was." A good portion of today's achievement could be credited to Jax Rawlins, because many of the people who attended her grand opening today came because of him. But a lot of those people seemed interested in returning to see works from the artists she'd booked over the next few months.

Mom walked into the main space with Chris at her side. "We had a wonderful time, dear. I'm so proud of you."

Piper smiled, and yes, a touch of heat flooded her cheeks. "Thanks. I'm proud of me, too."

"A job well done," Chris said. "It was a pleasure to finally meet you." He extended his hand to Piper.

"The pleasure is all mine." Standing on her tiptoes, she hugged the tall man.

"Mine, too." Mia copied Piper.

"We're going to head down to the ice art festival now. The judges are going to announce the winner in a few minutes." Mom narrowed her gaze. "Will we see you there?"

Piper chuckled. "Yes." She couldn't wait to find Cooper. "That reminds me, I need to grab something from the kitchen before I lock up."

"Good luck." Mom gave her a quick hug, and headed toward the elevator with Chris by her side.

"I'm going to head out, too." Mia turned to leave.

"It was nice that Kyle stopped by with the girls," Piper called. "I know you wanted them to be here."

Mia whirled around. Her expression was... Well, Piper couldn't tell if Mia was ticked off or happy about Kyle's appearance this evening. "Yeah. I guess it was."

"Piper?" Jax stepped off the elevator and into the hall. "Thank goodness you're still here. I dropped my cell phone and..." He stared at her sister. His gaze locked with hers. "Hey, Mia."

"Hi." Mia's cheeks flamed fire-engine red.

Jax's gaze jerked to Piper. "Okay if I look around for my phone?"

"Sure, but make it quick." She needed to find Cooper.

"Maybe Mia can help me?" His gaze landed on her sister again. "If you're not busy, that is."

Mia's lips parted and her eyes went wide. "Um... okay."

The air sizzled between the two of them.

One and done, huh? I don't think so. Oh, yes. This was getting more interesting by the second.

"Lock up for me." Piper grinned. "I've got to find Cooper."

"He's set up in front of the mansion." Jax shook his head. "I'll be honest. I don't think he's going to win this year. His sculpture... I mean it's cute, but..." He gestured to the front of the building. "You should judge for yourself."

Truth be told. Jax's opinion didn't matter. Nothing was more important than finding Cooper and telling him how she felt about him. She walked into the kitchen and grabbed the small cupcake box from the fridge where Elle had placed it earlier.

After Mom left this morning, Piper had called the Coffee Palace and asked Elle to prepare a very special, very personal chocolate cupcake with extra chocolate frosting. She and Abby had dropped it off during Jax's show. They couldn't stay long. With the ice art festival underway, the Coffee Palace was packed with customers. The same was true for Layla. If the parking lot was anything to go by, her restaurant was slammed.

How lucky was she to have such great friends that they'd take time out of their busy schedules to stop by and support her?

It wasn't luck. She'd opened her heart and received a wonderful gift in return.

Cooper's smiling face popped into her mind. Piper crossed her fingers. *Here's hoping.*

She exited the kitchen. Mia and Jax were nowhere to be found.

Piper grinned and exited the gallery. Once downstairs, she hurried around to the front of the mansion.

A throng of people milled about the area, but Cooper was nowhere to be found. Piper rushed into the crowd. Where was he? Had she missed him? "Excuse me." She turned sideways to pass through a swarm of humanity. "Pardon me." She squeezed by others. Her gaze darted around the mob, searching for Cooper's face.

"Cooper," she called, but there was so much noise she doubted anyone heard her. "Where are you, Cooper?" she yelled. How was she going to find him with all of these people clustered around her?

Her heart hammered as she continued weaving her

way through the multitude of people and shouting Cooper's name. Where was he? She needed to find him.

Piper wasn't sure how much time passed when a pair of strong hands grabbed her waist from behind and hauled her out of the crowd. She whirled around.

"Cooper." She threw her arms around him and planted kisses all over his face. "I've been looking all over for you."

He grinned. Wrapping his arms around her, he held her tight. "I've been looking for you, too."

"You were?" She luxuriated in the press of his body against her and the warm, minty scent of his breath on her face.

"I ran into your mom and she said you were here." Worry creased his brow. "I thought maybe she was wrong when I couldn't find you."

"I'm right here." She brushed her lips against his. She wanted to linger and savor his sweetness, but she needed to set the record straight first.

Piper grabbed his hand with her free one and led him to a spot a few feet away that was less congested. "I love you, Cooper Turner. With everything that I am and everything that I will be. I want to turn our fake relationship into something real and something lasting.

"I never dreamed that I could love someone as much as I love you." She shook her head. "I didn't want to. When I lost my father..." Piper swallowed hard. "I was afraid. Loving hurt too much."

"But you've changed your mind."

She beamed a mile-wide smile at him. "Yes. I've been miserable without you this past week. I've learned a life without love isn't living at all. It's just existing. That's what I've been doing for the last fifteen years.

Then you came along. You broke through all of my defenses without even trying."

Coop grinned and kissed her hard.

"I want to play in the snow with you. Cuddle on the couch and watch sappy romance movies with you. I want to argue with you when we don't agree—we'll keep that to a minimum—and make mad, passionate love with you." She grinned. "As often as possible. I want to make a life with you by my side, and I'm hoping you want that, too."

Her insides jumped and jittered as she waited for his response.

This brilliant, thoughtful, giving woman loved *him*. What had he done in this life to become so lucky?

"Yes. I want it all, as long as I'm with you." Coop was pretty sure he was sporting a goofy grin. He didn't care. Piper loved him. "I love you, too, Piper. More than words can say." He stroked his palm over her cheek.

"I screwed up, sweetheart, and I'm sorry. I saw you with Tom and… I was jealous. Plain and simple. I couldn't stand him being anywhere near you." Coop dragged his fingers through his hair. "There's something I never told you about Tom and Rachel."

"I know. Mia told me the night of Everett and Annalise's wedding. My question is, why didn't you? I thought maybe you were still in love with Rachel."

All his tension eased away. "No. No. I am not in love with Rachel. Any love I felt for her disappeared when I found out about her and Tom. As for why I didn't tell you about them…" Coop shook his head. "I felt like such a fool. They were together right under my nose for two months and I couldn't see it. What does that say about me?"

"It says you are a kind, loving man who chose to trust his partner and his best friend. They didn't deserve that honor."

He pulled her against him so that every inch of her touched every part of him. "Can you forgive me for being such a jackass to you at the wedding? I should never have implied…"

"You're right. You shouldn't have," she admonished. "I would never do that to you."

"I know." He kissed her because he needed the contact. "You're as honest as they come." Coop shook his head. "I knew I was in love with you, but I couldn't pluck up the courage to see if you felt the same way. I thought maybe you still liked Tom." There. He'd admitted the truth.

Piper eased back. "You thought I had a thing for *Tom*?"

He cringed. "You admitted you liked him in high school. It's why you were so upset the night of the Valentine's dance."

Piper shuddered. "That was before he acted like such a colossal jerk to me." She brushed her lips against his. "So we're clear, I have no interest in Tom Anderson. Now, you…" Piper nipped the corner of his mouth "…are another story. I have *immense* interest in you." She cupped his face with her palms.

A thud sounded behind her.

"Oh, no. Crap." She jerked away from him and bent to pick up something from the ground.

"What's that?" he asked.

Piper handed him the deformed cardboard container. "It's for you." She shook her head. "I'm sorry. It's a little smushed. I forgot I was holding it."

He lifted the top and smiled. A cupcake topper that

said Happy Valentine's Day sat in the middle of a huge, now-flat, mound of chocolate frosting flagged by two candy hearts that sat slightly askew. The words *Luv U* were written on one heart and *Forever* on the other. Coop burst out laughing.

Piper sighed. "That's definitely not the reaction I was expecting."

"No. I love it." He dropped a quick kiss on her pursed lips. "Looks like we're both on the same wavelength."

"What are you talking about?" she asked.

He grabbed her hand with his free one and walked her around to the front of his exhibit. Most of the people had moved on to view other sculptures. Only a few stragglers stood in front of his piece.

"Love Conversations?" She glanced at the name on the plaque as they passed by.

"You'll understand why I chose that name for my sculpture in a moment." Coop stopped in a spot that gave Piper the best view of his work.

She flashed a happy grin in his direction. "You made giant candy hearts carved out of ice. Oh my gosh. You even colored them." She touched the light orange and yellow hearts. "And etched words on the face. *Be mine. Always.*" Piper grinned and clapped her hands. "That's so sweet."

Coop handed the cupcake to his father who stood a short distance away with his mother, Jane, and a man he didn't know.

He reached inside his pocket and pulled out the small box he'd stored there for the last two days. The ring she'd spotted in the jewelry store window the day they'd made their deal.

His palms turned sweaty. His heart hammered faster than a racehorse galloping toward the finish line.

"Piper." Dropping to one knee, he cleared his throat. Mom gasped. He was pretty sure Jane did, too.

Piper gawked at him. "What are you doing, Cooper?"

He sucked in a deep, steadying breath. A few short weeks ago he couldn't imagine doing this ever again, let alone five weeks into a fake relationship. Now he'd never been so sure of anything in his life.

"Will you be mine always? I fell for you when I was thirteen years old." It was the truth. His brother was right about that. "But fate had other plans for us. Then, a few short weeks ago you walked into my life again, and turned my world upside down. I haven't been the same since. I love you with all my heart." He flipped open the top on the ring box and presented the diamond solitaire to her. "Will you make me the happiest man alive and marry me?"

"Yes." She gave him a watery smile. "I would love to marry you. I can't think of anything I'd like more."

Coop rose and smiled a mile-wide grin. "Love you so much, sweetheart." He lifted Piper into his arms and twirled her around.

"I love you, too. Now put the ring on my finger. Please." She bounced up and down.

"Bossy." He grinned.

"Euphoric. Ecstatic. And head over heels in love with you," she corrected.

She was as honest as they came. He'd never doubt that again.

Coop slid the ring on her finger.

"It's perfect. I love it." Piper grinned and raised her left hand in the air and waved.

Mom and Jane rushed over and hugged both of them.

"I always knew you two belonged together." Mom kissed his cheek.

"A Valentine's proposal." Jane clapped her hand to her heart. "How romantic. I'm so happy for you."

Piper twined her arms around his neck and brushed her sweet lips over his. "Best Valentine's Day ever, and it's all because of you."

He grinned. "It's definitely an improvement over that fateful night all those years ago."

"No skunk, for one thing." She waggled her brows.

He chuffed out a laugh. "Ha ha. You're funny."

"It's the new me." Piper chuckled. "Happy and in love. What do you think?"

He winked. "I'm liking it very much."

Piper smiled. "I can't wait to start our new life together. You and me. Forever."

He nodded. "Always. Through good times or bad."

"I love you, Cooper."

His heart filled to bursting point. "I love you, too." Best Valentine's Day. Ever!

* * * * *

Look for Mia's story,
The next installment in Anna James' new miniseries
Sisterhood of Chocolate & Wine
Coming soon,
Wherever Harlequin books and ebooks are sold.

And don't miss Layla and Shane's story,
A Taste of Home
Available now!

#3035 THE COWBOY'S ROAD TRIP
Men of the West • by Stella Bagwell

When introverted rancher Kipp Starr agrees to join Beatrice Hollister on a road trip, he doesn't plan on being snowbound and stranded with his sister's outgoing sister-in-law. Or falling in love with her.

#3036 THE PILOT'S SECRET
Cape Cardinale • by Allison Leigh

Former aviator Meyer Cartell just inherited a decrepit beach house—and his nearest neighbor is thorny nurse Sophie Lane. Everywhere he turns, the young—and impossibly attractive—Sophie is there...holding firm to her old grudge against him. Until his passionate kisses convince her otherwise.

#3037 FLIRTING WITH DISASTER
Hatchet Lake • by Elizabeth Hrib

When Sarah Schaffer packs up her life and her two-year-old son following the completion of her travel-nursing contract, she's not prepared for former army medic turned contractor Desmond Torres to catch her eye. Or for their partnership in rebuilding a storm-damaged town to heal her guarded heart.

#3038 TWENTY-EIGHT DATES
Seven Brides for Seven Brothers • by Michelle Lindo-Rice

Courtney Meadows needs a hero—and Officer Brigg Harrington is happy to oblige. He gives the very pregnant widow a safe haven during a hurricane. But between Brigg's protective demeanor and heated glances, Courtney's whirlwind emotions are her biggest challenge yet.

Get 3 FREE REWARDS!

We'll send you 2 FREE Books plus a FREE Mystery Gift.

FREE Value Over **$20**

Both the **Harlequin® Special Edition** and **Harlequin® Heartwarming™** series feature compelling novels filled with stories of love and strength where the bonds of friendship, family and community unite.

YES! Please send me 2 FREE novels from the Harlequin Special Edition or Harlequin Heartwarming series and my FREE Gift (gift is worth about $10 retail). After receiving them, if I don't wish to receive any more books, I can return the shipping statement marked "cancel." If I don't cancel, I will receive 6 brand-new Harlequin Special Edition books every month and be billed just $5.49 each in the U.S. or $6.24 each in Canada, a savings of at least 12% off the cover price, or 4 brand-new Harlequin Heartwarming Larger-Print books every month and be billed just $6.24 each in the U.S. or $6.74 each in Canada, a savings of at least 19% off the cover price. It's quite a bargain! Shipping and handling is just 50¢ per book in the U.S. and $1.25 per book in Canada.* I understand that accepting the 2 free books and gift places me under no obligation to buy anything. I can always return a shipment and cancel at any time by calling the number below. The free books and gift are mine to keep no matter what I decide.

Choose one: ☐ **Harlequin Special Edition** (235/335 BPA GRMK)   ☐ **Harlequin Heartwarming Larger-Print** (161/361 BPA GRMK)   ☐ **Or Try Both!** (235/335 & 161/361 BPA GRPZ)

Name (please print)

Address   Apt. #

City   State/Province   Zip/Postal Code

Email: Please check this box ☐ if you would like to receive newsletters and promotional emails from Harlequin Enterprises ULC and its affiliates. You can unsubscribe anytime.

Mail to the **Harlequin Reader Service:**
IN U.S.A.: P.O. Box 1341, Buffalo, NY 14240-8531
IN CANADA: P.O. Box 603, Fort Erie, Ontario L2A 5X3

Want to try 2 free books from another series? Call 1-800-873-8635 or visit www.ReaderService.com.

*Terms and prices subject to change without notice. Prices do not include sales taxes, which will be charged (if applicable) based on your state or country of residence. Canadian residents will be charged applicable taxes. Offer not valid in Quebec. This offer is limited to one order per household. Books received may not be as shown. Not valid for current subscribers to the Harlequin Special Edition or Harlequin Heartwarming series. All orders subject to approval. Credit or debit balances in a customer's account(s) may be offset by any other outstanding balance owed by or to the customer. Please allow 4 to 6 weeks for delivery. Offer available while quantities last.

Your Privacy—Your information is being collected by Harlequin Enterprises ULC, operating as Harlequin Reader Service. For a complete summary of the information we collect, how we use this information and to whom it is disclosed, please visit our privacy notice located at corporate.harlequin.com/privacy-notice. From time to time we may also exchange your personal information with reputable third parties. If you wish to opt out of this sharing of your personal information, please visit readerservice.com/consumerschoice or call 1-800-873-8635. **Notice to California Residents**—Under California law, you have specific rights to control and access your data. For more information on these rights and how to exercise them, visit corporate.harlequin.com/california-privacy.

HSEHW23